WRITTEN IN THE SCARS

MEL SHERRATT

Cover image by paperandsage.com

E-edition published worldwide 2015

To Sarah, thank you.

Chapter One

With a minute to spare before her shift was due to start, Donna Adams rushed into Shop&Save. She ran into the staff room at the back of the building and slipped her green overall over the top of her summer dress. Already she could feel sweat forming, although the glorious hot spell they were enjoying was supposed to break later.

'Made it by the skin of my teeth,' she sighed, joining her work colleague and supervisor, Sarah Hartnoll, behind the counter. 'Bloody hell, it's as hot in here as it is outside.' She glanced at the clock. 'Sorry, I would have been here earlier but I've had trouble with Mum not wanting me to leave. She was holding onto my arm for dear life, convinced that someone is trying to kill her again.'

Donna's mum, Mary, had been living in a self-contained flat for a few years since Donna's dad had died. More recently, she'd been diagnosed with dementia. After wandering off in the night, setting off the alarm to the front door, and being brought home by the police on three separate occasions, Donna had made the heart-breaking decision to move her into sheltered accommodation, where there would be someone to keep an eye on her all the time.

Sarah shook her head in sympathy. 'Never a dull moment in your life, is there?'

'Never.' Donna logged into the till and then looked up at the television monitor that was split into quarter views of the area in front of them. There were a few customers but thankfully no one was after their attention, and if she wasn't mistaken, Darren, their youngest member of staff, was stacking shelves in the far right corner.

The shop had four aisles, all covered by cameras, but it was well known amongst a certain group of people for being easy to steal from. Many a time she and Sarah had left someone to it rather than risk either a tongue-lashing or a hand raised to them. They had both learned the hard way over the years not to interfere with some customers.

'I still feel guilty every time I go and see Mum,' Donna added. 'But even if I had the time, I just don't have the energy to give her what she needs.'

'You should get Keera to do more.'

Donna stared at Sarah, before smiling at the elderly man who was walking towards them. 'Chance would be a fine thing with my lot,' she replied, helping him to fill his shopping bag before handing it back.

Donna had two children. A son, Sam, who was twenty-two and nineteen-year-old Keera, who had recently returned from a short time working in Ibiza.

Sarah held up a hand. 'I'd much prefer to hear all about the hen party on Saturday. Did you enjoy yourself or did you feel like the oldest swinger in town?'

Donna rang the money through the till. 'You might be laughing on the other side of your face when I tell you what happened.' She paused for dramatic effect once the customer had gone on his way. 'I met someone.'

'No!'

'Yes! His name is Owen, his eyes are so sexy – and his body is mmm-mmm.'

Donna smiled even more as she thought back to Saturday night. The hen party Sarah was referring to had been for a woman that Donna used to go to school with. About a month ago, Susan Parker had popped into Shop&Save by chance as she'd been driving through the estate. They'd been really good friends at school but had lost touch when Susan had moved out of the area. Once they'd recognised each other, they had got chatting and Donna had found herself invited to the night out. She'd declined at first as she wasn't sure she would know anyone else who was going, but Susan had mentioned a few names of women she knew, and said it would be great to catch up again.

In the week before the hen do, Donna had still had doubts about whether to go or not, but Keera persuaded her that she might have a bit of fun. And how glad she was of that now.

'How I got his attention is beyond me,' she continued. 'There must have been lots of women his age that he could—'

'Wait!' Sarah held up a hand. 'How old is he?'

'Thirty-five.' Donna dropped her eyes momentarily. 'He's too young.'

'No, he isn't.'

'I'm forty-two.'

'Don't say it like it's a disease!' Sarah scoffed. 'Besides, aren't we supposed to be as young as we feel? And at least you look after yourself. Half the women on this estate walk around in their pyjamas and slippers.'

'I suppose.' Donna sighed loudly. 'I'm not seeing him again, though.'

'Oh! He didn't want a second date?'

'Technically that wasn't a first, but yes, he did ask if he could take me out tomorrow night.'

'And you said no?' Sarah's tone was one of incredulity.

Donna shook her head. 'You know I don't have time – what with looking in on Mum and getting to work and then there's Sam, who couldn't look after a flea without—'

'The world won't fall apart if Donna Adams doesn't come to its rescue.' Sarah folded her arms. 'You should let that family of yours fend for themselves once in a while.'

'Leave everyone to their own devices?' Donna shuddered at the thought. 'It would be carnage!'

A young woman with the brightest of red hair came towards the till, and while Sarah served her, Donna stood staring into space. If truth be told, she hadn't thought of much else apart from Owen since Saturday evening. She could still recall the taste of him on her lips as he'd dipped his head to give her a long, lingering, goodnight kiss. A delicious shiver pulsed through her body.

'Earth to Donna, hello!' Sarah waved a hand in front of her face.

Donna giggled. 'Honestly, though. It's been such a long time since anyone's been interested in me, I just keep thinking that maybe it was too good to be true.'

'Will you listen to yourself? You haven't had a good seeing to in months – just get in there and bang him one if you get the chance.' Sarah picked up two mugs from beneath the counter. 'I'll make us a brew. And then I want to hear everything.' She glared at Donna. 'And I mean *everything*.'

Donna kept one eye on two teenage boys who had just walked in whilst Sarah went off to the staff room to make the tea. Sarah was just a few months older than her. Her hair fell to her shoulders, and she showed off pretty blue eyes below a blonde fringe. She wasn't particularly overweight for her height of five foot four but she did have a tendency to wear tight clothes that emphasised, rather than complimented, her shape.

Donna wished she had curves like Sarah's, but she was thin to the point of being scrawny. Most of the time she put it down to all the stress that came with her life, but a lot of it was to do with her erratic eating patterns and the fact that she was always on the go. Add that to the long-limbed build of a marathon runner and sadly she was never going to be as voluptuous as Sarah, no matter how much she would like to be. And, being a woman in her early forties, things had begun to sag that were beyond Donna's control.

Still, she could dream. Owen had made her night a lot more fun than she had thought possible.

Moments later, Sarah passed a mug of tea to her.

'I wish I'd been invited too,' she said, wistfully. 'You seem like you had a great time.'

Donna glanced up at the CCTV monitor again. The teens had been and gone with a couple of chocolate bars and a can of pop. There were only two customers in the shop at the moment, and they were in the middle of an argument. She turned to Sarah.

'It was one of those perfect nights where you don't expect anything to happen and then—' She was interrupted by the ring of her phone, rolling her eyes when she saw who it was. 'What's up, Sam? Oh – but you have his phone?' Donna looked confused as she spoke to the person on the other end. 'Yes, I'm his mother, his next-of-kin.' She gasped. 'What do you mean— is he okay? He what? Oh, no. I'm on my way.'

'What's wrong?' Sarah was already at Donna's side. She touched her lightly on the arm.

Donna took a few deep breaths, trying to keep her panic at bay. 'Sam's had an accident involving a chainsaw.' Her eyes glistened with tears. 'He's been rushed to A&E.'

Lewis Prophett sat on the bus, shoulder against the window, glad that the seat next to him was unoccupied so that he didn't have to make unnecessary conversation. Staring through the ripples of rain streaking down the glass, a brief summer storm just finishing, he looked out but didn't focus on anything.

It had been hard to make his way back to the Mitchell Estate after leaving the job centre. Before his marriage had ended a few months earlier and Lewis had returned home to live with his mum, the last time he'd been on the estate for any longer than a month was back in his teens. All he'd ever wanted to do when he left school was to get away from the place he'd grown up, even though it had meant leaving his childhood sweetheart behind. He couldn't wait to join the army, get a trade and make new friends.

Even after all this time, Lewis still felt like he was returning home as his eighteen-year-old self. He'd signed up because he felt that he didn't fit in anywhere and now here he was, feeling exactly the same again. He'd added his name to a waiting list with the housing association in the vague hope that a flat might come up for rent. Wow, so much to look forward to.

The army had been the perfect choice for Lewis and his twelve years spent there had been enjoyable. But since he'd come home to Stockleigh two years ago, everything had started to unravel. His wife, Amy, and their son, Daniel, who had been eleven at the time, hadn't known how to react to his mood swings. For a time, he and Amy had tried getting reacquainted but, after he had come home one day and raised a hand to her – not using it, but raising it in a threat – Amy had thrown him out. He knew things had gone too far, but he couldn't do anything about it. She wasn't willing to take him back after eighteen months of hell and he'd been back at his mum's for six months now. It seemed his marriage was over, as well as his career.

Twenty minutes later, the bus pulled in to Vincent Square in the middle of the estate and Lewis got off. The Mitchell Estate was made up of over fifteen hundred houses, flats and bungalows. Some were owned by the local council, a few were owner-occupied but most were rented from Mitchell Housing Association. The estate itself was split in two by a main thoroughfare, Davy Road. Above Davy Road was known locally as living 'on the Mitch' – the better part of the estate. Below Davy Road was known as living 'on the 'hell'. Lewis often wondered if any of it had true meaning. After all, they were only houses and people. Places shouldn't define people, although they often did. Take Afghanistan, for instance.

It was sad to see that the area had hardly changed since he'd been away. The square was still a dirty, untidy place for shops to be situated, and at least half of them were now boarded up. All around him, there were signs of anti-social behaviour. Rubbish bins were either missing or thrown onto the floor, litter scattered everywhere in the breeze. Fluorescent coloured graffiti was scrawled over roller shutters and doorways. To his right was the car park where he'd ripped open his knee after falling from his skateboard as a youngster, still looking in bad need of repair. The whole area felt like it had been forgotten, neglected. Pretty much how Lewis felt about himself.

He walked on past the local supermarket, Shop&Save. Lewis was surprised it had survived through the years, although shops he wasn't familiar with had sprung up alongside it – the nearest selling second-hand clothes and toys. Next to it was a drop-in centre for the locals to talk about careers. Lewis sniggered to himself, unsure why it wasn't already closed. From what he could remember, most of the kids he'd gone to school with had had no hope. Many of them still lived on the estate; most had done nothing with their lives. At least Lewis could say he'd seen some of the world.

He waited for a car to pass before crossing over Davy Road and made his way along Ronald Street. The houses either side were an exact same replica as his mum's and exactly the same as where he had been living with Amy until they had separated. Two bedrooms, semi-detached, postage stamp gardens, some with room enough to park a car on the front, most without space to swing a cat. He glanced at the houses as he went past. If you were lucky, you had a nice neighbour joining on to you. If you weren't, you'd be granted the neighbour from hell. Just lately, Lewis had had a few run-ins with one of the housing officers from the association. He'd been warned about his behaviour when he was drunk, shouting at the neighbours, arguing in the street. Of course he couldn't remember much of it the next morning, but the guilt would overwhelm him. So he'd return to the pub to try and drown out his sorrows.

Lewis sat down at the top of the steps that would take him down to the green and on to Graham Street, where his mum lived. Running a hand over his close-shaved head, he gulped in a deep breath. A tower of a man shouldn't feel panicked as he did. Gone was the Lewis that had left the estate as a teenager. He had hoped that it wouldn't take too long for him to adapt to civilian life again. But every night his dreams turned to nightmares as he relived what had happened. Damn the memories for coming home with him.

Moments later, Lewis stood up. Even though every footstep felt like he was going backwards rather than forwards, he shoved his hands in the pockets of his jeans and walked back in the direction he'd come from, heading for The Butcher's Arms. Drinking wasn't the answer, but he didn't want to stop either. Unable to live with what had happened, it was much easier to block everything out. Either that, or he would end up hurting himself, or someone else, and regret that too.

Because one thing Lewis couldn't erase was his guilt.

It was his fault that Nathan had been killed.

Chapter Two

The city of Stockleigh had a population of less than two hundred thousand residents. Based in the Midlands, it had pockets of crime and depravity alongside areas of affluence, like most cities.

Stockleigh's main hospital was situated near to the centre, five miles from the Mitchell Estate. Donna had raced to her car immediately after receiving the phone call about Sam, praying that the old thing would start but, even allowing for traffic on the ring road, it had taken thirty minutes to get there and find a parking space. She tore across the car park, through the automatic doors into the A&E department.

The waiting room was full to bursting with people sitting and standing everywhere. A man in paint-splattered white dungarees sat with a makeshift bandage around two of his fingers, while a girl of around ten years old, with what looked like a nasty bump to the head, was holding onto her left wrist with her right hand. Several people were sitting in wheelchairs, waiting to be seen. One man stood up on crutches, his left ankle off the floor.

Without a second's hesitation, Donna rushed to the front of a queue of people at the main desk.

'Samuel Harvey,' she cried. 'My son's been brought in as an emergency.' She turned to the woman beside her. 'Sorry, I— I just need to see he's okay.'

'We've all had accidents but we're waiting our turn to be seen,' a man in dark overalls, his right arm in a sling, shouted to her.

Donna turned to him with narrowed eyes. 'I don't need to be seen!'

'I'm just saying that—'

'He's nearly ripped his bloody hand off!'

A couple with a small baby sitting to her right grimaced at each other.

'Look, I just want to see if he's—' Donna's voice broke.

'You can come through the doors, here to your left,' the woman behind the desk told her. 'He's in cubicle nine.'

'Thank you.'

A buzzer went off. Donna opened the door and stepped into a corridor. Three trolley beds were queued in a line, their occupants all elderly, relatives and nurses fussing over them. Instantly, Donna was reminded of how frail her mum was and a sob escaped her. Why did this have to happen now? Didn't she have enough to worry about?

Fresh tears glistened in her eyes as she rushed to cubicle nine. As she drew level with it, she could see Sam lying on a bed, propped up with a pillow behind his head. His right hand was bandaged loosely and raised in the air, the third finger flopping down of its own accord. Dried blood sat underneath his fingernails, drips splattered over his other hand and there was a smudge of red across his chin. He'd been stripped of his clothes and put into a hospital gown.

'Sam!' Donna rushed to his side.

'Mum!' Sam's face creased up as he spotted her. 'It hurts like fuck.'

Donna ran a hand over his hair as if he were a child. 'Don't worry, son,' she soothed.

'But I might lose my finger.' His tears fell freely then as shock took over. 'I don't want to look like a freak.'

'Hey, come on now,' Donna soothed. She hadn't seen Sam cry since his dad had left when he was twelve. Although Joe Harvey wasn't his biological father, they had been close as Sam was growing up. Even after the truth had come out that his real father was someone else living on the estate, Sam had still wanted to think of Joe as his dad, despite not seeing too much of him now that he'd moved out of the area, remarried and had two further children.

Sam had Donna's long build and limbs, and his hair was dark like hers. Deep blue eyes were staring up at her, willing her to say that everything was going to be okay. For all his brave face and hard man attitude, Sam would always be her little boy. But he had some questions to answer, nonetheless. She waited for his tears to subside before speaking to him again.

'Are you feeling calmer now?' she asked.

Sam nodded, wiping at his eyes.

'Right then.' She leaned in close to him and whispered, 'Would you mind telling me how the *hell* this happened?'

Sam swallowed. 'We were doing a job – cutting down some trees and we wanted it doing quicker—'

'We being you and …'

Sam gnawed on his bottom lip. 'Scott Johnstone.' His eyes dropped.

'I might have bloody known!' In frustration, Donna raised her hand in the air and brought it down on the bed, narrowly missing Sam's thigh. 'He's only just come out of prison! You know he's trouble. I told you time and time again not to get involved with that good-for-nothing and what do you do? Lose half your hand and …' Stopping when she realised Sam was crying again, she searched around in her handbag for a tissue and handed it to him. 'Sorry. Go on.'

'We were on a bankside and it was covered with piles of bricks and rubble. Scott had the chainsaw. I tried to put a large piece into the barrow to wheel it to the trailer but it kept rolling out. So I picked it up and held it out for him to cut through.'

'Good God! And you didn't think that was a dangerous thing to do?'

'The blade snagged on a knot in the wood! When it came loose, it went over my hand. If I hadn't been wearing gloves, the doctor said it would have sliced all three fingers off as well.'

Donna whimpered at the mental image of her son being left with a disabled hand. Her knees went weak and she sat down on a chair.

'There was blood everywhere.' Sam glanced at her, tears spilling again. 'I'm going to be scarred for life, aren't I?'

'Let's wait to see what the doctor says.'

Watching as the numbers crept up on the blood pressure monitor by his side, Donna knew she'd have to keep Sam calm or scarring would be the last thing on his mind. She checked her watch: half past one. She'd have to try and catch Keera. Hopefully she could pop in to see if Mum was okay.

A man wearing a blue shirt, dark trousers and a bright lilac tie joined them in the cubicle. 'I'm Richard,' he introduced himself. 'I'm the consultant on duty.'

Donna tried not to show her surprise. He didn't look old enough to be a doctor of any kind. To her mind, he didn't seem any older than Sam. His bedside manner was welcoming though, his eyes behind black thick-rimmed glasses having a friendly sparkle to them.

Richard smiled at them both in turn before addressing Sam. 'You do realise you're the talk of the department? Everyone wants to see the chainsaw man.'

'I don't care. You need to give me something for the fucking pain!' Sam cursed.

'I will once we've looked you over.' Richard's tone was calm.

A nurse came into the cubicle to check the blood pressure monitor. Red-faced and sweating profusely due to her size, her stance gave the impression that nothing much would faze her. Donna couldn't help but frown: she barely looked old enough to be out of school either. Or was it just that she was getting old?

'I want something now!' Sam yelled, making them all jump. 'I can't fucking stand it!'

'Sam,' said Donna. 'Watch your language.'

'But—'

'Let us do our job and assess you,' said Richard, 'and we can get on to giving you the correct pain relief. Can you tell me what happened?' He reached for Sam's hand.

'Don't take the bandage off!' Sam screeched, pressing his body into the back of the trolley bed. 'It wouldn't stop bleeding before. I'll die of blood loss. I'm telling you, man, it gushed out.'

'I need to assess it.' Richard continued regardless.

'Sam, please,' said Donna. 'Try to keep calm.'

'Keep calm?' said Sam. 'Are you mad?'

Donna told the consultant what had happened as the dressing was removed. Afterwards, she peered at it in horror. There was a flap of skin hanging from Sam's index finger where she assumed the blade had stopped, and a wide open gash at the top of the third finger, about two inches in length. All she could see was a sliver of white in amidst the mess.

'Is— is that his knuckle bone I can see there?'

Sam tried not to cry out in pain.

Richard nodded. 'Yes, the blade must have sliced right through it.'

Donna covered her mouth to stop from gagging.

'Why is my finger hanging down?' Sam wanted to know.

'I suspect you've severed a tendon.'

'But you can fix it, right?' Donna asked.

'We need to clean it up first so that we can see more of it.' Richard's smile was reassuring. 'You'll need an operation for us to do that.'

'Wh— what?'

As Richard explained what would happen, Sam screwed up his face and groaned in agony. 'I can't do this,' he cried.

Donna tried to soothe him again. 'How soon?' she asked the consultant.

'It will be this afternoon or this evening. You'll probably be with us for a few days.'

Sam flopped back on the bed in resignation.

'I know it's hard, but try not to worry.' Richard smiled reassuringly at Sam. 'What's done is done, so let's get you as comfortable as we can. You're on the emergency list so you'll definitely be operated on before the end of the day. We'll move you to a ward as soon as we can and get you into a bed.'

The consultant gave Donna another smile before leaving them alone. She sat forward and rested her elbows on the bed, placing her chin in her hands. This was all she needed: as if she didn't have enough to worry about with her mum. She looked at Sam who was lying back, his eyes closed. He really should have grown up by now, be capable of standing on his own two feet. In a way, she supposed he was. He didn't live at home anymore, having moved in with a friend a few months back. Yet Donna knew she would never stop being concerned about her son. He couldn't cope on his own under normal circumstances. How the hell was she going to find the time to visit him and Mary as well as do her shifts at Shop&Save?

'I'm scared, Mum,' Sam spoke quietly. 'What if I have to have my finger removed?'

'Let's wait and see,' she told him.

Two porters appeared in the doorway.

'Which ward will he be on?' asked Donna as she stood up, reaching for her bag.

'Ward twelve, the emergency ward, for now.'

As she walked, behind the trolley bed, Donna checked her phone for messages. There was one from Owen:

Still up for meeting tomorrow night for a drink?

Donna looked ahead at Sam. Although it wasn't a major accident in the scheme of things, she'd have to put Owen off until she knew for sure that Sam was settled and getting better. Lord knew what would happen to him if he had to lose his finger. She sent a message back.

I'm really sorry, but I won't be able to make it. I have a family emergency. My son's had an accident. I'm at the hospital with him.'

'Damn you, Sam Harvey,' she whispered under her breath. 'Such bloody awful timing.'

Chapter Three

Once Sam was settled on the ward, Donna rushed into Stockleigh city centre to fetch him some essentials. The surgeon had finally shown up two hours after they'd been allocated a bed, so she'd come shopping to buy Sam pyjamas and slippers.

An hour later, she was on her way back through the estate, thankful that she had missed the school run so the roads were quite clear. Sighing in exasperation, Donna realised that she'd probably just have enough time to grab a quick bite to eat before heading back to the hospital for evening visiting hours.

Donna had lived on the Mitchell Estate all her life. It had its faults, with its anti-social behaviour and rowdy areas known for trouble but, for the most, she'd found it safe enough if you didn't venture out alone at night. She'd lived with her parents in Bernard Place on the top of the estate until she'd married her ex-husband, Joe Harvey, when she was twenty-one. Sam had been one by that time, and Keera had arrived two years later. After a rocky marriage that they'd stuck at for far too long to be healthy, Joe finally left twelve years later, after admitting to having an affair. It had been left to Donna to keep the family together and they had survived. Not lived – but survived.

As she drove along Davy Road towards her home in Trudy Place, Donna caught her reflection in the rear-view mirror. Her hair was in need of a wash after she had run her hands through it for most of the past few hours and her make-up was now non-existent, leaving her skin looking sallow. Her eyes felt dry and ready to close and it wasn't even five o'clock yet.

Finally home, she parked outside the house and raced up the path. The cul-de-sac had seen some comings and goings over the years, yet when Joe had left, she'd never felt the need to move on as well. Even though some people didn't stay around for long, Donna knew and liked most of the neighbours, and the others she tolerated, or else complained about to the housing authority.

The cul-de-sac was made up of forty semi-detached houses, with two blocks of flats at its head and a large grassed area that caused no end of trouble with the kids using it as a football field. Today, it was awash with people enjoying the August sunshine. Donna could hear squeals of delight coming from a few children who were playing with water bombs.

'All right, Donna?' Rita Manning, her next door neighbour shouted over to her.

Donna looked over the waist-high hedge. Rita was sitting on the front door step, wearing a long black vest that showed several rolls of fat and a denim skirt that was far too short, pale white legs stretched out in front of her.

'I'm fine.' Donna continued towards the house.

'Only I heard your Sam's been having a cutting time.'

Donna stopped in her tracks and turned to Rita. 'Keep that out of my business.' She put a finger on her nose. 'It's got nothing to do with you.'

'All right, keep your hair on.' Rita took another drag before flinging her cigarette butt into the wilderness that was once a garden. 'Can't say anything around here.'

Donna ignored her and went into the house. News as usual had travelled fast and Rita was only after the gossip. Maybe she should have told her that Sam had lost his hand and seen how much she would have exaggerated it by the time the gossip came back to her. Knowing Rita, Sam would be on a life support machine with no legs, as well as having a missing hand, rather than just an injury to it. Rita could spread gossip around anywhere, truth or lie.

'Keera? Donna shouted, closing the front door behind her. 'Are you home?'

'Yes.' Keera appeared in the kitchen doorway. 'How's Sam?'

'I left him swearing at the top of his voice, saying they're all a bunch of sadists.' Donna joined her daughter in the kitchen, plonking her car keys down on the table.

'Bloody typical, especially as it's his fault.'

Donna listened as Keera moaned about Sam, knowing it was a light-hearted jibe. She was only trying to make her feel better. And, despite Keera thinking that Sam got away with too much, Donna would always defend her son. She was well aware that she let him get away with more than she would Keera, and knew for the most part that it infuriated Keera, too. Still, they were quite close, even though they were half siblings, so maybe Sam would confide in her if he needed any help.

She listened as Keera made a cup of tea. Looks-wise, the two of them were similar in many ways and just by glancing at Keera, Donna was reminded how old and tired she looked in comparison to her fresh youth. Keera was thin and petite, her hair and skin dark like her father's. At the moment, her hair was cut into a short bob and dyed a vibrant red, with the odd black streak here and there. Even though it was hot enough to melt foundation off, she wore a full face of make-up. The tan from her recent stay in Ibiza was clearly visible in her skimpy clothing; Keera never missed an opportunity to show off.

'I had to buy him pyjamas.' Donna lifted a carrier bag before putting that down on the table too. 'I don't think Sam has worn them in years but I'm not having him walking around in those hospital ones. They make him look like he's escaped from an institution.'

'He belongs in one.' Keera shook her head. 'Fancy doing something as stupid as that. Was he any better when you left?'

'Actually, he was in a right state.' Donna pulled out a chair and sat down. 'I don't know what on earth possessed him to mess around with chainsaws but the surgeon said if they can't repair the severed tendon, his finger will hang down uselessly and get in the way. If that's the case, he said they'd be better removing it.'

'Ohmigod!' Keera sat down too. She reached for her mum's hand, giving it a quick squeeze. 'When will they know for sure?'

'He's on the emergency list for surgery – tonight, as soon as they can fit him in.' For the umpteenth time that day, Donna's eyes brimmed with tears. 'Whatever they can or can't do, Sam is going to be permanently scarred. We're going to have to be there for him. It could start him off on a downward spiral and I don't think I could cope with another one.'

Sam had gone off the rails in his late teens, causing Donna ample grief from the police as well as the neighbours. Several times, Josie Mellor, the housing officer from Mitchell Housing Association, had called them both in to see her, threatening eviction from their home if things didn't stop. But Sam had continued to cause a nuisance, mixing with the wrong crowd and getting into more trouble. Donna had been worried that he'd end up in prison if he wasn't careful, but the death of one of the local girls, Rachel Bradley, in 2012, had led to the lowest point for Sam. Rachel had been stabbed by another young girl. They had both been rival members of gangs, and fighting each other for top dog had got out of hand. Rachel had been running from Stacey and was murdered in her garden, seconds from the safety of her front door.

Until that moment, Donna had never told anyone who Sam's dad was, not even Joe. But because Pete Bradley had conned her into doing a dodgy favour for him at the same time, the truth had come out that he was Sam's father too.

It had all come about when Pete had wanted to get his own back on a friend of his, John Williams. He'd persuaded Donna to pretend that Sam was John's son. She had known John from school so it was easy to make up the tale.

She wasn't quite sure now why she had gone along with it, and afterwards she'd been quite ashamed, because Sam had then gone on to rob John's house after Pete paid him. Pete's wife, Gina, had heard overheard Sam talking about the burglary and had put two and two together as to why. When questioned, Pete had admitted having an affair with Donna. He and Gina had separated soon after that.

Having thought that Joe was his biological dad, Sam had taken his anger out on Donna, not speaking to her for over six months. He'd started to drink heavily and dabble with drugs.

It was Keera that had managed to persuade Sam to visit their mum again and they'd had a good talk about everything. There had been tears and anger from them both, regret on her part too. But she had only done what she'd thought was best at the time. Once Sam saw this, credit where it was due, he'd got help and cleaned himself up. Donna had thought that with his volatile nature he would revert to his normal habits over time, but thankfully he hadn't. He still wouldn't get a proper job, though.

'Apparently, he's been very lucky.' Donna's eyes brimmed with tears. 'The blade sliced through the knucklebone. He was wearing the right gloves for the job, though Lord knows where he got them. But the protective meshing inside them, plus the fragments of his bone, will need to be cleaned out of the wound during the operation.' She shuddered. 'Then the surgeon will try and stitch back the tendon to see if they can save his finger.'

'Euw, sounds hideous,' said Keera. 'And painful. Are you going back to see him this evening?'

Donna nodded, seeing Keera's shoulders drop. 'What?'

Keera blushed under her mother's stare. 'I was going to ask if I could use the car if you weren't going out.'

'Well, I am.' Donna paused. 'Although I won't have time to call on Nan. I don't suppose you could—'

Keera shook her head. 'I'm due in work at seven.'

'But, it's only just gone five …'

Keera stood up. 'I'm not sure of the buses.'

'Fine,' Donna snapped. 'I'll go on my way out. I'll just have to quickly grab a bite to eat. I'm starving – haven't eaten anything decent since this morning.'

'Okay, okay!' Keera sighed. 'I'll go!'

After Keera left the room, Donna put a hand to the back of her neck. Sitting around on hard chairs in the hospital waiting room for most of the afternoon had given her a headache. She moved her head from side to side, trying to ease the tension. Why did this have to happen now?

Although Donna was desperately lonely at times, her family kept her busy enough not to think about it too often. Not that it was always a blessing, especially when she was curled up in bed alone at the end of a very long and tiring day. There had been a few men over the years since Joe had left, but nothing serious enough to last long term and tempt her into marriage again. Her longest relationship was with Daryl Collins. She'd been with him for three years but finally that had come to an end too and she'd been single for two years since.

Which is why, she supposed, when she'd got a bit of attention from Owen, she'd let in a little glimmer of hope that things might be about to change. And although her plans were on hold rather than cancelled completely, she hoped Owen would understand.

Surely, she deserved a chance at happiness just as much as anyone else?

Chapter Four

When Lewis had left The Butcher's Arms after downing a few pints, he'd taken himself off to bed for a couple of hours. Waking up a little worse for wear, he went downstairs into the kitchen. Recently refitted by the housing association, standard white units and black-marble effect worktops gave it the same uniform look as the houses he had passed on his return home today. It pleased him to see clean lines; he'd never been one for things out of order.

On the side of the fridge, held in place by a Help the Heroes fridge magnet, was a photograph. It had been taken in the back garden on a sunny day, the summer before his dad had died. The two of them were laughing, arms around each other, beer bottles raised in the air. Lewis swallowed. They had been so close, sharing most of his time on leave together. Sometimes he couldn't bear to look at this picture. It reminded him too much of what he missed.

His mum, Laura, was at the sink, washing a few dishes. From where he stood, he could see her sagging shoulders. His dad, Michael, had died suddenly after a heart attack eighteen months ago; such a quick and brutal death. Here one minute and gone the next. Even though Lewis had left the army, he hadn't been able to make it back to his parents' house in time. It had been too quick for Laura to have the chance to say goodbye to Michael either.

Lewis knew when she turned to him that she would put on a brave face. How alike he and Michael were. He knew he must remind her of what she had lost every time she looked at him. It must be so hard for her to have him around so much now, too. He cursed himself inwardly for being so selfish. If only he hadn't been so angry all the time, he might still be living with Amy.

Laura emptied the water from the bowl and wiped her hands on a tea towel. Lewis helped himself to a biscuit from the barrel.

'I hope you went to sign on before going to the pub,' she said, flicking on the kettle and grabbing two mugs.

'Don't worry,' he replied, his tone sharper than he'd intended. 'I'll be on my way as soon as I can find a permanent job.'

'That's not what I mean and you know it,' Laura chastised. 'You can stay here for as long as you like. Tea?'

'Please.'

Lewis went through to the living room. He sat down in the armchair closest to the large bay window, the sun streaming in as it did throughout most of the day. He'd always sat there as a child, with his feet up beside him most of the time, and his mum had always sat on the settee. The remaining armchair had been his dad's. From a young age Lewis had never sat in it and he wouldn't sit in it now. He stared at the chair, almost despising it as he realised it seemed to belong in the house more than he did.

All at once, images came before his eyes. Blood, injured men, noise, shouting, calls for backup amongst the gunshots. His heartbeat ratcheted up at an alarming rate, sweat breaking out on his brow. The colour drained from his face and he breathed deeply to stop the panic building. One, two, three, four, five – five, four, three, two, one. Over and over he counted, but it didn't help. His vision blurred around the edges of the room and he couldn't focus on his dad's chair anymore.

'Lewis?' Laura put down the two mugs she was carrying and came towards him.

Lewis held up a hand. 'I'll be fine,' he managed to say, trying desperately to concentrate on a rhythm that wouldn't have him gulping for air, clenching and unclenching his fingers as they began to tingle.

'Are you sure?' Laura's eyes rested firmly on his.

Lewis couldn't speak for a while, but eventually the tightness in his chest began to subside. His eyes flicked upwards towards his mum, recognising the worried look that he had continually seen on Amy's face for the past two years.

'I just got a bit panicky, that's all,' he tried to reassure her. 'I'm not sure why.'

'Did you have a flashback?'

Lewis had confided that he'd been suffering from them when he'd moved back in with his mum. It didn't seem fair not to.

He nodded. 'They come when I least expect it.'

'Well, you're safe here. That's all that matters.'

He tried not to snap at her thoughtless remark. How could Laura understand what he was feeling? She'd never wanted him to join the army. Dad had been okay about it – said it was a good career to get under his belt and better than anything he would find if he stayed on the estate. But what had he known? Yes, he'd had twelve good years but look at him now, he was on the scrapheap. Lewis had no job, and although he had some transferable skills, the things he had learnt didn't suit anything apart from being in the army as a medic, and he had no one to help him get through the mess he was in. His family lived less than a mile away, yet he couldn't visit for fear of antagonising them. He'd lost the love of his wife and was a stranger to his son.

Worse, he'd given up years to serve his country and what did he have to show for it? Nothing.

Lewis stood up. 'I – I think I'll go to my room.'

'I'm off to work in half an hour anyway.' Laura handed him a drink. 'Take this with you but be sure to bring down the mug afterwards. I remember how you used to hoard everything in your bedroom before you went in—'

'I was a teenager. I've done a lot of growing up since then.'

'In some ways more than others.'

'What's that supposed to mean?'

'You don't have to snap at me all the time. I'm trying my best to understand you but, most of the time, I feel like I can't do, or say, anything right without you biting back. 'Laura sighed loudly. 'I'm on your side, son.'

'I suppose you're going to say you understand why Amy doesn't want anything to do with me now.'

Laura shook her head. 'I know that Amy misses you, and so does Daniel. He called round this morning.'

'Did he?'

'Yes. When I told him you were out, he stayed for a while. I wasn't certain if he wanted to be here when you got back or not. Why won't you go and see him?'

'Because I have to see Amy and I— I don't want to go to the house that I should be living in.'

'At least he wants to see you,' noted Laura. 'Maybe you could meet him somewhere else.'

'Tell him to stop creeping around when I'm not here, and come when I am. Surely that's simple enough. He only has to send me a text message. Kids his age are always on the phone.'

'But can't you see? He doesn't know how you'll react if he does that.'

'I'm his dad.'

Laura shook her head. 'I'm just not getting through to you, am I?'

Lewis left the room as an awkward silence descended. He took the stairs two at a time. Opening the door to his bedroom, he held back his anger as he flopped onto the bed. He lay on his back, hands behind his head, staring at the blue skies beyond the window. Outside, everyone was enjoying the hot spell but all he wanted to do was close his eyes and forget that life existed beyond these four walls. Sunny days such as this one brought back memories of Helmand Province, when he would have been with his regiment, his buddies. Sweat drenching him as they walked in full protective gear outside the camp, his hand hovering over the trigger, ready to shoot at a moment's notice. As a medic, he had seen action regularly, most of it following him home. Even now, as he closed his eyes and curled up on his side, Lewis missed the camaraderie, the daily routine, the teamwork. He even missed the arguments and the odd fight breaking out between the squad.

He squeezed his eyes shut, resisting the urge to scream out loud and punch the wall beside him. Hell, he missed Amy so much. Yet what happened here with his mum wasn't a patch on what had gone on when he'd been living with her. She'd done her best to help him too. But if he'd been angry, or scared, then he'd taken it out on her. If they weren't arguing and shouting at each other, they'd be giving each other the silent treatment. Daniel had seen most of this, and after being called in to see his teacher because he was struggling to concentrate at school, Amy had put her foot down. No wonder she'd had enough.

Lewis felt like he was heading for a meltdown but he didn't know how to stop. He needed to sort his life out sharpish because right now, he couldn't see the point in it.

And that felt like a very dangerous situation to be in.

Chapter Five

High Lane was on the edge of Stockleigh and about three miles from the Mitchell Estate. Situated at the end of a row of terraced properties was The Candy Club. There weren't many people occupying the houses now - most had been boarded up as they had become inhabitable due to lack of maintenance, or as a result of compulsory purchase orders by the local authority - but the massage parlour had been around for longer than a lot of the residents who had chosen to stay.

Although she had told her mum that she was working behind the bar at Sparks' nightclub, Keera was employed at The Candy Club as a masseuse. It had been her friend, Estelle, who had told her about the vacancy, and about the extras she could do to make a bit more money, if she were that way inclined.

'Sorry I'm late,' Keera cried as she entered the dimly lit reception area. She gasped for air before speaking again. 'I'm done in. I had to run to get here on time – and it's so hot out there!'

The room wasn't entirely welcoming, with deep red flock wallpaper that had been up since the first time it had been in fashion. The floorboards creaked underneath the threadbare carpet and the settee on the far wall seemed as battered as many of the clientele.

Ramona Wilson was sitting behind a wooden reception counter, flicking through the pages of a magazine. Keera had known Ramona for years before she'd become her supervisor. She was twenty-one, and even though they hadn't been in the same year, they'd gone to the same high school. Having given birth to three children before she'd been Keera's age, she'd yet to rid herself of the baby fat, no matter how many times she went to the local slimming club. Her mousey brown hair was tied back with a band, pink lipstick on her thin lips, and her eyes sparkled as much as her silver eye shadow.

Ramona raised a perfectly manicured hand to wave away Keera's comment. 'Chill out, you're not at school. And besides, you don't have any clients waiting to see you yet. You can be a little late, under the circumstances. How's Sam doing?'

'Not good.' Keera sighed loudly as she pushed her bag into her locker, which was located in the tiny staff room behind the reception. She came back through and carried on speaking. 'He needs to have an operation. They won't know until then if he'll keep his finger.'

'Might stop him from putting it in too many pies.' Ramona laughed loud at her joke as she leaned forward, her large chest straining across her red blouse. 'Seriously, is he okay, Kee?'

'They're operating on him tonight,' Keera replied, knowing there was no malice intended in Ramona's words. 'I couldn't use my mum's car as she's off to visit him this evening and I had to call on my nan so I wasn't sure of the bus timetable.'

'Couldn't your mum give you a lift?'

'God, no.' Keera shook her head, her bob swishing from side to side. 'She doesn't know I'm working here; neither does Sam. And if they ever find out, I'm not sure which one would lynch me first!'

'Even though you're a good girl?' Ramona raised her immaculately plucked eyebrows.

'Like they would believe that.' Keera scoffed. 'Which room am I in?'

'Number five.'

Humming to herself, Keera jogged upstairs and along a narrow corridor, stopping at the third door to her right. Her thoughts returned to her brother. It was going to be a long night for Sam, and Keera prayed that they could save his finger. She didn't want him to spiral out of control again either. Despite him being an idiot most of the time, he had calmed down lately. And family stuck together: she was a firm believer of that. At least once he'd had his operation, the surgeon would know the outcome.

She pushed open the door, marked with a '5' written in black paint, and stepped inside. Even after three months working there, the faint whiff of cheap disinfectant mixed together with coconut oil never failed to assail her nostrils every time she went into a room. Although she knew some of the women dished out more than a massage, there were certain lines that Keera would never cross. She would have turned the job down outright if she'd been told that she had to do any more than rub a few backs to earn a decent wage.

Her phone beeped and she picked it up. It was a message from Ramona, letting her know that her first appointment was here. Keera texted her back, marvelling at how technology allowed her to do her job and still feel safe. Despite its decrepit state, Ramona had set up a system on the computer. She'd told Keera it had worked out well for her as she knew which girls were with which clients and hadn't then got to sit on the reception desk checking everyone in and out all the time. Essentially, though, Ramona knew which clients the girls were with so if anything went wrong, or she hadn't heard from anyone by the time she should have, she would raise the alarm. It was a sure fire way of keeping a check on the girls' safety.

Keera looked over her list of appointments to see who her first client was. Ugh, Martin Smith. She'd only seen him a couple of times and had hated every minute of both occasions. The dirty bastard always needed a bath. Damn the man for asking for her again. He wasn't a regular that Keera wanted to have, thank you very much.

Still, despite what anyone thought of The Candy Club, working there wasn't as bad as she'd first assumed. And it was far safer than the last job she'd been doing.

Sam lay in the hospital bed, trying to get some sleep. It was half past eleven and he still hadn't had his operation. Except for the occasional snore coming from the man in the bed across from his, the ward had been quiet until three nurses situated on the station at the end of the bay had started discussing last night's television. They'd been there for ten minutes now. He wanted to scream at them. Why couldn't they be quieter?

The throbbing from his hand was like nothing he'd experienced before. Even with the maximum pain relief he could have, he could still feel it pulsing as if it was going to explode, as if someone was shoving a hot poker into his hand and twisting it round for sheer enjoyment. Twice it had swelled underneath the bandaging and the nurse had had to loosen it off.

The anaesthetist had been to see him an hour ago, letting him know that he was the second name on the emergency operation list and they would be with him as quickly as possible. He'd gone through the procedure with him but Sam wasn't interested in that. Instead, he'd caused a fuss, saying he needed more pain relief. He'd been administered as much as they could give him, but the pain was so intense that it hadn't made much difference. In the meantime, he'd been unable to eat or drink for several hours. He'd kill for a pint, and to be having it in the pub with his mates. As well, he needed to speak to Scott Johnstone to see what had come of the job they'd been doing.

Glad the ward was in low light, Sam fought back tears. Why had he done that stupid job? If it weren't for the fact that he was broke and needed some quick cash, he'd never have agreed to it. Scott had never used a chainsaw before but he'd reassured him that it would be a doddle – a few hours' work for a good crust.

Except when it had come down to it, it *had* been dangerous, and it had brought him to people's attention. God knows who would come sniffing around once they heard what they'd been up to. The land was private. They shouldn't have been on there, despite what he'd told his mum earlier. They were clearing it for better access to the building suppliers that Scott was planning on robbing. Their aim to look like they were local council contractors had even fooled one of the neighbours when he had come across to have a chat. Nosy git.

The nurses had moved away now, and the man across from him was finally quiet too. Sam wished he could allay his fears by getting a bit of sleep but he knew that wasn't possible. He'd never had an operation before, and just the thought of it was enough to set his heart racing. He'd read all sorts of tales in the news of people being awake on the operating table but unable to let anyone know and feeling every single thing. Sam shuddered. Why couldn't they come for him now and get it over and done with?

He glanced down at his hand again, the warmth radiating through the dressing. What the fuck was he going to be left with after this operation? Shit, if he lost his finger he wouldn't be able to look at his hand ever again. And it was his right hand – he wouldn't even be able to sign his name.

More importantly, as he lay in the still of the ward, he couldn't help thinking about how vulnerable he was without two hands to put up a fight. He could count on the fingers of his good hand just how many people might want to get their revenge, especially after he'd started to work with Scott Johnstone. He'd found himself in more than one sticky situation over the past few months. Luckily, he'd got away with everything so far, but why the hell had he thought he could run with the big names?

One thing was certain. No matter what state he left the hospital in, Sam would need to watch his back for the foreseeable future.

Chapter Six

Visiting hours were around the clock on the emergency ward, so after spending most of the evening at the hospital with Sam, Donna had been thankful to finally get home for the night. The recent bout of hot weather had meant tempers had risen along with the heat, and a spate of late-night barbecues had resulted in many drunken arguments, but the cul-de-sac was fairly quiet as she locked up her car.

Once in the house, she made toast and coffee and then sunk down on the settee. What a day. During the last couple of hours, Sam had really tried her patience with his moaning and groaning, but she'd kept her thoughts to herself. He was clearly in a lot of pain and the last thing he would want to hear was his mum saying it was all his own fault.

She'd just finished the toast when her phone rang. Reaching for it quickly, the caller display showed 'unknown number.' She worried that it could be the hospital, or something wrong with her mum, Mary.

'Hello?'

'Hey, it's me, Owen.'

'Oh, hi.' The relief Donna felt was immense. 'I didn't recognise your number.'

'I'm on my landline. I just wanted to see how you were – and how things were with your son. It's Sam, isn't it?'

'Yes.' Donna was pleased that he'd remembered Sam's name. 'He's in a bad way but he's going to be fine. It will take a miracle for them to sort his hand out to look anywhere near decent but the surgeons seem fairly confident that he won't lose his finger.'

'That's good.' A pause. 'I also wanted to say thank you for thinking of me when you were in such turmoil with your family.'

What do you mean?'

'I could tell by your text message that you were disappointed that we couldn't meet.'

'Could you?' Donna giggled.

He laughed. 'You won't get rid of me that easily.'

Donna liked the sound of that. She checked her watch to see it was nearly half past eleven. 'You certainly left it late to ring me,' she said, trying to stifle a yawn.

'On the contrary, I think it shows how much you've been on my mind.'

'Oh, please. You've only just met me.'

'I know. I can't explain it either.'

Despite being exhausted, the sound of Owen's voice soothed her. She felt her skin flush at how his words made her feel.

'How are you?' she asked.

'I'm busy.'

Donna smiled. 'I take it you're at home now?'

'Yes.'

'Which is?'

'Not far from you.'

'You mean on the Mitchell Estate?'

'Yes, in Percival Crescent.'

Percival Crescent was at the top of the estate and one of the better streets. Donna remembered a boy she'd had a crush on at school living there. At the time he'd gone out with her best friend, Shaunna, and had broken her heart.

'That's not far from me,' she said. 'Have you lived there long?'

'Do you always ask so many questions?'

'I usually have someone answering back, so I guess I'm used to trying to get in the last word.' She yawned again.

'I should go.'

'I'm sorry.'

'Don't be. When will I be able to see you?'

'Soon, I hope.'

They said goodnight, and Donna disconnected the phone. She grinned. How lovely that Owen was thinking of her, despite the time of the call. Her mind flipped back to Saturday night, recalling how his short-sleeved shirt had given her a glimpse of his tanned, muscly arms, how well he fitted his tailored trousers, how she had to look up to catch his smile. Later, the fingers of his large hands had interlocked with her smaller ones. His eyes had smiled as he'd laughed along with her – at what, she couldn't recall. But she clearly remembered them sitting close together on a settee in the club, Owen throwing back his head as he laughed at something she had said.

She really couldn't believe her luck when she had met him. There had been fifteen women in total at the hen party. They'd gone around town for a few drinks but then as the night wore on, someone had suggested a club. That was when Donna had really felt her age. All the young women with their toned legs and firm breasts, dressed to kill in mini-skirts and high heels.

But, feeling quite tipsy by then, she'd got on the dance floor with the rest of the women. She'd been there for a few songs when one of the men behind her had lost his balance after flinging himself around. He fell backwards into them, catching her across the side of the neck with his hand. Her natural instinct had been to turn around and Owen, who had been with the group, had apologised for his friend. He'd led her away from the dance floor, offering to buy her a drink to compensate. They'd stayed together for the rest of the evening.

Her phone beeped and a text message came in.

I can't sleep thinking of you.

She sighed wistfully as she stared at the screen. When he'd asked to see her again, Donna hadn't really hesitated, despite what she had told Sarah earlier. She just hadn't wanted to tell anyone that she had arranged to meet Owen again in case he stood her up. Even now, two days after meeting him for the first time, it seemed wrong that someone as good-looking as him would be after someone like her. Seven years wasn't too much of an age gap – not an age gap at all if she swapped their ages around. But still, Donna knew he could do a lot better than her.

She thought back to the men she'd dated. Okay, there had been a few before Joe had come along but none that had been long lasting except her marriage – and that had turned out to be a disaster, except for the kids.

She and Joe had grown apart quickly, yet his infidelity had rocked her to the core. And despite the years since, she'd never quite been able to trust anyone else enough for them not to feel stifled, often becoming jealous and keeping her men on a tight leash. She didn't have physical scars but she did deal with the mental ones on a regular basis. Joe Harvey might have swept a young Donna Adams off her feet but he had definitely been the wrong person for her.

So could Owen be her Mr Right, after all these years? She hoped she'd have the time to find out soon.

Lewis peered at his watch, trying to focus on its face. He pulled it in closer, but could only see one hand: it looked like it was nearing midnight.

The Butcher's Arms was the only pub on the estate that was still open. There had been the White Lion until a few years ago but it had been boarded up for a couple of years and then burned to the ground when someone set it alight. If Lewis remembered rightly, the youth responsible hadn't survived the fire he'd started.

The pub had been made over since he'd come out of the army but it still couldn't hide its grubbiness. Deep red carpet already had signs of wear and tear, stains and cigarette burns. The curtains were red too, thick velvet that reminded him of a pub from *Life on Mars* that he'd been recently watching on catch-up TV. Why hadn't they thought to make it over into something modern rather than keep it in the tired and traditional state that it was in now? If the brewery had thought about it, they would perhaps have had more of a steadier clientele. But then again, maybe that was indicative of the estate – nothing would ever make it a nice place to live, so what was the point in trying?

He left the pub, groaning as he pushed on the door. Mum would be on the warpath if he didn't get home soon. The fresh air hit him and he swayed slightly, struggling to stand up. He couldn't remember how long he'd been in the bar, or how much he'd had to drink, but it hadn't worked to dampen his anger. Even before he'd walked a few minutes, he struggled to recall the name of the bloke he'd been talking to that evening. Had it been Peter, Patrick, Paddy? He didn't really care though.

'Stupid nosy bastards,' he muttered under his breath, crossing over Davy Road. What was it with people on the estate? Twice he'd had a go at someone for saying too much, pushing things that little bit too far. Everyone wanted to talk to the returning soldier, hear his tales of blood and death. Had he killed anyone? What was it like? Didn't they realise he didn't want to talk about it? Lewis wanted to forget it.

But, even so, he didn't know what else to talk about. What could he contribute? How much his wife hated him and how much his son didn't want to be with him anymore? No one wanted to hear that. It was too much like normal life.

Normal life, he sniggered, tripping over a raised flagstone on the pavement. He didn't know what that was anymore. Was it waking up every night, covered in sweat, praying that the nightmare wasn't real? Was it waking up in a single bed back at his mum's house, his wife and child asleep somewhere else? Was it being unable to hold down a job for longer than a few months at a time? Well, yeah, he supposed that last one could be classed as normal for some.

He staggered down the pavement, from left to right, right to left. The night was quiet, and most of the houses either side of the road were in darkness, except for the odd light on here and there. He almost lost his footing again, causing him to stagger to the left and bump into the side of a parked car. Cursing loudly as the wing mirror dug into his hip, he pulled up his foot and kicked at it. When it hung by a wire, he pulled it until it came away. His breath coming in fits and starts, he slammed it to the floor, stamping his heel on it, relishing the crunching sound it made underneath the soles of his boots.

'Hey, what are you doing?'

Lewis turned around in a circle but he couldn't see anyone.

'You can't just damage other people's property like that.'

He looked again for whoever had spoken. Finally, in the

shadows, he spotted someone on the doorstep of the house he stood in front of. 'Go back inside and mind your own business, you nosy cow,' he told her.

'I beg your pardon!'

'You people, you're all the same.' Lewis pointed at her, swaying as he stepped forward. 'Wind your neck in and bugger off back inside.'

'You can't speak to me like that.'

'Kicking this is much better than taking it out on a person.'

'I've a good mind to report you in the morning for—'

'Yeah, yeah, you do that.' Lewis brushed aside the comment with his hand and walked away. Silly bitch – what did she know?

He continued in the direction of Graham Street, hoping that his mum wasn't waiting up for him again. She'd done that the last few times, greeting him with folded arms and a firm stare, before giving him a telling off the next morning. It was worse than being with Amy. She'd given him the stare too. Well, he wasn't a child anymore. No one told him what to do now that he had come out of the army. So screw his mum – and screw Amy.

When he arrived home, music was blasting out from a house several doors away. Every window at the front of the property was open, a number of youths on the front lawn chatting loudly. Lewis resisted the urge to go over and punch someone's lights out: for once he knew he was too drunk to fight. Instead, he pushed open the garden gate, negotiated the last few steps, and finally managed to get his key in the lock of the front door.

He went straight upstairs and sat on the edge of his bed, dropping his boots noisily onto the carpet. Muttering obscenities to himself, he flopped to his side and collapsed, fully clothed. Maybe sleep would come to him now that he had alcohol in his system. Shut him down for a few hours so that he could get some rest. Not that he would feel rested after the sleep of a drunk, but anything beat sitting on the edge of the bed watching the sun rising every morning.

The room began to spin, taking him back to a time when he was in a helicopter with the rest of his regiment, going out on a mission. The noise of the blades, the beating of his heart as adrenaline coursed through him, praying that they would all return. The crunch of their boots as they walked for miles, eyes everywhere, finger on the trigger awaiting any eventuality. The blood pouring from the bullet wound in Nathan's neck …

Not even alcohol could block out those kind of bad memories.

Chapter Seven

At ten o'clock the next morning, Josie Mellor walked up the pathway of seventeen, Graham Street. It was the second time in as many weeks that she had visited this property. She knocked on the door and glanced around as she waited for it to be answered, fitting into her old role as easily as if she'd never been away from it.

For the past three years, Josie had been on a secondment at The Workshop, an enterprise centre on the estate. She'd been in charge of overseeing it when it was refurbished, and then had been based there working on a domestic violence initiative, funded by the government. Although The Workshop was surviving, now that her funding had dried up, she'd soon be returning to her original role as housing officer, so had started taking over a few cases in preparation.

She knew she'd miss being based at The Workshop but, on days like these when the sun was in the sky and the weather was glorious, Josie was glad she could work outside. Being out on the patch was never easy but at least she had regulars who she could keep an eye on once more. Good and bad ones - like Margaret Sidworth with her untidy garden next door at number nineteen.

In contrast, the garden of number seventeen was tidy, the driveway cleared of weeds and general rubbish. Parked on it was a bottle-green Land Rover, gleaming in the reflection of the mid-morning sun. Flowers were dotted around a dug-over border around the edge of a small patch of freshly mown grass. A hanging basket next to the door sprouted multi-coloured lobelias, almost tumbling down to a small wrought iron bench in front of the living room window.

Josie knew from experience how much you could tell about someone from the state of his or her garden. Not necessarily from the house, if paint was peeling from a door or if someone had a broken window or was in need of new windows altogether. In her mind, there was a world of difference between untidiness and poor maintenance.

She glanced over the fence at next door again. The garden she was in made the adjoining property's stand out for its lack of maintenance. She tutted: the weeds in number nineteen's garden were higher than the small patch of grass left in the middle, the hedges were overgrown too. The weather had been wonderful for three weeks now, there was no excuse. But then again, Margaret, who lived there with her teenage son and daughter, would find sunning on the doorstep far more important than tending to the grass.

As she waited, she wrote down details to pass on to the environmental enforcement officer when she was next in the office. He'd need to visit to get Margaret to take action.

A woman opened the door behind her. Laura Prophett's greying blonde hair had been tied back from her face, making her look more youthful than her actual age of early fifties, but her puffy eyes and faint smile betrayed her worry. Despite that, she was dressed in colourful summer clothes.

'Hi, Mrs Prophett,' Josie smiled. 'Might I have a quick word?'

She was shown into a living room that was as tidy and respectable as the garden. The wall that housed the chimney was covered with wallpaper of large black flowers on a white background, the remaining walls painted white. The three piece was black leather, a three-seater settee and two armchairs, dented where bottoms had settled over the years.

Josie sat down when invited, pushing her hair out of the way behind her ears. She'd long ago swapped her glasses for contact lenses, showing off deep blue eyes below a thick, blunt fringe. Her friend, Livvy, had given her a well-needed makeover a few years ago and, despite trends coming and going, she'd kept her hair shoulder length because it suited her so much.

'You've come about Lewis, haven't you?' asked Laura.

When Josie nodded, Laura's shoulders sagged.

'I've been trying to get him out of bed for the past hour. But whatever he's done, he won't come down to face the music.' There were tears in her eyes. 'I've tried to be patient too, but he just goes up like a bottle of pop if I suggest anything he doesn't like. Then the next minute, it's "I'm sorry, Mum. It's just taking me time to adjust." It's like living with Jekyll and Hyde. I dread seeing him in the mornings now. It puts me on edge for the rest of the day and I don't want it when I'm off to work.' She glanced away sheepishly. 'Sorry, mouth overload.'

Josie knew that Laura worked at Poplar Court, a sheltered housing block for dementia sufferers. Patience was a virtue for her role as a housing officer but so much more was needed when it came to working with the elderly. Sometimes Josie would hold back her annoyance if she knew someone was trying to get one over her, using age as an excuse. But most of the time, she dealt with genuine cases of hardship and people unable to cope.

'Are you aware of what I've come to see you about?' she asked now, hoping to move things along.

'He hasn't hurt anyone, has he?' Laura sat upright.

Josie shook her head. 'There was a spot of trouble last night. It's the damage he's caused to a car that's my main concern. We think he kicked off someone's wing mirror and smashed it while it was on the floor. The description I was given from the complainant matches Lewis so I though I'd check it out before the complainant went to the police.'

'The police?' Shock was clear in Laura's eyes. 'I can't believe he'd do that. He's always precious about how hard people work, and how people on this estate will come along and take what isn't theirs because it's easier or sometimes, just because they can. Are you sure it was Lewis?'

Josie shook her head. 'I can't be certain, but I think so.'

The last time they had discussed Lewis, Laura had told Josie that she thought there was something on his mind, something he wasn't telling them. Josie had hoped that between them they could get to the bottom of it, knowing how much a difference it could make if Lewis would confide in someone. But, so far, no one had been successful in getting him to do that.

'Do you think he will ever get help?' she asked.

Laura looked up, her eyes glazed with tears. 'Until he realises he has a problem, I don't think so, but …

'When we spoke last time,' Laura continued, 'you mentioned Post Traumatic Stress Disorder. I've been researching it online. It's often triggered by an event after the trauma, isn't it?'

'Yes,' nodded Josie. 'Some soldiers do come home and adapt to life without any problems, although a lot are suffering because of events on the job.' She saw Laura raise her eyebrows questioningly. 'Without any problems they *tell* us about, should I say.'

'Do you think it was more than Michael's death that he seems stressed about?' Laura lowered her voice, fearful of Lewis overhearing.

'It's possible, I'm sure.' Josie paused, wondering if she should voice her concerns. 'Maybe when he came home, back to Amy and Daniel, with support from his family and his parents, he was able to cope a lot better. But as soon as he lost his dad … well, maybe he can't confide in anyone else?'

'I often wondered what they talked about when they disappeared into the shed at the bottom of the garden. Sometimes they would be in there for hours. I always thought perhaps he was sharing happy memories of his time in the army – Michael was so proud of him. But I never stopped for a moment to wonder if he was counselling him through his trauma.'

'And was it soon after Michael died that Lewis's drinking spiralled out of control?' Josie probed.

Laura nodded. 'But I don't know if he'll ever realise that.'

'It's probably the reason he's drinking more, to block something out of his life. He can't face what's inside his head on his own.'

'I never thought he would turn to alcohol,' Laura admitted. 'He used to be the life and soul of a party without a drop of beer. He was always happy-go-lucky. I … I wish we could get that back.'

'He hasn't mentioned anything at all?'

Laura shook her head. 'All I know is that something happened when he was out on a tour and he says it was his fault. And when I question him about it, he clams up. He doesn't want to talk to us.'

'Really? Not even to Amy?'

Laura shook her head. 'And that's the saddest thing. Amy and

Lewis were good together. They were both so young when Daniel came along and when Lewis went in the army, I thought that the relationship would collapse. But they proved me wrong. Amy is like a daughter to me, and I miss having her around. I do go to see her and Daniel, but it's difficult. I feel like I'm taking sides and I don't want to do that.'

'He'll come around, in his own time.'

'I hope so.' Laura was quiet for a moment. 'It's like he's come home as a stranger. That's when he's actually in the house, and not down the pub causing trouble.'

'It must affect you, too, as well as Amy and Daniel?'

'I guess so, but I'll be okay. I just wish his father was here to support us both.' Laura sniffed.

Josie glanced at the photo of Lewis to Laura's side. The face of a soldier grinning into the camera stared at her, almost making her smile back at its immediate warmth. Lewis wore his desert gear, rifle in hand, helmet on head.

'He's your only child, isn't he?' she asked, already knowing but wanting to make small talk to ease the sombreness in the room.

Laura nodded slightly.

'And deployed to Afghanistan three times?'

'Yes, and I don't think my Lewis came back at all when he left the army.' She pointed to the ceiling. 'What's upstairs in that bed isn't my son.' Laura shook her head, a lone tear escaping down her cheek. She wiped it away quickly before continuing. 'I just wish I could help him find his way back.'

Josie sighed. She had her doubts that it was possible, but she wasn't about to give up on Lewis yet.

Chapter Eight

While Josie talked to his mum, Lewis lay in bed upstairs. With his head pounding and mouth dry, even though he'd had a long drunken sleep the night before, he couldn't see much point in getting up. If he went downstairs, the bloody housing officer would most likely tell him off again like a five-year-old, even though he knew he fully deserved it. Why the hell had he kicked off that mirror? He wasn't a vandal.

He rolled over on his back. He hadn't closed the curtains the night before, and the sun's rays cast a bright image of the window across the carpet. The stretch of good weather coming was supposed to last for the rest of the week, if the long-range weather forecast was to be believed. It wasn't anywhere near as hot as it had been in Afghanistan, though. How Lewis wished he were there right now, having a laugh with Nathan and the gang.

When he heard the front door open again and voices in the hallway, Lewis padded over to the window. Out of view, he watched as Josie walked down the pathway, stopping to close the gate behind her. She was okay, as far as authority went. He'd met her a few months ago now, when she'd called at the house after a complaint had been made against him. That was about the noise he'd made coming home one night. He'd been drunk then, too.

Lewis scowled. Alcohol wasn't the best option but if it helped him to get rid of the images inside his head, then the neighbours would have to put up with a little noise here and there. It wasn't as if he caused a riot every day.

He waited for Josie to drive off before going to take a shower. Once freshened up and dressed, he went downstairs to face the music.

Laura was standing with her back against the worktop when he walked into the kitchen, her arms folded. 'Afternoon,' she said, eyebrows raised.

'Morning.' Lewis opened a cupboard and pulled out a box of cereal, then a bowl.

'You need something more substantial than that.'

He shook his head. 'I'm not that hungry.'

'You need to soak up the alcohol I can smell on your breath.'

Lewis sat down at the table and poured milk over his cereal.

'What did she want?' he asked.

'She says you vandalised a car.'

'Ah.'

'Did you?'

'No.'

'You're lying, aren't you?'

He nodded.

'For crying out loud!' Laura tutted. 'You can't go around taking your anger out on innocent people.'

'It was a car, not a person!'

'Nevertheless, it belongs to someone who has worked hard for it.'

Lewis looked up sheepishly. 'Don't you think I regret it?'

Laura sat down across the table from him. 'You can't go on like this.' She reached for his hand. 'Whatever is troubling you, son, I'd like to support you. To listen, and to—'

'What, Mum?' Lewis snatched his hand away. 'Help me get through it?'

'Well, yes,' she nodded.

'You can't help me. No one can.' Lewis put down his spoon. 'What happened was my fault.'

'But what *did* happen?'

There was a pause before Lewis spoke again.

'I don't want to talk about it.' He shook his head.

'If you tell me what's bothering you, maybe I can support you.'

Lewis's laughter was cruel. 'Stifle me, more like.'

'Stifle you?' Laura sat back in her chair. 'How can you say that? You haven't lived at home for twelve years, I've taken you back after the break-up of your marriage—'

'It's only a separation. I'll get her back.'

'—and in the space of a few months my whole way of life has been affected. It was bad enough losing your dad and being on my own, but I'm beginning to think that I'd rather it be that way. You have the nerve to say that *I'm* stifling *you*?'

'I can just as easily move out again, if that's an issue,' Lewis bristled.

'Of course it isn't. But you can't continue to—'

Lewis stood up abruptly, the chair scraping across the floor in his haste. 'Look, Mum. I appreciate what you're trying to do. Honestly, I do. But no matter how much you want to help me, you wouldn't want to be inside my head right now.'

'Son.' She touched his arm this time.

'If I want to get Amy back, I have to do this my own way.'

'But Amy doesn't want to—'

'Leave me alone!'

Laura recoiled, her face paling at the anger in his voice.

Lewis marched out of the kitchen and left the house with a bang of the front door. Margaret, who was sitting on her doorstep smoking a cigarette, threw him a filthy look.

'What are you staring at?' he shouted, before slamming shut the gate and running down the street.

Why wouldn't anyone listen? He deserved to be unhappy, couldn't they see that? Why should he be happy when Nathan…

Only when he had left the house far behind did his steps slow enough for him to catch his breath. What was the point in running? He couldn't escape his problems, his fears. The guilt would come with him wherever he went. It would haunt him for the rest of his life. And he couldn't talk to anyone about it. Because then everyone would know what had happened and whose fault it was.

Once he'd calmed down a little, Lewis went across to Vincent Square. In Pete's Newsagent, he found a pile of envelopes that he could buy individually and brought one. Next, he went into Shop&Save and withdrew sixty pounds from the cash machine inside the doorway.

Once he'd popped the notes into the envelope, he walked back to Davy Road, hoping he'd be able to recall where he had caused the damage last night. Stopping suddenly, he drew level with a car parked outside a house. It was a Fiesta, in fairly old shape now. The passenger side mirror was missing, wiring hanging out of a hole in the door.

Embarrassment flooded through Lewis at the thought of what he had done the night before. Feeling his skin reddening, he walked up the pathway and knocked on a door.

It took a while for the door to be opened. An elderly woman with short, thinning grey hair stood looking through the half-inch gap allowed by the safety chain on the door. Over the top of her glasses, she eyed Lewis with contempt.

'Didn't you cause enough trouble last night?' she snapped.

'I did and I'm sorry.' Lewis thrust the envelope through the gap in the door. 'I came to give you this.'

'What is it?'

'Money for the mirror.'

Her hooded eyes narrowed. 'I can't take that.'

'Why not? It was my fault.'

'Yes, I know but that doesn't make it right.'

Lewis frowned back. 'What would make it right?'

'You only needed to apologise.'

'But it cost you money.'

The door was shut in his face. Lewis was about to leave when he heard the chain being removed before the door was opened up fully. The woman couldn't have been a day under eighty and immediately reminded Lewis of his nan who had passed away when he was in his late teens. She wore navy trousers and a two-piece pale blue cardigan and jumper. He could see from her posture that she was unsure on her feet. In his drunken state the night before, he hadn't noticed the stick she was leaning on.

'I would have clouted you with this if I'd had it near me,' she said, rising it an inch from the floor.

'I'm not sure what I would have done if you had,' Lewis admitted.

She glared at him for a moment, then, seeming to relent, she handed back the envelope. 'How about you do me a favour instead of giving me this?' She pointed to her garden. 'I do my best to keep everything tidy but I struggle with those hedges. I don't have any family to help, so I don't suppose …?'

Lewis looked at them. It wouldn't take longer than a couple of hours to cut them down to a decent size. He glanced up at the clear sky. It was perfect weather for it and it would give him something to do.

'Unless you're too busy in your day of causing trouble?' the woman added with a sly grin.

'Lewis's brow furrowed. 'Why are you letting me off?'

'Because you came to make amends. I see people for what they are and not for what they do. Sadly, most people aren't like me.' She looked up at him, despite being two steps above the level of the path. 'Besides, it's not my car.'

Lewis grinned. He'd been wondering about that.

'Well, I suppose it will pass a few hours away,' he said.

'Perfect.' She held out her hand. 'I'm Elsie, by the way.'

'Lewis. Lewis Prophett.'

'Well, Lewis Prophett, once you've finished the hedges, perhaps I can persuade you to run the mower over the lawn and we're quits.'

Chapter Nine

Of all the wards that Megan Cooper helped to keep tidy on her shifts at the hospital, number twelve was her favourite because of the variety of people she got to see. It was a holding bay for emergency patients who needed surgery for injuries caused that day. Once the operations were done, patients were either discharged or moved to a more specialised ward for further treatment. It was also her last ward to clean before she went home for the day.

The ward was mixed, with beds segregated for males and females, fitting six in a bay. She turned the corner into the first bay, mopping the floor as she went, her tiny frame lugging the cleaning trolley behind her. There were three patients that morning. To her right, two elderly men were sitting in chairs beside their beds chatting to each other, their arms waving around as they spoke. She tried to work out what was wrong with them but there didn't seem anything obvious. They looked too well to be in hospital but she knew that people could change in an instant on this ward as they were being monitored.

On the other side of the bay, sitting on top of the covers in the middle bed, was a man that looked familiar, although Megan couldn't think why at first. Even though he was scowling, she could tell a smile would light up his face if he ever let it. He didn't look too much older than her nineteen years; she would bet his spiky black hair wouldn't usually look so messy too. He wore pyjamas, his legs crossed at the ankles, new slippers on his feet. His right hand was lying on top of the covers, a bandage around it.

In the other, he held a newspaper. He dropped it to the bed as he caught her eye.

'Hi, there.' Megan smiled broadly. 'I think I remember you from school. It's Sam, isn't it? Sam Harvey?'

'Yeah.' His eyes narrowed.

'I'm Megan, but you probably won't remember me as I was a couple of years below you, I think. Did you have a sister? Keeley or something like that?'

'Keera?'

Megan nodded. 'How are you feeling today?'

'Like someone has tried to rip my fucking hand off.'

'Oh, dear. What happened?'

'Had an argument with a chainsaw.'

'Euw.' Megan grimaced.

'It's not that bad!'

'It's never that bad, you see?' She smiled. 'Do you need an operation?'

'Had one last night.'

Megan continued to mop the floor as she saw Sue, one of the staff nurses on duty, walking towards them. She hoped she wouldn't get into trouble for chatting, like she often did. But Sue smiled as she walked past to make up a bed that had been recently vacated.

'Give him a run for his money, if you can,' she shouted over as she pulled back a sheet. 'He did nothing but moan last night.'

'You'd moan if you were put through so much pain.'

'Is it any better this morning?' Sue stopped what she was doing. 'The doctor will be around soon and we can sort out more pain relief if possible.'

'I'm okay, thanks.'

Sue nodded and continued stripping the bed.

'It was too swollen to do everything,' Sam explained to Meg. 'I might have to have another operation. I have to wait and see.'

'Well, you might be moving wards soon then.'

'Haven't a frigging clue. All I know is that it hurts like fuck.'

Megan looked at him with a frown. 'You swear a lot, you know.'

'And?'

'Some people, they curse so much in conversation that they

don't even realise they do it all the time. It can offend people without you realising.'

Sam bit on his bottom lip. 'Have I offended you?'

'Me?' Megan shook her head, her blonde ponytail swishing at the back of her head. 'Not at all. But—'

'Well then, mind your own business and stop interfering.'

'I was only –'

'You were trying to be a busybody, like a lot of people here. But what do you know? You haven't had an accident and you aren't stuck in here either. So forgive me if I swear every now and then without thinking.'

'Hey, you said a few sentences *without* swearing!' Megan glanced at him from below her fringe.

Sam's frown changed into a smirk. Then it morphed into a yawn.

'Sorry, I have a tendency to yackity-yack for too long,' Megan smiled.

'No, I'm just tired.'

'That'll be the anaesthetic,' Megan nodded knowingly. 'It knocks you about for a couple of days afterwards. You'll just be getting used to it as they'll be sending you home.'

'Oh, ha ha, very funny.'

Megan beamed as she wheeled away her trolley. 'It's far better than being a grumpy chops and swearing at everyone.'

When she heard a noise behind her, she turned back to see that the plastic cup which had been on the cabinet beside the bed was now on the floor, a small pool of water beside it.

'Oops, how clumsy.' Sam pressed a hand to his mouth, a look of innocence on his face.

Megan frowned, catching Sue's eye as she did. Sue was hiding a smirk. Had Sam knocked the cup off deliberately?

She wheeled the bucket over and proceeded to mop up regardless. Picking up the cup, she shoved it in the rubbish bag attached to the handle on the trolley.

'What did you say your name was?'

Megan turned round and tapped her name badge with a finger.

'Well, Megan,' Sam whispered. 'You have a mighty fine arse from where I'm sitting.'

Megan tried not to smile but she couldn't help herself. Even when he frowned, she still felt herself drawn to him.

'Pity it's out of bounds for you then, isn't it?'

She flounced off, feeling happy to have the last word.

It was five thirty. Donna looked up as Keera rushed through the living room to get her bag.

'You off out already?' Donna asked.

'Yes, and I'm going to miss the bus and be late again, if I don't leave right now.' Keera's eyes flitted quickly around the room. 'Have you seen my black cardigan? The one with the short sleeves?'

Donna pointed to the table. 'Over the back of the chair where you left it.'

Keera sighed with gratitude. 'There it is, thanks, Mum. Right, I'm off, see you later.'

'Give me a ring if you're stopping out?'

'I'm not stopping out.'

Donna shrugged. 'You never know – you might meet a nice fella and want to have a good time.'

'Chance would be more like it.' Keera rolled her eyes. 'They're usually three sheets to the wind by the time I'm ready to have some fun.'

Donna smiled. 'See you later, love. Don't forget you said you'd pop over to see Nan in the morning.'

'I won't!' The door slammed behind her.

Donna's eyes skimmed over the familiar room, and the numerous photos of her family. They were the most precious things in her life. No amount of material things around her would replace them.

Unlike a lot of the families on the estate, she didn't have much but what she had was clean and tidy. A navy blue settee was pushed against each wall, with a large bay window looking out on to the avenue. The settees had taken ages to pay for but they were hers now and the perfect colour to mix and match rugs and curtains in the latest fashionable colours to keep the room up to date. The large flat screen television had been a present from Sam: she hadn't asked where it had come from.

Her mobile phone rang. She wondered if it would be Owen but anticipation turned to disappointment when she saw who it was.

'What do you want?' she said.

'Don't be like that.' It was Sarah. 'You know you love me really.'

'Oh, all the time. Who hasn't turned in now?'

'Maxine – she's rung in sick. You know I wouldn't normally ask for help under the circumstances as I know you have a lot on your plate right now, but I don't have anyone else to ask.'

Donna sighed. Why couldn't everyone just get on with their lives and give her a bit of peace? But she knew Sarah would be feeling terrible for asking her, which meant she must be desperate. And they had helped each other out so much over the years that she didn't mind so much. Donna could always do with a little extra money, too.

'Pretty please!' Sarah spoke into the silence.

'Okay, okay. What time do you want me there?'

'Half an hour?'

'I'm not staying too late, though.'

'Nine o'clock finish do you?'

Donna sighed. 'I suppose so.'

'Thanks – you're a life saver!'

Donna put down the phone with another frustrated sigh. Why did she always give in so easily? She could do with a few hours to herself really. It was what she needed after running around after her family all the time.

She wished she could learn how to say no, but everyone knew her weak spots. Sarah's comment was laughable. She wasn't a life-saver. She was a mug!

Chapter Ten

Donna ended up booking Wednesday off as a holiday from Shop&Save – not that she received much holiday pay, but she couldn't fit everything in. She'd spent most of it on the ward with Sam, listening to him moaning about everything and anything until she had finally told him to stop feeling sorry for himself. But now she was feeling guilty for her outburst. After visiting Sam she'd done a bit of shopping and raced over to see Mary.

Since her condition had worsened, she tried to visit every day. With a nudge, Keera would visit once or twice a week, and Sam maybe once a fortnight, with a really big shove. As usual, most things were left up to her, especially the fetching and carrying.

Poplar Court was only a few minutes' drive away on Leonard Drive. Donna had been thankful of this on the times that she had been called out by the warden to tend to Mum when she had been ill, or more recently, confused enough to keep pressing the emergency call-out button.

Only a few years old, it was a massive complex spread out over several acres, backing onto fields. The building itself was set out in an L-shape, housing one hundred and ten small self-contained flats, run by the city council, with shared facilities on the ground floor. There was a gym, hairdressers, small supermarket and coffee shop.

Once she had arrived at Poplar Court, Donna pressed her key fob up to the electronic remote panel, pushing the door as a buzzer went off. The flats accommodated elderly people, single or couples.

Mary was on the second floor so for speed, Donna took the lift.

Mary's flat was near to the end of a wide corridor. When she reached flat 209, Donna stepped into a windowless hallway with four doors off it. The kitchen and bedroom were to her left, the living room and bathroom to her right. Each room was decorated to a high standard and Donna hadn't let it slip. Unlike some of the other families, she wanted her mum to live in cleanliness.

In the living room, Mary was sitting in the armchair watching the television. Donna never knew from one visit to the next if Mum would recognise her but she lived in hope. Some days, Mary would smile up at her and Donna's heart would lift. But then she would call her by a different name or ask her to change her bed-covers, or ask when her dinner would be ready, thinking Donna was one of the carers. Other times, Mum would start talking about days gone past and when Donna joined in she would laugh for a while. Then there would be days where she hadn't got a clue who Donna was, and it felt like a slap in the face because she was a stranger to her own mother.

'Hi, Mum, it's only me,' she smiled, bending to kiss her on the forehead.

Mary looked up at Donna, a blank look in her eyes, a faint smile on her thin lips. She was a small woman in her late sixties, yet even though she looked frail, she was extremely strong when challenged.

Mary used to have the same colouring as Donna and Keera, but her hair was white now, her skin almost transparent. Sometimes she had a sparkle in what Donna could see of her eyes beneath the hooded lids, but most of the time she looked as she did now. Just lately, Donna had seen her lose more and more of her fighting spirit. It was as if the dementia was taking every last bit of her mum.

Donna perched on the arm of the chair. 'How are you today, Mum?' she asked. When there was no reply, she sat for a moment, staring at the television screen but not really watching it.

A head popped around the doorframe. 'Oh, hi, Donna,' a young woman said. 'I didn't hear you come in.'

'Hi, Megan. I've only been here for a few minutes.' Donna glanced at the clock on the wall. It had been from her childhood home and she remembered it fondly through the years. The times she'd cursed at it when she'd been late. The times she'd sat watching it, waiting for someone to ring her when she was a teenager with a crush on a boy from school. She was surprised it was still working, and Donna knew even though it was old-fashioned, when Mary did eventually leave them, it would be the one thing she would treasure. Time stood still for no one.

'I saw Sam this morning,' Megan added. 'Sorry to hear he's had an accident.'

Donna frowned. How did she...?

'I clean at the hospital, too,' Megan explained.

'Blimey, you're a worker.' Donna was impressed.

'I do a few hours there in the mornings and then come here for a few hours most afternoons. My mum has osteoarthritis and is barely mobile, so it suits us both. It gives her independence because I can pop home at lunchtime to see if she needs anything.'

'Ah, yes, I remember you telling me that,' Donna nodded, instantly feeling sorry for the young woman. Megan didn't look a day over twenty and had a lot of responsibility already. A bit like herself, she surmised. Yet, for her young age, Megan seemed to have a sensible head on her shoulders. Donna had known her for around six months, since she'd managed to get extra help in for Mum from social services. Denise Barker, the warden at Poplar Court, had assigned Megan to help out more regularly. She wished Keera would share the burden more too, with a little less attitude.

'How is he?' Megan continued. 'He seemed in a lot of pain when I saw him.'

'He's coping, I suppose.' Donna sighed. 'I feel like all I do is visit people and go to work in between at the moment.'

'It will get better once Sam leaves the hospital.' There was a slight pause from Megan. 'Won't his girlfriend help him out too?'

'He's single at the moment. He shares a flat –' Donna stopped herself from saying *with another layabout* '– with a friend. I'm hoping he'll feel able to cope on his own when he gets discharged but if not, he'll be back under my feet again, I expect. Not that I'd mind too much,' she said, hoping that Megan didn't think she was being harsh.

'Well, if he starts moaning too much, you should send him

round here. He still has one good hand – I bet Denise could put him to good use.'

Mary smiled when Donna looked down at her, but the vacant look was still there. Donna smoothed down her hair like she had done to Sam on the day of his accident.

'Right, I'll leave you in peace,' Megan said, a few moments later. 'I'm finished here for today.'

'Bye, Megan.'

'See you tomorrow, Mary. Lucky thing – you have me again. Bye, Donna, see you soon.'

Alone at last, Donna spoke into the silence.

'I wish we could have a proper chat, Mum,' she said. 'I loved it when you used to talk things through with me. Even though we didn't always see eye-to-eye, I always felt like I had someone on my side.' She paused, wondering if she should voice her excitement about what had happened at the weekend. Even though she knew that conversations would always be one-sided now, and there would be no advice forthcoming, she had shared so much over the years.

It had been so exciting when Donna and Joe had first been married. In their early twenties, with the first throes of love to keep them happy, they'd been full of hopes and dreams for a great future together, and for many years they had been content. But that had soon petered out once the kids had got older, and complacency had stepped in.

Now Donna couldn't remember a time when she'd last had a laugh with anyone, a real belly laugh where tears had poured down her face and her ribs had ached from the effort. All she seemed to do was worry – about Sam and Keera, about her mum, about getting enough money to pay the bills. And realising she'd have to do this all on her own made her feel totally alone. It was no wonder she was dreaming about Owen.

'There's this man I've met, you see,' she found herself saying to her mum. 'I don't know if he's too young for me or if I should just do what Sarah says and have a bit of fun. You know only too well how empty my life is of fun right now.'

Donna looked at her watch and stood up quickly. She was going to be late again if she didn't stop feeling sorry for herself and leave right away. She bent to kiss Mary on the forehead, sighing when her eyes never moved from the television screen.

'Bye, Mum,' she said, wearily. 'See you tomorrow.'

A few minutes later, as she made her way back to her car, her phone beeped. It was a text message from Owen.

Hey, how are you? You got time to meet yet?

Donna sniggered. She'd barely had a minute to herself since she'd spoken to him. But Sarah's words came back to her. If she didn't make time for herself, then she would never have any fun. Before she could change her mind, she picked up her phone and replied to his message.

I might be able to make it later in the week, if you're free?

Chapter Eleven

About to start her evening shift, Keera welcomed in her first client with a smile. Derek Paige was a taxi driver and, during the few times she had seen him, she had learned that he was forty-eight, divorced with two children who he never saw due to their mother emigrating to Australia when they were young, taking them with her. Since then, he'd had a few relationships but nothing ever as serious as marriage proposal status.

For a man of his age, Derek was really distinguished. He reminded Keera of Richard Gere in *Pretty Woman*, one of her all-time favourite chick-flicks - although he sported some mean-looking tattoos all over his arms and back. And he was clean, unlike Martin Smith.

Keera had taken an instant shine to Derek, and it seemed to her that the feeling was mutual. He hadn't asked for extras yet, which she was glad about, because she would hate to turn him down. Although she didn't want him to be disappointed and then ask for one of the other girls, she just couldn't get past the thought of doing anything sexual – she wasn't that desperate for money.

'So, Derek, am I allowed to say "just the usual?" to you now that this is your fifth visit to see me?' she asked as he took off his jacket and hung it on the back of the door.

'Well, you are my favourite,' he replied with a grin.

Keera found herself blushing, dipping her eyes as she patted the couch. 'What are you waiting for? Strip off and jump aboard.'

She turned away as he removed his T-shirt. When he was lying face down, she grabbed a small plastic bottle, then poured oil into the palm of her hand and set to work.

'So, how have you been since I last saw you?' she asked as her hands moved up and down his back.

'Not too bad, thanks.'

'Work good?'

'I suppose.'

'What's your best night then? Friday? Saturday?'

'I don't work at weekends, so it's Friday for me.'

'How come?' Keera pummelled at the skin around his spine next, delighted when she heard a moan.

'I don't need the money – nor the hassle. I finish around midnight, too - saves catching the drunks. They give me the most abuse.'

Keera laughed to herself. This job wasn't much different than being a hairdresser. She asked the questions and the men answered, often telling her more in return. She was a confidante, in many respects.

Men were always trusting her with their secrets. She kept them to herself, too – unlike Tracy Tanner, who told the rest of the women anything juicy so they could all laugh about it. Keera didn't like that, even though she often found herself joining in with the laughter. Tracy had a way of telling stories that cracked everyone up.

'What brings you here, Keera?' Derek asked. 'I mean, you seem too nice to work in a place like this.'

'I'll have you know all the girls here are nice, Mr Paige,' she admonished.

'Oh, I didn't mean … Sorry, that was rude.'

'I know what you mean. It's the first job that I came across when I got home. We hadn't long been back from San Antonio – me and my friend, Marley, that is. We were supposed to be staying there for the summer but it all went wrong within the first month, so we came back.'

'Is Marley a good friend of yours?'

'Yes. I've known her since junior school. We left high school with a few exams between us, so with only the crappy jobs to look forward to – if we were even lucky enough to find jobs in the first instance – we wanted to have a bit of fun.'

'I don't blame you. Living around here is hardly thrilling.'

'Tell me about it. We were so desperate to get away that we decided to go and work abroad.'

'As holiday reps?'

'No.' Keera shook her head, although he couldn't see her. 'I could never do that. All that being at everyone's beck and call all the time – that wouldn't be much fun either, even if we could chill in the sun on our days off. We got jobs working in a bar. Serving drinks, waiting on tables, you know. Boring stuff but we had a laugh. For the first time in our lives, we felt free. But then it all went wrong.'

'Oh?'

Keera shuddered at the memory, still so clear in her mind. She didn't like to revisit it so her words came tumbling out. 'We'd been living in a tiny apartment near the bar. Early one morning, the owner let himself in. He accused Marley of ripping him off and stealing his money. He was in such a drunken rage that before we could stop him, he dragged Marley into the bedroom and wedged a chair under the door handle so that I couldn't get in.'

'You don't have to tell me—'

'I screamed until help arrived,' Keera continued, 'but by then Marley had been beaten badly. The only thing that stopped the bastard from raping her was that he was too pissed to get it up.'

'Was he arrested?' Derek turned his face so that he could see hers but she gently pushed his shoulders down and continued to massage his back.

'The police took him away,' she told him. 'We weren't sure what happened to him because we flew home a few days later. But I hope he got what he deserved.'

Keera sighed. She didn't blame Marley for wanting to go home. In actual fact it had creeped her out just as much and she was glad when Marley had suggested it. She didn't want to live in fear of being attacked next and she certainly wouldn't have stayed there on her own.

'Even coming back here was better than staying there,' she continued. 'Marley's parents live in Manchester now, so we can't see each other much at the moment. Still, we text and call each other – and we chat over Skype.'

Keera missed Marley as much as Ibiza: the camaraderie in the bar, dozing in the shade of an umbrella on the beach while they caught up with their sleep after working until three a.m. every night, chilling out with a group of friends they'd made who worked the bars too, always around for happy hour before starting over in the bar, the music blasting out enough to make their ears ring. If it weren't for what happened, she would go back tomorrow.

'Don't you have any other friends? I'm sure a young girl such as yourself must have lots of them.'

'Yes. There's a group of us who meet in the local pub, but it's not the same without Marley. I feel like I've lost my shadow.'

'And now you're working here!' Derek's tone was singsong.

'Don't say it like that!' Keera slapped him playfully on his shoulder. 'A friend told me there were jobs going. And before you say it, I'm not naïve. I know what some of the girls get up to but I have my limits.'

'And so you should.'

Keera stopped for a moment. She couldn't believe how much she had opened up to Derek. She wasn't usually that forward. He obviously had a comforting affect on her. She wouldn't talk to any old client!

'Blimey,' Keera grinned. 'I thought I was supposed to listen to your problems, not the other way around.'

'I like that you find me so easy to talk to.' Derek smiled as he sat up. He stretched his arms to the ceiling before stepping off the bed.

Even long after Derek had gone, Keera couldn't stop thinking of their conversation. She could get off the estate if she wanted to but she hadn't got the qualifications needed to get anything more than a menial job.

Keera knew she wasn't like a lot of the women who lived on the estate though, always scrounging off the social or getting by on knock-off stuff from the bloke they were shacked up with at the time. She'd wanted to earn her keep since she'd left school. It was one thing her mum had instilled in her after her dad had left. The need to provide for herself, to never rely on anyone else.

When Derek had asked her what she fancied doing, she couldn't answer, because she hadn't got a clue. And that had upset her. She didn't want to be one of the people who went through life without a purpose, like her mum. Life was too short to be running around after everyone the way she did.

And, unlike her brother, Keera wanted to work to pay her way. She wanted money in her pocket, a decent flat, nice clothes, and good holidays.

She wanted a future, something to look forward to – but she wasn't going to get that around here, now was she?

Chapter Twelve

Megan was pleased to see that Sam was still on her rounds when she went into work the next morning. He'd been moved to number seventeen, one of the more recently refurbished wards. It still had that sense of newness about it and was a pleasant place to be, rather than having the old feel of ward twelve.

Most things were fresh and shiny, as if not used before. There were only a few scuffmarks on the painted cream walls, the curtains decorated with retro patterns, flashes of yellow, coral and beige. Megan often wondered if the nicer surroundings helped people to get better; if the older wards prolonged illnesses by leaving their patients in a state of despair.

She gave Sam a friendly wave.

'How are you feeling?' she asked, as she dragged over the cleaning trolley.

'All the better for seeing your pretty face.'

'You're a relation to Mary Marshall, aren't you?'

'Yeah, she's my nan. Do you know her?'

Megan nodded. 'I work at Poplar Court in the afternoons. She's a resident there, isn't she? She hasn't been there long.'

'God, you're a nosy one.' Sam's tone was jokey, so Megan smiled.

'I know your mum, too,' she admitted.

'Lucky you. Do you still live on the estate then?'

Startled by his bluntness, she decided to be nonchalant. 'Yes,' she said. 'You?'

'If I told you, I'd have to shoot you.'

'Really?' She raised her eyebrows.

'I live in Benedict Road.'

Megan knew it was near to where she lived in Rosamund Street. 'That's on the 'hell, isn't it?'

'Just about.'

'Ouch – I live on the mitch.' She said it without thinking, then cursed inwardly for giving personal information out when she didn't know him very well.

Sam laughed.

'What's so funny?'

'I should have realised.'

'Why?'

'Because if you didn't live on the Mitchell estate, you'd be a nurse rather than a cleaner.'

Megan pouted. 'I don't think that's fair, and it isn't true, either.'

'You don't want to be a nurse?'

Megan shook her head. 'I'd hate to work with all that blood and sick and poo.' She wrinkled up her nose. 'Not me, no sirree.'

'Isn't that what you clean up anyway?'

'Sometimes but not often.' She began to mop again. 'Only if anything happens when I'm on my rounds. Other than that, someone else gets to do it. I have set rounds, you see.'

'Well, in that case ... Oh, fuck.'

Megan looked up to see a policeman walking towards them. As he stopped at Sam's bed, she moved away to give them a bit of privacy.

Sam swore under his breath.

'Mr Harvey.' PC Andy Shenton nodded in greeting as he stopped in front of him. 'Mind if I pull up a chair and have a word?'

'Yes, I do mind. I'm waiting to see the doctor and you're only going to give me grief – like every other time I see you.' Sam went to fold his arms, then realised with the bandages on that he couldn't.

'Likewise,' said Andy. 'How's the hand?'

'Hurts like fuck.'

Andy pulled a chair from a stack of three and sat down next to the bed. 'I suppose you know what I'm here for?'

Sam said nothing.

'Do you want to tell me what you were doing on private property?'

'We weren't – I mean, I wasn't.'

'So you were on your own when the accident happened?' Andy raised his eyebrows.

'Yeah, I was.'

'Oh, come off it, Harvey.' Andy folded his arms next. 'Do you really think I'd believe you attacked yourself with a chainsaw? You were with Scott Johnstone, weren't you?'

Sam frowned. How the hell had he got that information so quickly?

'I checked the hospital CCTV to see who brought you in. Nice of him to abandon you on the car park, though.'

'That says nothing,' said Sam. 'I could have gone home and then Scott brought me here when he saw the state I was in.'

'What were you doing there?'

'I'm not admitting to anything.'

'We have a witness who said—'

'Okay, okay.' Sam sighed. 'We were clearing land.'

'To plan a getaway?'

'What?'

'Let's face it, if things had gone better than they had, you might have been going home that night with a van full of … let me take a guess, electrical goods to sell on? That would be quite some tidy profit.'

Sam shifted on the bed. He'd better be careful what he said, there was too much of a notion there already.

'Are you arresting me?' he wanted to know.

'Just routine questions for now,' Andy smiled.

'We were just helping a mate to clear his land.'

Andy got out his notepad, smiling at a nurse as she walked past the bottom of the bed. 'This mate of yours, was he there?'

'No.'

'So he didn't actually know you were clearing it?'

'Of course he did. We were helping him—'

Andy threw that day's copy of the local newspaper down beside him on the bed. 'While you were in here, it looks like your fellow criminals decided to do the haul without you.'

Sam snatched up the newspaper and read the heading on the page it was turned to.

Robbery of electrical goods.

The sneaky bastards. They had only gone and done the job even though he was in hospital.

'Still, like you said, it had nothing to do with you.' Andy stood up. 'Wouldn't be like you, profiting from anything like that.'

Sam couldn't look at him. His features were stuck in a glare.

Andy made his way to the end of the bed. 'I'm off to catch up with Johnstone now, see what he knows about things. I've missed him while he was inside. 'Course, if you hadn't had your accident, I might never have found out who was cutting back the trees.'

'Wait!' Sam called after him but Andy kept on walking.

When the policeman had gone, Sam got off the bed and headed down the corridor. The television room at the end of the ward was empty, the TV switched off, so he dived in out of the way. He sat down with a thud on a small settee.

That bastard! After all Sam had gone through to clear the land so they could get decent access to the back of the industrial estate, Scott had gone ahead and done the job without him.

Why hadn't Scott been in touch? Was he trying to keep it from him? Sam got out his phone, keeping it on his knee while he punched in Scott's number with his left hand.

'Yeah?' Scott answered.

'I've just seen the paper. You did the job without me?' Sam's tone was incredulous.

''Course we did.'

'So when were you going to tell me about it?'

'You've been under a lot of stress, what with the accident and—'

'Don't fucking patronise me!' Spittle flew from Sam's mouth. 'You'd better save my cut or else.'

'Looks like you've already had one.' Sam heard Scott snigger. 'You were the stupid fuck that nearly cut his hand off.'

'But you're the one who caused the accident!' Sam felt his body tense as he sat forward in the seat.

'You're no good to me now, so you're off the team.'

'What the—' Sam stood up and paced the room. 'You're chucking me because I've had an accident?'

'You won't be able to do much for a while. You can always join us again once you're back to normal.'

'Things will never be normal again because of you. I'm scarred for life!'

'Stop with the whining. It can't be that bad.'

'What would you know?' There was a silence between them. Sam couldn't trust himself to speak or else he would lose it.

'You'll get your cut,' Scott spoke eventually.

'I'd better, because if—'

'Of course, it will only be equivalent to what you did, which wasn't much.'

'What?'

'You only did half the job so you only get half the pay.'

'I nearly lost my fucking hand because of you!' Sam lowered his voice as two nurses walked past the room and glanced in. 'That money is my compensation. I want what's mine.'

The door to the room opened and a woman in pink stripy pyjamas and fluffy white slippers walked in, pushing a drip in front of her. She smiled shyly, then let it drop as she caught his eye.

'I want my fair share,' he repeated.

'You're no use to me as damaged goods.'

'What did you say?' Sam gasped but the phone had gone dead. Glaring at the woman before storming out of the room, he flounced down the corridor and back to his bed. Damaged goods? How dare Scott say that to him? It was all his fault. He'd make him pay.

But in the back of his mind, Sam knew he'd do no such thing. Scott Johnstone was above his league. He'd realised that as soon as he'd hitched up with him after Scott had been released from prison. Maybe this might work out better for him.

He lay down on the bed. 'Fuck!'

'Language, Sam, please!' A nurse turned to him with a sigh.

'Yeah, pipe down,' said the man in the bed opposite. 'My dog makes less noise than you.'

'Piss off,' Sam said.

'Mr Harvey! Show some respect.'

Sam glared at the nurse before turning on his side, his back towards them. He wished he could go home, just walk right on out of there and sort this mess out. He could if he wanted to, discharge himself. But he knew that it would be to his own detriment. He didn't want to be disfigured if another operation could save his finger.

He'd just have to bide his time until he was able again, and think about how to get out of this mess.

Chapter Thirteen

Donna had her head down when Owen walked into Shop&Save, so didn't even notice him coming in. It wasn't until he came to the till that she looked up.

'Hi!' she almost croaked, then coughed to clear her throat.

'Well, hello.' Owen handed her a newspaper and a bar of chocolate. 'Fancy seeing you in here.'

'Fancy.' Donna felt her skin flushing immediately. Christ, what was it with her and this man?

'It's a bit late for a morning paper,' she added. 'It's nearly lunchtime.'

'Precisely why I thought you might like to go and grab a bite to eat?' He placed a few coins in her outstretched hand, lingering to curl her fingers around them. 'If I don't come to you, you'll never find time to meet me. I can have you there and back in an hour, if they can spare you?'

'I … I … well, yes, I suppose they can.' Donna ran a hand through her hair, glad that she always made an effort to look smart, even if she did have to wear a green overall.

'Come on, Donna,' a voice came from behind them. 'Hurry up, won't you? I've got a bet on a horse at twelve and I want to be back at the bookies to watch it.'

'Wait your turn, Bernard.' Donna ran Owen's things through the till. 'It's not often you're kept waiting, is it?'

'I'll be dead at this rate before you're done.'

'That doesn't sound like a bad thing,' Donna muttered under

her breath. Owen was trying to keep his face straight as she shooed him away. 'If I can get off, I'll see you in … thirty minutes?'

'If you can get off?' It was his turn to speak quietly. Owen moved closer so that only she could hear. 'Now, that sounds like something I'm very interested in seeing.'

Understanding his meaning, her skin flushed even more. As Owen pulled back his head and roared with laughter, she noticed black hair curled up over the top of his T-shirt again. She gulped: she shouldn't be having the thoughts that were running through her mind right now.

'Away with you,' she told him.

'I'll be waiting outside.'

He winked at her before leaving, making her blush again. 'Right, then, Bernard,' she turned to him all of a fluster, 'your usual is it?'

'Yes, and about bloody time.'

Donna served him and sent him on his way.

When she'd finished refilling a shelf nearby, Sarah tapped her on the shoulder. 'Who was that I saw you talking to?'

'That was the guy I was telling you about.'

'You mean … *him*?'

'Yes, it was Owen.'

'Ohmigod, he's divine.' Sarah practically squealed. 'Are you sure he's interested in you?'

'Oi, you cheeky cow. Yes, he is.' Donna grinned. 'Actually, I can hardly believe it myself. It's a bit strange, don't you think? Someone like him wanting to go out with someone like me?'

'What on earth do you mean by that?'

'I'm not exactly a catch, am I? Forty-two years old, living in rented accommodation, with nothing to call my own.'

'Aw.' Sarah gave Donna's arm a gentle squeeze. 'You will always have hope, my friend.'

'I will. He's asked me out for lunch!' Donna smiled. 'That's okay, isn't it?'

'I'm sure I can cope without you for an hour or so.'

'I'm only down for a half hour break as I—'

Sarah interrupted her. 'We may be busy and rushed off our feet but if you want an extra thirty minutes, I won't tell anyone you've been gone longer than you should.'

'Oh, thanks!'

'It's only fair. You always help me out whenever we're short-staffed. Now, freshen up in the back room and go and spend some time with your dream man.'

'Before I wake up, you mean.' Donna laughed as she walked off.

After his mum had mentioned that Daniel had been around to see him, Lewis had arranged to meet him for a burger. As it was the school holidays, half of Stockleigh must have been in the takeaway shop they went to. Everywhere he looked there were children. Mothers shouting at them to behave, babies screaming, toddlers making a noise. Lewis could feel it grinding on his nerves already. He tried to shut everything out as he gave his order and waited for it to be prepared.

Daniel had gone to sit down while Lewis stood in the queue for food. A couple of minutes later, he sat across from him and passed him his burger and chips. Despite the surrounding noise, Lewis could still feel the silence between them as they ate.

'Is that good?' he asked Daniel, after he'd eaten a few bites of his nondescript burger.

'Yeah, thanks.'

Lewis laughed. Teenagers, they'd eat anything you gave them.

'Do you want to come for tea later, Dad?'

'Not right now, Dan.'

'Why not?'

'Well, was it your mum's idea?'

Lewis watched as Daniel went the colour of the tomato ketchup bottle on the table.

'You haven't asked her, have you?'

Daniel shook his head. 'But I know she'd like you to.'

'Next time, maybe.'

Daniel wasn't perturbed. 'Why won't you come home?'

'Your mum can't live with me as I am now.'

He picked up a chip and stopped before putting it in his mouth. 'Then why don't you get some help?'

'It's not that easy.'

Daniel wiped his hands of salt and pulled out a few pieces of paper from his holdall. 'I've been looking things up on the Internet. There's an organisation called Combat Stress. They might be able to help.'

Lewis looked at him in surprise as he slid them across the table to him. He didn't know what to say.

'Thanks, I'll check them out later.'

Daniel seemed to be pacified by this and went back to eating his chips for a moment.

Lewis bit into his burger, but put it down again. He'd suddenly lost his appetite. If his son could see he needed help, what message was he giving off to him? And since he'd last met Amy, he'd sunk into a depression again. It seemed like every way he turned, there was no hope.

'Mum misses you,' said Daniel. 'I hear her crying at night sometimes.'

'Mum misses the old me,' Lewis told him.

'You can be like that again.'

'It's not that easy.'

'It is … if you want it to be.'

'Give it a rest, yeah?'

Daniel lowered his eyes, nervously picking at his food.

Lewis cursed inwardly, seeing his son's embarrassment. Struggling hard to keep his temper under control, he reached across and pinched one of Daniel's chips.

'I'll be okay, Dan,' he told him, before popping it into his mouth.

Megan was doing her final check on Sam's ward before leaving for the day. Seeing him sitting on a chair by the side of his bed, she went over to him with a fresh jug of water. She wondered if she dared ask about the visit from the police. She knew she shouldn't pry, but she liked to think that she and Sam had a little bit more rapport between them than when she spoke to other patients. Besides, she wanted to know.

'I'm sure I spotted Keera earlier,' she said, as she popped the jug on top of the bedside cabinet. 'She was in the main corridor. I was going to say hello but she was too far away. Has she been to see you today?'

Sam snorted. 'You really want to know why the police were here earlier, don't you?'

'Not unless you want to tell me.' She kept her back to him, feeling her skin begin to flush at her fib.

'Well, it was nothing to do with me. It's a mate of mine they're after.'

'Oh.' She turned to him with a smile. 'Nothing for you to worry about then.'

'Not yet.'

Megan looked at him, hoping he would elaborate, but he remained quiet.

'My sister doesn't really care,' he said eventually.

'Why?'

'She only visits because Mum gets on to her.'

'So your mum obviously cares?'

'What's your point?'

'I see a lot of people in these wards.' Megan began to wipe around the surface, picking up the two get-well cards and placing them back again. 'Some patients don't have anyone to visit them. So despite your moaning because you feel sorry for yourself, you should really be grateful that they come to see you at all.'

'You need to mind your own business.'

'And you need to smile once in a while. You look lovely when you do.' Megan bit her bottom lip as she realised she had spoken her thoughts aloud.

'Ha, I'm sexy and I know it.' Sam treated her to a rare smile. Up close, he had soft features beneath the hard exterior he portrayed, and gorgeous eyes that lit up his face.

'At least I made you smile,' she replied.

'Are you paid to talk shite?'

Megan's shoulders dropped. 'Of course not – I just like to make people feel happy.'

'Why? Because it brightens up your day?'

'Actually, I'd like to think that I brighten up someone else's day when I have a chat with them.'

'How could I feel bright with this?' Sam held up his hand and then flopped it down in despair. 'No girl's going to look at me when they see this, are they?'

Megan bristled. She wanted to say how shallow she thought he was. Did he think people only saw his hand?

'It won't be like that forever,' she said instead.

'You want to bet? I know it won't ever be right again.'

'But it will get better and stronger.'

'I'll still be scarred for life.' He tried to fold his arms and then, when the splint on his hand got in the way, he pouted.

'Will you ever stop feeling sorry for yourself?' Megan sighed. 'I've a good mind to get you out of your bed and wheel you along to the next ward. They're dying in that one. Fancy being in there?'

'Do you talk to every patient as much as you do to me?'

'That depends. I can't help being a chatterbox but I know some people don't like it. I learn who I can chat to and who I can't.'

'And I fit in to the category of people that you can chat to?' Sam scoffed.

'I like to think so.'

'You're so irritating.'

Megan sensed his anger escalating. 'I'm sorry, I was only—'

'You're a pushy cow, I'll give you that.' He lifted his hand. 'Wouldn't this bother you if you'd been left with this scar?'

'I think scars define us.' Megan continued mopping.

'What would you know?'

'What would I know indeed,' she muttered, moving away. Despite her efforts to cheer him up, Sam was struggling to cope, and it was making him miserable. It was entirely natural for him to feel that way. This was all new to him. He hadn't had to live with it all his life.

But he was wrong about one thing. Scars did define people. She knew only too well.

Chapter Fourteen

It was nearing lunchtime as Megan arrived back home. It had just been the two of them for the past seven years, since her dad had left them. In her early thirties, Patricia Cooper had found out she had severe osteoporosis in her knees and back and would have trouble walking for the rest of her life. Her father had taken care of Patricia for a while but then it had become too much. He'd obviously wanted a life of his own, without an imperfect daughter and a wife.

Megan had never forgiven him for that. She often wondered if he'd deliberately walked out on her too. She had heard that her father was living with another woman now and they had a young daughter. She hoped he looked after her better than he had his responsibilities with Megan and her mum – he'd shirked every one of them as soon as the going got tough.

'Hi, Mum, it's only me,' she shouted through as she pulled out her key and closed the door behind her. Throwing her bag over the bannister, she went through to the living room. Although it hadn't been decorated with fresh wallpaper in a long while, Megan had gone over the walls every year with cream paint, keeping it neutral and brightening up the room with artificial flowers and coloured candles.

'Hello, love,' Patricia smiled up at her from the armchair in the bay window. She had the same bright eyes as her daughter, almost the same hair colouring –minus the grey that was creeping in – although hers was cut short so as not to be too much bother.

She hunched forward and tried to push herself up. Having put on a lot of weight due to her immobility, Patricia struggled to stand by herself.

Megan took hold of her hands and gently pulled her up. 'Do you want to walk around a bit?' she asked.

'No, I'll just stand.' Patricia sighed. 'It's good to be out of that chair.'

'How was your morning?'

'Not too bad, love. Those tablets that Doctor Sanders gave me last week seem to be easing the pain a little.'

'That's good to hear. Do you need anything? It's so hot that I'm going to take another shower before I go to Poplar Court. Would you like help to get changed?'

'No, thanks. I'm fine.' She pointed to an empty plate. 'Those ham sandwiches were lovely, thanks.'

Megan scooped up the plate and two dirty mugs that were by the side of it. They'd got their routine down to a T now. If Patricia wasn't feeling able to move around, Megan would make sandwiches, fill the kettle and leave mugs and a beaker of fresh milk on a small table by the side of the chair. Patricia would be able to make herself a couple of drinks and eat until Megan could next get her anything she needed. She wasn't yet unable to make the downstairs loo but she did struggle with the stairs. The less she moved, the less pain she would be in.

Last year, they'd had help to move her bed downstairs into the room at the back of the house. Patricia's old bedroom upstairs had been turned into a sitting room for Megan. The arrangement suited them both. Patricia could stay fairly independent and so could Megan.

Once she'd washed the few dishes and made her mum a fresh cup of tea, Megan went upstairs to her bedroom and began to remove her clothes. She flicked the venetian blind closed a little to take the glare of the midday sun away. Her uniform was sticking to her, and her make-up sliding off in this heat wasn't good.

As she cleansed her face before heading to the bathroom, she thought about Sam. Megan enjoyed her job at the hospital because she didn't really get to see many people on a regular basis, so she could stay fairly anonymous. Yet there were often patients that stood out for different reasons, people that she'd seen and spoken to. This week, from the moment she had seen Sam, she hadn't been able to get him out of her mind. He was the best looking man she'd seen in a long time, which was hard to take as he wouldn't look twice at her if he saw her bare face.

She glanced in the mirror, one lone tear falling over the port wine birthmark that had been revealed after she had removed her make-up. It started at the side of her face, just below her hairline, travelled across most of her cheek, part of her nose and eyelid and finished in her jawline. Sometimes Megan couldn't even bear to look at herself when she wasn't wearing any concealer and foundation. She wished she was brave enough to accept it as part of her but after nineteen years of putting up with her disfigurement, even though she hid it as best as she could, she'd had enough.

Megan hated being defined by a stain on her face, and envied the people who made YouTube videos about how they coped with their birthmarks – all the staring and the laughing and the gawping. People didn't realise how hurtful it was. How hard it was to be different.

For the past eighteen months, she had been saving every penny she could towards treatment. Their family GP, Doctor Sanders, had told her on numerous occasions that laser surgery wouldn't make a difference, that her scarring was too deep and that it might worsen the condition; that it would raise the surface of the skin so that it would look like acne underneath her make-up. But Megan didn't believe him – wouldn't believe him. There were new things coming on the market all the time.

If she couldn't have the surgery, she hoped one day to be able to wake up with someone who would roll over and cuddle up to her, not at all bothered by the discolouration of her skin. Seeing beyond it. Seeing past the birthmark and seeing only her.

In all honesty, she didn't think this would happen, but that's why the surgery was so important to her, despite her knowing it was probably not going to be successful. If she did have the surgery, Megan would be the same as everyone else. Until she was rid of the birthmark, she wasn't free to live her life as she wanted.

So even if Sam did fancy her, she was off-limits to him. She was off-limits to anyone until she'd had her surgery. Then she would give her heart gladly – no matter how much she was drawn to Sam Harvey and his smile.

Donna shielded her eyes from the sun as she walked across to Owen's car. She slid into the leather seat of his BMW and buckled up the seatbelt.

'I'm not sure there is anywhere you can take me for lunch around here,' she said, 'unless you want to suffer from food poisoning.'

'Don't worry about that.' He smiled. 'I have the perfect place.'

A few minutes later, they pulled up in a nearby country park, Raven's Mount. It was one of the nicer places in Stockleigh, but somewhere she hardly ever came to, despite it being practically on her doorstep. Twenty-five acres of fields and hills, a haven for dog walkers and hikers.

Donna turned to Owen with a puzzled expression.

'Come on,' he said. 'I'll show you my favourite spot.'

'Sounds good to me.' Donna got out of the car and was pleasantly surprised to see Owen grab a large blue cooler box from out of the boot.

'A picnic!' she grinned with delight as he handed her a tartan blanket.

'With the weather as it is, why not?'

He took her hand and they walked a few minutes to a spot under the shade of a large oak tree. It was far enough away from a group of children playing football, and the other couples looking for privacy, just like they were.

Donna shook out the blanket and sat down on it. Owen sat beside her and took out item after item from the box. Then he produced a bottle of wine.

'I can't have much because I'm driving and you can't have much because you have to go back to work,' he said. 'But we can have a glass each and you can take the rest home with you.'

Donna grinned. It seemed like he'd thought of everything. She looked inside the box and spotted a tub of coleslaw.

'You won't find any,' he said, removing the wrapping from a sandwich and popping it onto a paper plate.

'Sorry?'

'Cutlery. I didn't bring any.'

'Oh.'

'I didn't forget it. I just thought it wasn't necessary. We can use our hands to feed each other.'

Donna couldn't help but laugh. It all sounded a bit *50 Shades of Grey* to her but still, what would she know? She couldn't remember ever being taken out for a picnic.

She relaxed back on her arms, legs out in front of her, and looked across at Owen. 'Thanks, this is lovely.'

'As are you,' he whispered, passing her a glass.

She held it up and studied his face as he filled the glass with wine, wondering again why it was that Owen was with her. What did he see in her to treat her to a picnic in the middle of her working day?

He smiled at her again and, shutting the thoughts from her mind, she decided that she wasn't really bothered in the whys any more. All she was concerned about was the here and now.

'Do you have the day off work?' she asked.

Owen wiped his mouth with a napkin before speaking. 'I run my own company. I'm into IT and all that dull geeky stuff that is boring to talk about. So I kindof snuck off early.'

'Do you work from home or do you have an office?'

'I work from home.' He stretched out a hand. 'This could be my office if I had brought along my laptop.' He patted his trouser pocket. 'I have my phone, so all I need is on there too. Very portable. But switched off for the duration of our picnic.'

'I wish I could do something exciting.' Donna sighed, thinking of how she used to dream of doing more with her life when she was younger, before Joe left and the children were small. 'All I do is go to work and visit my mum. How boring am I?'

'And Sam – is he your only child?'

'No, I have a daughter too; Keera. She's nineteen and, thankfully, looks after herself.'

'Is she as beautiful as her mum?'

Donna felt her skin redden. He couldn't mean it, could he? He was being coy, surely.

'She's a lovely girl,' she said, eventually. 'She's a hard worker, unlike her brother.'

'So you get on quite well?'

Donna paused. 'Well, we're not the kind of mother and daughter who go shopping together, or even spend a night in watching a movie, but, yes, I suppose we do.'

'But you worry about her?'

Donna wondered whether to confide in Owen about what had happened to Keera and her friend, Marley while they'd been in Ibiza, but decided against it. 'I worry about them both. And my mum – family is very important to me.'

'You seem to have so much to do.'

'I don't mind.'

'You should certainly take more time for yourself.'

Donna dipped her eyes momentarily but met his stare eventually. 'How about you? Do you have family?'

Owen shook his head. 'No, my parents died years ago, and I was an only child.'

'Have you ever been married?'

'No.'

'I'm divorced.' Donna posed the question to get him to open up about his past, but Owen didn't respond. They sat in silence as he took out two cream cakes from their packaging.

He handed one to her. 'It's a bit warm for this too, but we can share it.' He bit into the other one, the cream spurting out all over the plate.

He looked at Donna with such innocence that she laughed. Another scene reminiscent of *50 Shades of Grey* buffered into her mind.

All too soon, it was time to head back to work. With a sigh, he dropped her off outside Shop&Save.

'I'm so glad we finally got to spend some time together,' he said, kissing her lightly on the cheek.

Donna could only nod her agreement. She was still sinking deep into his eyes, wanting to pull him into her arms. Should she lean forward and kiss him back, so she could feel his lips on hers?

'I know what you're thinking,' he said. 'Again.'

Donna raised her eyebrows.

'Proper kisses – full, passionate, breathless kisses – are saved for first dates.'

'But we've already had a first date, technically speaking.'

Owen smiled. 'Technically speaking, we're on our second date right now.'

Donna nodded. As he leaned closer, she parted her lips in eagerness. But he stopped an inch away from her.

'Hold that thought until next time,' he teased and planted a kiss on her nose.

As Donna got out of the car, she couldn't help but smile. She tried not to turn back as she moved away, knowing that Owen would be watching her as she hadn't heard his car move away.

After a moment, a horn papped and she did turn. Owen waved before driving off.

Donna waved back, staying still until the vehicle was out of sight before racing across the square toward the shop. Wait until she told Sarah!

Wow, what was happening to her? Her heart seemed to be beating out of her chest.

She didn't know where Owen had been all her life but she was so happy that he was here now.

Chapter Fifteen

Donna rushed back into Shop&Save in the nick of time, grabbing her overall and putting it on quickly.

'So, how was it?' Sarah asked. Before Donna could speak, she held up her hand. 'You don't need to tell me how much you enjoyed it. It's written all over your face.' As there were no customers in the shop, she beckoned her closer. 'You didn't have sex in the car, did you?'

'No, we did not!" Donna laughed.

'Where did he take you?'

'We had a picnic at Raven's Mount.'

'No! I haven't been there in years. Was it nice?'

'Yes, it was so romantic.' Donna's skin flushed yet again and she held a hand to her chest. 'Oh, Sarah, he's even more gorgeous up close and personal. There was definitely some sexual tension rising.'

'Was that the only thing rising?' Sarah giggled.

'I couldn't see!'

'What did you talk about?'

'Oh, you know, this and that.' Donna pulled on her overall again.

'This and that?' Sarah looked disappointed. 'Please tell me you arranged to see him again?'

'Well, yes, but it will depend on our Sam and when he is coming out of hospital as—'

'You're putting your family first again!' Sarah shook her head in exasperation.

'I'm not. He's picking me up tomorrow night - as long as nothing comes up in the meantime.'

Sarah raised an eyebrow. 'If nothing comes up? That's what you're hoping for, isn't it?'

Donna slapped her bottom as she moved past her.

Sarah turned back with a look of regret on her face. 'It's my day off tomorrow so I won't get to know any gory details. That was bad planning. I'll text you.' She winked. 'Seriously, I hope you have a lovely time with him. He seems keen.'

'He does, doesn't he?' Donna nodded fervently, pushing any doubts to the back of her mind. 'Makes a change after being on my own for so long.'

'You've moved on a lot since that idiot you were with last, though. What was his name, again?'

'Daryl.' Donna giggled. 'How the hell I put up with him for three years was beyond me.'

'You're too nice, that's your problem. People walk all over you.'

'They do not!'

'I meant it in a nice way. Your heart is in the right place, and he took advantage of your good nature.'

'I suppose.' Thinking about her relationship with Daryl, Donna realised now that he'd merely been after a roof over his head and someone to look after him, rather than a partner. The sex had been practically non-existent after the first year, which had surprised her, yet still she stayed with him until he left her.

When she'd been with Joe, their relationship had been friendly too, even if the love had gone. Because of this, she often wondered how he was doing. She hadn't seen him in years, even though he had been a big part of her life, especially when Keera was younger.

They'd grown apart but maybe they could have stuck together if he hadn't had an affair. Still, all she wanted to look forward to now was Owen. Having a bit of fun with him was definitely what the doctor ordered.

'It's just a date,' she told Sarah.

'A date that could lead to lots of things.'

'Oh, I'd settle for a good shag, if I'm honest. It's ages since I've had a fella between my legs.'

'When you've finished chatting ladies,' a voice came from the side of them. For the umpteenth time that day, Donna blushed – until she realised it was Mr Turner, eighty-one years old with a hearing aid that never worked properly.

'Yes, Sidney, what can I do for you?'

After her shift at Shop&Save finished that afternoon, Donna decided to visit her mum before going to the hospital. Hopefully Sam would be discharged soon, which at least meant she wouldn't have to trek as far to see him. The flat he was sharing with his friend was only two streets away from Trudy Place, so it would make things a little easier for her.

She'd said she would look after him if he wanted to move back home for a while but he'd flatly refused. Sarah had ticked her off for offering, saying he could cope on his own, but despite his age, Donna needed to know he would be okay. And it wasn't so much the physical scars she was concerned about, as the mental ones.

As she sat in traffic, she wished that she could tell her mum about the picnic with Owen. It would be lovely to see Mary's face light up but the mum she used to have was gone. Half the time she didn't even recognise Donna, let alone was able to understand something like this.

She wished her mum was her old self. If things were different, Donna knew she'd be happy for her, although she wouldn't have told her Owen's true age unless things became more serious later.

At Poplar Court, she spotted Mary sitting in the window of her flat and waved but there was no response.

'Hi, Mum,' she greeted as she let herself into the small hall. In the living room, she smiled at Mary and perched on the arm of the chair next to her. 'It's a lovely day out there.' She took her hand. 'It's still so hot. Would you like to go outside for a while?'

'Ow! Stop!' Mary pulled her arm away quickly.

Donna frowned. 'What's wrong, Mum?'

Mary rubbed at her arm. She didn't speak but her head shook from side to side.

'Let me look.' Carefully, Donna pulled up the sleeve of Mary's cardigan. There was a bruise there, the size of a small apple, dark and nasty. Donna sighed.

'Oh dear, Mum, what have you been up to now?' Before she could continue, a knock came at the front door. At least now she might be able to shed some light on what had happened. 'That will be Megan, I expect.'

'No!' Mary seemed aghast, her head shaking again. 'I don't like her.'

'Don't be daft, Mum. Everyone likes Megan.'

'Hi, Donna,' Megan smiled as she came in to them. 'Morning, Mary. How are you today?'

'Hello, love.' Mary smiled up at Megan.

Donna sighed. This was the woman Mary had just said that she didn't want to see!

'Megan, do you know how Mum got this bruise on her arm?' she asked.

Megan came over to look. 'Oh, I hadn't noticed, to be honest. It looks recent though, sore too.'

'It's one hell of a size.'

'They do bruise easily at that age.'

'Yes, I know, but–'

'Would you like me to put something on it?'

'I can do it.' Donna glared at Megan. 'I am capable of doing things, you know.'

'Oh, of course. I didn't mean …' Megan blushed. 'I'll keep an eye on it for you, if you like? Though, if it gets too painful, we might have to take her to A&E to have an X-ray.' She looked up at Donna. 'I mean, you'd take her.'

'Yes, I can do that at the same time that I go and visit Sam. Kill two birds with one stone.' Donna looked away. Christ, why did Megan have to make her feel so guilty?

Megan wasn't perturbed. 'Let me keep an eye on her today, and if she gets worse by this evening, I'll get someone to give you a call.'

'Thanks,' Donna replied, hating how inadequate she felt. 'I'm sorry to snap. It's nothing personal. I just— I just don't have time to do everything.'

As Megan went through into the tiny kitchen, Donna sat with Mary for a few minutes before getting up again. 'I have to go now, Mum.' She bent down to kiss Mary on her forehead.

Mary grabbed her hand, her grip stronger than she looked

capable of. 'Don't leave me here,' she whispered. 'They're mean to me. They hit me and make me eat my dinner until I'm sick. They make me lie in the bed so long that I have to wee myself.'

'Don't be silly, Mum.' Donna feigned a smile.

Mary began to cry. 'Please take me with you. I hate it here. I hate it, hate it!'

As she left Poplar Court minutes later after calming Mary down a little, Donna didn't know what to think. The outburst played on her mind. No one really knew when to believe what a dementia sufferer was saying, whether it was true or not. How would they know? Often Mary would accuse Donna of abandoning her. It wasn't fair, Donna did her best.

But she would keep an eye on Mary's bruises for a while, check each time she visited to see if there were any more.

Chapter Sixteen

Lewis was at the Job Centre in Stockleigh. Thursdays were his signing on days. He'd thought that after coming out of the army he'd never have to go on the dole; that he'd be able to get fixed up with a permanent position straight away. Everyone would need a strapping fella like him, his dad had said. Who wouldn't want to employ someone who was a team player, organised and reliable?

But being ex-army had worked far more against him than to his advantage. At first Lewis had volunteered at the army recruitment centre after coming home but, after a few weeks there, he had felt too claustrophobic to be in an office. He knew he'd never be able to work indoors, in a factory or doing long shifts in a shop.

So far, he'd spent six months on a nightshift doing security at B&Q, until that contract had ended. Just recently he'd been given the boot as a doorman at Sparks nightclub because he'd lashed out at someone having a go at him. As a bouncer, he was supposed to keep his cool, to defuse heated situations, but this one fella had riled him up a little too much. So now he was back on the dole, missing the banter and routine of a full-time job.

Signing on was even more of a degradation. Even though the building itself was a fairly new-build, it still had an oppressive atmosphere.

Once he'd been to the reception, he was shown to the first floor. The room was open plan, with coloured chairs in different areas in the middle and desks around its edge. There were people everywhere, of all ages; some even had children in pushchairs. Looking around, Lewis saw people he knew would never hold down a job, as well as others he thought didn't want to work.

He sat down on the row of green chairs that he had been directed to, resting a clipboard on his knees as he began to complete another round of paperwork. His head was pounding after drinking too much again the night before. The weather was hot and clammy, making the drink go down easier when it was outside in a beer garden – or what was called a garden at least. Technically it was a just a yard leading on to an alleyway.

He'd called Amy yesterday evening, on his way home from the pub, but she hadn't wanted to talk to him. He'd asked to speak to Daniel but she said he had gone to bed. He'd tried to keep her on the line but she'd hung up after a few seconds.

He wiped perspiration from his brow, pools already forming on his T-shirt. He wore long shorts with his desert boots, supposing he looked quite trendy, and felt smug knowing they were the real thing, not some knock-off crap from the local market. These boots had seen action – too much, really.

He wondered whether it was worth going to see Amy after he'd signed on. Face to face, she wouldn't be able to turn him away, unless she slammed the door when she saw who was on the step. He smiled, knowing full well that she wouldn't do that. He was the angry one, not Amy.

Amy was his saving grace. They'd first met at school. Lewis had been fifteen and Amy fourteen. They'd known each other for years, having attended the same schools, but all at once they noticed each other. It was at an end-of-year disco as they messed around to the sounds of 'Hit Me Baby One More Time' and 'Livin' La Vida Loca'.

He'd been with a group of his mates, caught Amy's eye with his stupid dancing and they'd started to laugh. The music slowed down as Lonestar's 'Amazed' was played. They were still dancing around each other and it took a step to pull her into his arms. He could remember their first kiss as if it were yesterday, the taste of strawberry lip-gloss lingering on his lips afterwards.

Theirs was a childhood romance that had blossomed, as things do at that age. They'd lost their virginity to each other on a cold, wet afternoon when his parents had been at work and they should have been at school. Amy knew from the beginning that he wanted to go in the army and would be joining up as soon as he could. He'd been in the local cadets as soon as he'd been old enough to join. Despite knowing he wouldn't be around all the time, it hadn't put Amy off.

Just after he'd started his training, she'd found out she was pregnant. It wasn't an ideal time, as they were both such a young age as well as the fact that Amy would have to cope on her own, but they'd decided to go ahead with the pregnancy and Daniel had come along. Amy had done a great job of bringing him up almost single-handedly. Lewis was so proud of his son, and of Amy too.

When he'd come back home for good, he'd thought everything would settle and routine would take over, but it was the routine that he missed from the army that made him so antsy.

What had he got to show for all those years in service now? Would he have been better being here with Amy and Daniel and working on their lives together rather than being away for long stretches?

'Lewis Prophett!'

Lewis got up, keeping hold of his clipboard, and went over to a desk. A bored looking man, who looked like he should have retired by now, pointed to a seat in front of him. He sat down on the hard plastic chair.

'Name,' the man said.

'You've just shouted it out,' said Lewis.

'Address,' the man sighed, as if Lewis was an intrusion into his day.

Lewis folded his arms. Well, at least he didn't have to be stuck in an office with this jerk all the time.

Keera thought she was lucky to be working at The Candy Club. It wasn't like some of the massage parlours around the city. She was paid per client, so it was worth her while to get repeat business from likeable clients such as Derek. All the men were vetted, albeit as discreetly as possible. And after their recent scare in Ibiza, Keera was glad of this.

She could always tell what kind of a day men had had by their stance as they came into the room. Even if they came in with a mopey face, she tried to make them leave with a smile. She was here to do a job, provide a service, so she might as well enjoy it. And as she'd got to know which clients were talkative and which were non-responsive, she'd learned to play music when the silence became too intense. Keera had chosen a tune for each client and played it as they came into the room. Just her silly little game, but it didn't do any harm to anyone.

Around half past ten that evening, she found herself with a bit of time for a break. Reaching for her mug, she decided to grab a coffee and a chat with Ramona.

Keera smiled to herself as she went down the stairs. She couldn't stop thinking about Derek who had been in again earlier, and what it would be like if they fancied each other. She had often fantasised about having a sugar daddy – someone giving her money when she wanted it, not having to go out and earn a living, although she reckoned it would be hard to live with the constant criticism. Everyone would talk about them if it were to happen because of the age gap.

Derek also brought to mind her father, Joe. She often wished he'd been around more as she was growing up. She knew her mum and dad hadn't been happy but there was never any violence, nor many arguments she could remember. They just seemed to drift apart.

She could hardly recall doing anything as a family when she was younger. It had always been Mum who had taken them out. Dad apparently had been working – she obviously knew better now – and it saddened her that he'd gone off and created a new family, as if she and Sam weren't good enough.

As she was about to go down into the reception, she heard loud voices. A male voice she didn't recognise shouted out.

'Get me my fucking money.'

'I don't have it.'

It was Ramona. Keera could hear the tremble in her tone. Then she heard what sounded like a slap. Without hesitation, she put down the mug and barged into the room.

A man had gone behind the reception counter and pushed Ramona up against the back wall. One of his hands was around her throat.

Keera ran at him and jumped on his back. 'Leave her a-fucking-lone!' she yelled. In her haste, she lost a shoe as she clung to him.

'Get off me, you mad bitch,' the man cried.

As he dropped his hands to try and shake off Keera, Ramona grabbed a wooden bat from underneath the desk.

'Get out,' she told him, 'or I swear on my life, Steve, I will call the police.'

'You know him?' said Keera.

No one answered her.

Steve sneered. 'I'll go when I get my fucking money.'

Ramona fumbled in the till and passed him a few notes. 'Take it. It's all I have.'

Keera shook her head. 'Ramona, you can't—'

Steve snatched the money. 'Not enough here.' He glared at Ramona.

'That's all you're getting,' said Keera. 'Now piss off.'

Steve's eyes fell upon Keera and he looked her up and down with interest. She stared back at him before purposely doing the same. He had long hair, straggly and thinning on top, beady eyes and a large nose. His dirty denim jacket looked like it was from a charity shop, two sizes too small, with rips that hadn't been made purely for fashion. His jeans were skinny, leading down to cowboy boots that made the look a bit trendier, although that probably wasn't his notion.

'You need to mind your own fucking business.' He pointed at her. 'Don't push your luck by doing that again.'

'Then don't come threatening Ramona.' Keera wasn't intimidated by his stare. 'I know people too.'

Steve laughed. 'I know who you are, Keera Harvey.'

Keera swallowed. If he knew her name, then he must know her brother. If he said anything to Sam, she would be in big trouble.

'Oh!' Steve grinned as he clocked her expression. 'He doesn't know you work here, does he?'

'He doesn't need to know,' said Ramona. 'This is between you and me.'

'How is he, by the way?' Steve's grin was nasty. 'I hear he's had an accident.'

'He's fine,' said Keera.

'Maybe so, but I don't think he'll be fit to pull his weight for a while, not with an injured hand.'

'He's—'

'I'll be back by the end of next week,' Steve interrupted. 'I want the rest of my money by then.' He turned to face them again just as he got to the front door. 'And if you don't have the money, then I'm going to ask her darling brother for it.' He pointed at Keera.

As soon as he was gone, both women's shoulders dropped with relief.

'Ramona, are you okay?' Estelle came barging into the room. 'I was erm, a bit tied up so couldn't get down here straight away.'

'I'm fine.' Ramona waved a hand. 'It's nothing to worry about.'

'You sure?'

Ramona nodded.

Once Estelle had gone back to her client, Keera turned to Ramona. 'You're not okay, are you?'

Ramona shook her head as she rubbed at her neck, red blotches already appearing under her skin.

'Who the hell was he?'

'He's my brother.' Ramona dropped her eyes with embarrassment.

'Oh!' Keera stood wide-eyed. 'I thought he was after protection money or something.'

Ramona shook her head. 'The Mitchell estate might be a shit place to live, but it isn't the East End of London.'

'What did he want money for?'

'I owe him five hundred quid. I should have given it to him ages ago. I suppose he thinks he's waited long enough. But thanks for helping out.'

'I could lend you some, if it gets him off your back?'

'No, thanks. I won't let him have all his own way. He comes round here too often, trying to push his luck. I know when I'm not here some of the girls can't cope with him and give in to his demands. I must owe them a fortune, too.'

'The cheeky bastard!'

Keera sat with Ramona for a while until she felt it was safe enough to return to her room. But it left her with a bitter taste in her mouth and she cancelled her last client to sit with Ramona until the end of the evening. She wasn't certain that Steve wouldn't come back.

If things were different, she would have called on Sam. He would help to sort Steve out. But Sam was still in hospital and his fighting days were clearly over for some time. More to the point, no one knew she was working here – and she didn't want anyone to find out, let alone her family. What would Sam think? Worse, what would her mum think?

So if Steve Wilson needed money, then she might have to get it for him. She couldn't risk him opening his mouth to Sam.

Chapter Seventeen

At work on Friday morning, Donna spent a depressing hour stacking the shelves with baked beans and packets of noodles, all the time worrying about her mum and Sam. This had been one of the longest weeks of her entire life. Sam would be out of hospital soon, and how would he cope with one working hand? He wouldn't be able to do anything but the basic of tasks. She'd have to do his washing and ironing, as well as help to keep his flat in good order. After visiting Sam's place and finding it a tip, Donna knew she couldn't trust his flatmate Brendan. Honestly, she could clean and tidy for hours and it would hardly make a dent.

Her phone beeped the arrival of a text message. It was from Owen.

I can't stop thinking about you. Can't wait to see you when you get chance.

Thank goodness she had their date to look forward to. She replied quickly.

Me too.

Really?

Really.

Then come outside the back way.

Donna nearly dropped her phone. Owen was here? How the hell had he got into the yard behind the shop? He must have jumped over the wall.

'I'm just going out the back for a break,' she shouted through to Sarah, trying to look nonchalant even though she could feel her skin burning. 'Darren can man the tills if they get busy. It's stifling in here.'

Donna opened the back door, squinting as her eyes grew accustomed to the light. Once outside, she breathed in the hot air. The weather was still treating them to bright blue skies, bringing thoughts of cocktails and barbecues at the weekend. Knowing her luck lately, it would invite fights from the neighbours, drunken layabouts, loud music or a thunderstorm.

Owen stepped from behind an industrial bin.

'Oh, very romantic,' Donna grinned, her stomach flipping over at the sight of him in cut-off denims and a pale blue polo T-shirt. Sunglasses hid his eyes but he removed them as she drew closer, throwing her a smouldering glance before pushing them into the neck of his shirt. He stepped forward, reached for her hand and took her round the corner of the building out of sight of anyone.

'I'm sorry, but I can't wait any longer.'

He bent his head down and kissed her, his touch so light and feathery that it felt as if it were a breeze across her lips. She gazed into his eyes, saw the lust reflected in her own as he moved in to kiss her again. This time he stayed where he was, moulding his body to hers.

Donna held him tightly, hand at the back of his neck. Desire rushed through her as he pressed her into the wall hard enough for her to feel every inch of his body next to hers, and not be mistaken by how much she was turning him on.

A moan escaped her. In seconds, the man had woken up feelings she had put to bed a long time ago.

'Well, that was worth waiting for,' he grinned when they finally broke for air.

Donna couldn't speak. Already, she missed the heat of his body, the strong sense of it being pressed against hers.

'Say something?' said Owen.

'I don't want to,' she replied.

He frowned but as she brought his face towards hers again, she knew he understood her meaning. She kissed him this time, her tongue probing, darting, but tentative. When it touched the tip of his, she moaned again. If this was what he did to her with his kiss, she could only imagine what else he would do to her, once they had the chance.

They broke free again, each breathless, just staring at the other. Owen remained close to her, as if he didn't want to move.

'I know it isn't the most romantic of places,' he nodded in the direction of the yard, 'but I was driving past and I – well, I had to see you. I haven't been able to stop thinking of you since we met. You do something to me that I've never experienced before.'

'You're full of shit, do you know that?' Donna regretted the words as soon as they had left her mouth. She shouldn't think every man was out to hurt her. It was just scars from the past coming back to haunt her.

'Oh, God, I'm sorry,' she added as Owen looked at her, his eyes questioning. 'I didn't mean to say that out loud,' she tried to explain. 'Let's just say that life hasn't exactly been good to me in the love stakes, and sometimes I'm scared to let go in case I get hurt.'

'I won't hurt you, Donna,' he whispered, moving his lips close again. He cupped her face in his hands, his eyes never leaving hers for a second. 'I need you to believe that.'

She wanted to. Oh, how she wanted to.

'You do believe me?' he asked.

She lowered her gaze from his. 'I have to get back to work. If not, Sarah will come looking for me soon.'

Owen nodded and dropped his hands. 'See you later,' he grinned.

She smiled before walking away. But then his hand grabbed her and she was in his arms again. And suddenly she was falling under his spell. The smell, the taste, the sex of him – everything was pulling her nearer. She didn't want the moment to end. Every inch of her body was on fire, expecting more than he could give, wondering how it would feel to receive it all.

They broke free again, with difficulty. Embarrassed laughter followed.

'Go,' Owen said, and patted her bottom before pushing her away.

Donna almost floated back into the shop. She waved a hand in front of her face to try and cool her down. That man certainly knew how to stoke her fire. One minute he was wooing her with a picnic: the next he was treating her to a stolen moment of passion. She couldn't wait to see him again.

She was wondering where they would go when she joined Sarah behind the counter.

'It's still hot out there, I see?' asked Sarah.

'Hmm?'

'Your skin is flushed already. You need to put some lotion on if you sit outside for too long.'

Donna put a hand to her cheek and nodded. Let Sarah think it was the sun that had caused her skin to redden. She didn't want to say anything about Owen. It was her special moment, and she didn't want to spoil it by talking about it.

She felt she was on the cusp of possibilities, of hope, of love and laughter and shared dreams and future plans and wishes. And she didn't want the feeling to disappear.

It was so exciting to have a little light in her life at last.

Chapter Eighteen

Josie had been surprised to get a call on her mobile from a tenant in Russell Place. Even though she still had a few weeks left at The Workshop until she returned to the estate full-time, she'd rung the individual and reassured the irate woman that she would investigate the matter further.

It was another complaint about Lewis Prophett. Lewis and his wife, Amy, had been tenants since they'd moved into one of the estate's rented properties just after their son, Daniel, had been born. Despite her youth and the hardships of living alone with a baby when Lewis was overseas, Amy had been a model tenant. Josie heard lots of negative things about young mums with babies but Amy did everything right. The house was always tidy, the baby had been immaculate and Josie was pleased that she hadn't gone the same way as some of the mums on the estate.

While Lewis had been in the army, there hadn't been any complaints relating to the property. So it had concerned Josie when she'd started hearing about Lewis causing problems these past few months. It seemed that Amy didn't know how to handle him and his moods. It appeared that no one did.

She knocked on the door. Amy Prophett opened it with a look of resignation, her shoulders drooping. She was a small woman in contrast to Lewis's tall stature, and thin where Lewis was bulky. Her blonde hair was tied back revealing a clean, make-up free face. Her eyes didn't smile, even though her lips did.

She let Josie into the property.

'Who's complained this time?' Amy asked as Josie followed her through to the kitchen. 'Honestly, I wish people would think before they ring you. I could tell you lots about the residents in this street, but I don't. I keep myself to myself.'

'Oh, take no notice of anyone who complains,' said Josie. 'I couldn't give a tuppence unless there was a riot or he'd damaged our property. I just wanted to see if you're okay. I know Lewis has been having trouble lately, but how are you?'

'Me?' Amy raised her eyebrows. 'You're the first person who's asked that in a long time! Everyone always wants to know how Lewis is.'

'I can imagine, but it must take its toll on you and Daniel?'

Josie saw Amy bristle at the mention of their son's name.

'We get by. Dan's doing well now,' Amy told her. 'He's picked up at school again.'

'Not asking to join the army now?'

Amy shook her head. 'I think he's come to his senses after seeing what it's done to his dad.'

'Want to talk about it?'

Amy pointed to a chair and they both sat down at the table. 'Lewis came over yesterday after he'd been to the job centre. He was distraught that he couldn't find a job, felt like he was going to be on the scrapheap forever. I tried to tell him that he'd get fixed up soon, but he's got it into his head that if he finds his feet again and starts to settle into a routine, he could come back here and we could start over.'

'And that's not an option anymore?' Josie probed.

Amy shook her head. 'Not unless he gets help. I can't see what we had working again if he doesn't. I know it would take us time to readjust after being apart for so long, but it isn't just that. I could cope with us pussyfooting around each other if he hadn't been so angry all the time. I only had to put a cup down in the wrong place and he'd start shouting at me.'

'He took his frustration out on you?'

'Yes, and it was hard to live with. I took it for a while but then, when it started to affect my sleep and I was constantly in a state of worry, especially when he began drinking heavily, it started to feel like a war zone right here in our home. It wasn't good for Daniel to see either. I was worried about him, too.'

Josie could see guilt in Amy's eyes as she glanced her way before continuing.

'In the end, I used to sigh with relief when he left the house, but dread the sound of his key in the door when he came back. And Lewis kept telling Dan to be quiet. He's just a boy – they make noise – but Lewis was always jumpy every time he heard a bang. Dan stopped bringing his friends around.' Her smile was faint. 'It had always been open house. I miss having lots of kids around here. Some have started to come again since Lewis left, but now they're older, they want to be out, don't they?'

Josie nodded. 'So when he came to visit?'

'He wanted to prove to me that he'd changed, but because he couldn't get a job, he kept saying he'd failed. He accused me of not understanding. I *don't* understand him, if I'm honest. Trouble is, I don't think I want to understand anymore. I don't want my marriage to be over but I think I'd prefer to think that Lewis is still away in the army, rather than have the constant worry of what he will do next.'

'He lost a support group when he left his fellow soldiers behind,' said Josie.

'*I* should be his support group now.' A lone tear fell down Amy's face and she flicked it away quickly. 'But he won't talk to me. I don't know what else to do.'

When Josie left the house, she walked down the path and put her face up to the warm rays of the sun.

She didn't know what it was about him, but Lewis's plight touched her heart. So many of her residents didn't want to be helped, pushed her away, or called her a 'jobs worth.' So many more were just out for what they could get. Lewis was different. He was hurting.

But this was so far out of her jurisdiction that she felt out of her depth. She wished she could help him, but he needed to *want* that help. There seemed no point in barging in with her opinions and advice leaflets.

Perhaps she could do some more research on PTSD, try and get in touch with someone that Lewis could talk to.

Her shift over for the day, Donna went to see Sam at the hospital. He'd had his second operation that morning. Thankfully, the surgeon had managed to attach the severed tendon again so he wouldn't lose his finger. They'd stitched it up as neatly as they could and now it would need lots of physio to get it working again.

It was only after leaving the hospital, as she rushed off to visit Mary, that she started to look forward to her evening. Tonight was finally going to be the night. Owen was picking her up at seven thirty and they were going out for a meal. The prospect of her evening had got her through the stresses of the day; every man and his dog had been moaning about the weather being too hot. They should try standing in a shop all day where the only air conditioning was the door being open, Donna thought to herself.

As she let herself into Mary's flat, shouting out a greeting, a head popped around the kitchen door.

'Oh, hi, Megan,' she smiled as the young girl came out, carrying a beaker of juice for Mary.

'Hi, Donna, how are things?' Meg handed the drink to Mary, cupping her hands around the base of the beaker to attempt to get Mary to do the same.

'Fine, thanks. You?'

'Good, thanks. And Mary is doing well, aren't you?' Megan gave Mary's arm a quick pat before standing up straight again.

Mary sucked away on the beaker, causing Donna to grin at the funny noises she made.

'How's Sam?' Megan enquired.

'As well as can be expected, thanks. He's had another operation today, though. If all goes well from now, he'll be able to come out after the weekend.'

'That's good.'

Donna detected a slight blush on Megan's cheeks. She caught her eye and the young woman looked away as her skin reddened further. Donna couldn't help but smile. It looked like Megan had a crush on Sam.

'You should look in on him if you have time,' she encouraged. 'He's spoken about you a lot this week.'

'Oh, I— well, I'll see if I have time after my shift.' Megan looked at her watch. 'Talking of which, I need to go. Bye, Mary, and see you tomorrow.'

Donna showed Megan out. At the door, she stopped her.

'Thank you for looking after Mum so well,' she said. 'I know she's in safe hands with you.'

Megan beamed. 'I like her, she's a lovely lady. And besides, I like to speak to people as equals. Mary might not remember me tomorrow, and she may not even like me tomorrow, but that shouldn't affect the way I treat her. Manners and understanding cost nothing.'

Once Donna had closed the door, she went back into the living room with Megan's words ringing in her ears. What an old head on young shoulders. She hoped that she did have a soft spot for Sam. He'd do well to find someone like her.

'I don't like her,' said Mary suddenly.

'But that's Megan. Everyone loves Megan.'

'Not me,' said Mary. 'She's horrible, that Laura.'

Donna sighed. Laura Prophett was another of Mary's carers. 'That's Megan, Mum, not Laura.'

Mary looked up with a smile. 'Can we go home now? I wish I had my old bedroom, with the pink wallpaper and the cushions on the bed. Can you remember that cushion, Donna? You bought it for me. It said "World's Best Mum" on it.'

Donna's face lit up and her eyes brimmed with tears. For an instant, she had her mum back. She had remembered something about her past, instead of it being locked away forever.

'I do, Mum,' she replied, hastily wiping away the tears that had spilled. 'I bought it for you for Mother's Day when I was seventeen.'

'I loved that room.' Mary looked up at her with an expression of fear. 'Please take me back. I don't like it here.'

Donna squeezed Mary's hand, wishing that she could make everything right for her mum again. No matter what she did, she couldn't help feeling guilty. Mary was well looked after at Poplar court. Despite what Mary had said, Donna felt relieved to leave her, knowing that she would be safer there as she couldn't do much harm to herself. If she brought her to live with her, Mary wouldn't rest, and Donna would have to give up her job to look after her and then where would the money come from? No, she couldn't do it.

'I'll take you back, one day, Mum,' she fibbed.

It was the best she could offer. She thought about the accusations that Mary had made. She had seemed quite lucid at the time so maybe Donna shouldn't dismiss it so easily, especially with that bruise on her arm.

But, for her own sanity, she had to, because it had come from her mum's illness rather than fact.

Chapter Nineteen

'See you tomorrow, Ramona,' Keera shouted as she left the building after her shift had ended. It was her last one after working six in a row and she was looking forward to a night off the following evening. She'd arranged to meet some of the gang in The Butcher's Arms. Even though Marley had said she might come down to stay with her for a couple of nights, she'd found some temporary work in Manchester so she couldn't make it this time. Keera sighed, realising she'd have to make do with having a laugh with some of the others. She liked Regan, and Summer too, but they weren't Marley.

Outside, it felt like a storm was approaching and she was glad of it. She couldn't wait to get home for a shower. The air needed clearing; her skin still felt hot and sticky. When she'd come to work that afternoon, it had been nearing eighty degrees and the air felt tropical. Even now the temperature didn't seem to have dropped a lot, although it was nearing midnight.

Keera crossed the street and walked down the road towards the bus stop. A wave of guilt rushed over her as she realised she hadn't done anything to help out again. She'd told Mum she would call in to see Nan and then hadn't made the time. Still, Mum always made it clear that she was coping okay on her own whenever she tried to talk to her.

Thoughts of home made her think of her brother. She wondered how Sam had got on after he'd had his second operation. He was always moaning about his lot but he was going to be twice as bad after his accident. No doubt he'd be telling anyone who would listen how much pain he was in. He was such a drama queen.

'Well, well, well, look who we have here.' A shadow passed in front of her. Keera gasped when she saw who it was. It was Steve Wilson - a very drunk Steve Wilson, by the way he lurched unsteadily on his feet.

He staggered a step towards her. 'Do you do extras, love?' he slurred.

'Piss off.' Keera tried to go around him.

'Where are you fucking going?' He blocked her with an outstretched arm. 'I reckon you owe me after the trick you pulled the other night.'

'Had I had known Ramona was your sister, I would have punched you in the face too,' said Keera, never one to keep quiet. 'You shouldn't treat family like that. I've a—'

Steve pushed her against a boarded-up shop window. His face was in hers, greasy hair hanging limp, breath smelling like something had just thrown up in his mouth. His eyes tried to focus on her but he was finding it hard to keep his head still.

'Get off me!' she cried. But the more she struggled, the more he pressed himself to her.

'I'd watch what I was saying, if I were you.' He pointed a finger up close to her face. 'That mouth of yours is only good for one thing.'

'Leave me alone.' Keera glanced behind him. The street ahead was deserted. She couldn't even scream out. No one would hear her until it was too late, even if anyone came to help at all.

'Does Sam know that you get paid for sex too?' Steve licked his lips.

'I don't do sex.'

He pressed his hand to the bulge in his trousers. 'But you're going to do me, my sweet one, aren't you?'

Keera turned her head to one side to rid herself of the stench of his breath. How did she get herself into these situations? It wasn't on, just because she worked a shit job. God, she couldn't wait to get away from this dump.

She'd have to try and fool him.

'Okay,' she nodded, 'but we'll have to be quick.' She heard him undoing his zip and put a hand over his. 'Not here! We'd get arrested if anyone saw us.'

'Oh, yeah,' Steve grinned, cottoning on at last. He took her hand and walked with her up the street. Keera tried not to recoil from his touch, suppressing her instincts to pull her hand away and make a run for it. He might catch her up again and who knew what damage he could do then? She'd seen how Steve had come at Ramona and that was his sister. She knew he wouldn't care what damage he did to her.

Steve stopped as they drew level with an entry.

'This will do.' He smiled lasciviously. 'No one will stop us down there, out of sight.'

The alleyway didn't have any lighting. With every step they took, it became darker and darker as they left the street lamps behind. A few more steps down into it and Keera felt the adrenaline kick in as he pushed her up against the wall again. Trying not to pull away when he dipped his mouth towards hers, she let him get closer. Just a little bit closer.

With as much strength as she could muster, Keera slammed her knee up hard into his groin.

'Don't think you can get the better of me, you dirty shit,' she cried.

As he dropped to the floor, she pummelled her fists into his head.

'Gerroff me, you mad bitch,' he yelled.

He grabbed for her leg but she stepped out of his way. Before he could respond again, Keera made a run for it. But when she turned, she hadn't realised how dark it would be. For a moment, disorientated, she panicked. Then, spotting a sliver of light to her right, she raced towards it, not stopping until she was out on the main street again.

Quickly looking behind to see if he was following, she breathed heavily when he was nowhere to be seen. Then she ran on to the main road. A few cars passed by. Up ahead she could see people standing outside Percy's Kebabs.

When she'd convinced herself that he wasn't following her, Keera slowed down to a walk. Relief washed over her and she grinned manically. She had got away! Lord knows what he would have done if she had given him a blowjob like he wanted. He could have taken more.

But as awareness began to sink in, Keera burst into tears. She'd lost her bag in the struggle. Worse than that, she didn't have any money, nor her phone, nor her house keys. She'd have to go home through the estate.

She made her way along the road, all the time reliving what had just happened, shivering when she thought what *could* have happened.

Then realisation dawned. She had made things far worse for her and Ramona. She'd worked on instinct hitting out at Steve, never thinking of the repercussions for her friend.

And now there was nothing to stop Steve from telling Sam either.

Chapter Twenty

Donna opened her front door, stepped inside the hallway and let out a blissful sigh. With a huge grin, she slipped off her strappy heels, massaging her toes to get some feeling back into them. As she stood up straight again, she caught sight of her reflection in the mirror at the bottom of the stairs. She put a hand to her cheek. Wow, was that really her? She hadn't looked this, well, sexy, in a long while. Her eyes shone back at her, her cheeks flushed, her lips reddened.

'Owen, what have you done to me?' Donna asked herself, before grinning again.

Finally, she'd had some 'me' time. It was a novelty to focus on happiness instead of glaring in despair at her wrinkles.

Humming to herself, she went through to the kitchen and opened the fridge. Even though it was past midnight, her hand rested on a half-open bottle of wine. She took it out and poured a large glass, went through to the living room and sunk down into the settee.

She couldn't stop smiling, thinking of Owen and how the night had gone. He'd taken her to an Italian restaurant that had recently opened. Sarah would be green with envy when she told her. The food had been excellent, the company even better, and by the end of the evening, a little tipsy on wine, she'd opened up to Owen a little bit about how hard her life had been lately. Owen had held her hand across the table, squeezed it when he'd noticed tears in her eyes. Still, she'd soon stopped thinking of bad times when he'd dropped her off and drew her into his arms. She pressed a hand to her mouth, her lips still tingling from his kiss.

An incoming message beeped in on her phone. Thinking it would be from Keera, she opened it and was surprised to see it was from Owen.

I had a great time. It was hard to leave you. You looked so sexy. x

She smiled as she quickly typed a message back.

You didn't look bad yourself! I enjoyed it too. x

The ringtone blasted into life, making her jump in the silence of the room. She answered the call.

'When can I see you again?'

The huskiness in Owen's voice made her skin instantly break out in goosebumps. She shivered.

'You said later next week,' she replied.

'I can't wait that long.' His voice sounded pained.

'You'll have to.'

'Are you alone?'

'Why?' She held her breath.

'Well, I could come back to yours for a … coffee.'

'You've only just dropped me off about ten minutes ago.' She giggled coyly.

'So I can be back in ten minutes.'

Donna paused. He wouldn't want coffee. But what if he was disappointed in her once he saw her body? She wasn't a twenty-year-old woman with beautiful skin and a figure to die for. Her breasts weren't pert, her stomach wasn't flat. She'd had two children, for starters.

'So – are you alone?' he asked again.

Could she do this? She reminded herself she was forty-two, not seventy-two.

'Wait one second,' she told him quickly. With the phone still in her hand, she thundered up the stairs to check that everything looked in order, just in case Keera had come home early unexpectedly. But the house was empty.

'What are you doing?' Owen asked as she came down the stairs a little slower than when she'd raced up. 'You sound out of breath? Are you getting excited, Ms Adams?'

'Cocky little shit, aren't you?' Donna heard a roar of laughter. 'If you must know, I'm checking to see that the house is empty.'

'And is it?'

'It is.'

'So …'

'Coffee it is.'

Donna disconnected the phone and slipped her heels back on, praying that the wanton look of earlier was still there. She checked one more time in the mirror. Yes, there it was.

Keera hugged herself to stop from crying as she walked. Her teeth were chattering so much that she couldn't control them. That creepy bastard, Steve Wilson.

She shuddered as she thought back to when he'd led her up the alleyway half an hour earlier. She knew if she hadn't kneed him in the balls that she would probably have ended up being exploited by him for sexual favours whenever he felt like it. Did he think just because she worked in a massage parlour that she was scum of the earth and would do anything? She wouldn't – for anyone. No one owned Keera.

She jumped as she heard a car door shut ahead, its occupants saying goodnight loudly. The car drove off and she was alone again. She hurried as fast as her feet would carry her.

All of a sudden, Keera wished she was with her brother. But she couldn't even phone him, because she'd lost her phone in the scuffle with Steve.

If he hadn't had his accident, she could have told him what had happened. She might have been able to get Steve off her back for good, and maybe Ramona's too. Steve would back down if Sam had a word with him, she was sure. Bullies always stood down when tackled. But she couldn't tell Sam about it now. He'd be in more pain if he tried to fight it out for her.

Keera was glad to see Davy Road, knowing that she was close to home, even though it was the longest road on the Mitchell Estate. She made a mental note to check with the other girls, see if Steve had taken advantage of any of them in the same way. If he had, she was going to do her utmost to stop him. The bastard shouldn't be allowed to get away with it.

Working at the massage parlour wasn't the best of jobs, but it was a job. Just because she and the other girls chose to do it didn't mean they deserved to be treated like pieces of meat.

She heard a car drawing level with her. Her footsteps quickened as it drew into the kerb beside her. Heart racing, Keera kept her eyes straight in front of her and walked on when she heard the window going down.

'Keera?' A familiar voice shouted. 'It's me - Derek! Are you okay?'

Relief swept through her as she stopped.

'I know it's a warm night,' he smiled, 'but surely you know better than to be walking around the estate on your own.'

Keera burst into tears.

'Hey, don't cry.' Derek reached across and opened his door. 'Jump in and I'll take you home.'

Keera slid into the passenger seat, thankful to rest her feet after the long walk home. She could already feel blisters forming, and knew that she had rubbed away the skin on the heel of one foot at least. But she was safe.

Derek made no move to drive.

'What's happened?' He looked concerned as he turned slightly towards her. 'I'm used to seeing your smiley face all the time.'

Keera wiped her eyes with the back of her hand, unable to speak as she caught her breath.

'Has someone hurt you?' he probed.

Keera shook her head. 'They tried to.'

'Who was it?' Derek pursed his lips. 'I've a good mind to—'

'I'm fine. It's an occupational hazard.'

'What do you mean?'

'Let's just say that someone's going to wake up with bruised balls in the morning.'

Derek didn't smile, not even at her attempt to laugh it off.

'Who is it?'

'No one you know.'

'All the same, I—'

I lost my bag,' she interrupted. 'Everything was in it; my phone, my keys, my purse. That's why I was walking home.'

'You mean he stole it? The bloody lowlife scum …'

'He pushed me up an alleyway and it was so dark. When I

made a run for it, I must have dropped it. I didn't want to chance going back when I realised.'

'The bastard.'

Keera nodded vehemently. 'I hope he won't see it. He was really drunk. It might still be there tomorrow. I'll have to get up early and go to look.' She shivered, involuntarily. 'I just wanted to get as far away as possible in case he had another go at me. He would have wanted to get his own way.'

'Buckle up,' Derek told her as he pulled away from the kerb. 'I'll take you back for it now.'

'No,' said Keera, 'I can go myself in the–'

'It won't take a moment.' Derek was already turning the car around. 'Maybe he'll still be there too.'

As he drove back the way she had just walked, Keera's shoulders relaxed. Thank goodness Derek had turned up.

Knowing she was safe with him, she rested her head back on the seat.

Chapter Twenty-One

Waiting for Owen to return felt like hours but in reality was only a matter of minutes. And then there he was, in Donna's doorway, in her hall, in her bedroom, in her arms. He pressed himself to her, his hands on her back pulling her into him as his mouth found hers again. There hadn't been much room for exploration inside the car but here, in the safety of her own home, she gasped at the thrill of his tongue reaching out to find hers, pushing gently, rhythmically in and out so that her legs felt weak and she literally sank into his body.

His smell overpowered her senses again as his mouth dipped lower, tiny butterfly kisses all over her chin, her neck, the top of her chest. Her body jerked with pleasure.

Tentatively, she ran her hands over Owen's shoulders as he pushed down the strap of her dress to expose her collarbone, running his tongue lightly from its edge and up towards her mouth, slowly, tantalisingly slowly, until he found her lips once more.

His hands moved to the middle of her back, fingers lightly brushing her skin, teasing, testing as far as he could go. She knew she wouldn't back down, lost in the power of lust.

His mouth still on hers, she felt the zip to her dress slide down, shuddered with desire as he slid the material down her body. Once it was at her feet, she stepped out of it and he tossed it to one side. She stood in front of him in just her underwear.

'Beautiful,' he whispered.

Donna knew she was far from that but right now she didn't

care. His flattery was all she needed. She reached behind to undo her bra, thankful that she had put on her best lace. She let that drop to the floor, her eyes firmly on his, defying him to look away.

He stared at her for a moment but as she stepped into his arms again, his eyes dipped, followed quickly by his mouth.

She groaned as he took her nipple in his mouth, his tongue circling it, gently biting it. She arched her back, then decided to grab the bottom of his shirt. She needed to see him too. Trying to concentrate as her passion soared, her skin on fire with his touch, she undid the buttons and slipped his shirt off his shoulders, gasping at the firmness of his chest. She pulled at the sleeves and the shirt joined her dress on the floor.

He pushed her gently down onto the bed. As he kissed her again, he lay next to her.

And then he stopped.

She looked into his eyes with confusion.

'Do you want me to continue?' he asked, his voice low.

'Do *you* want to continue?' Oh, God, please don't let him change his mind now that he had seen her naked.

'Yes, but...' Owen sat up and reached for his shirt.

'What's wrong?'

He turned to her with a look that made tears well in her eyes.

'I'm a little scared,' he admitted.

'Of me?' She spoke quietly.

'Of what's happening to me; of the intensity of my feelings for you. This has all happened so quickly.'

Donna sat up, bringing her knees to her chest as she felt exposed. 'I'm not sure I understand.'

He sighed. 'You're not the only one scarred by someone else.'

'Oh.'

'Oh.'

'But I'm not her.'

'Right.'

'And incidentally, you're not him.'

'So...' he glanced at her, 'technically, it's just you and me.'

'Yes.'

'And the moment.'

Donna sat still, unable to breathe. Had the moment passed? Had he worked himself, and her, up to the heights of something new, something promising, for it all to be taken away at the last minute?

He turned to her slightly. 'You don't know what I'm capable of.'

'I thought I'd been about to find out.'

He moved towards her again, covering her body with his own. The relief was immense when his mouth found hers once more and his hand roamed over her breast before moving lower. She reached down for him too, trying to concentrate on giving him pleasure as her body craved more.

Finally, he pushed himself into her. Moving together, she felt familiar waves rush through her. Oh, this was so good.

With a groan, Owen thrust one last time and she pulled his buttocks towards her to feel him as close to her as she could.

As her breathing began to return to normal, Donna realised that the moment had gone better than she had first hoped.

Afterwards, Owen leant on his elbow and ran his fingertips over her stomach. 'That was special,' he said.

Donna couldn't help but well up again. She smiled, hoping her tears wouldn't fall.

'I enjoyed it too,' she replied.

'So we can do it again, sometime?'

'Absolutely.'

He pulled her into his arms and, as they lay together in silence, all she could think of was how vulnerable Owen was. What had his last partner done to make him feel that way?

She would have to find out more, make him realise that no matter what had happened, she would never do anything to hurt him.

Donna knew that during her earlier years, she had been brash. She'd had a loud mouth that said a lot of things she'd since regretted. She might have been hurt by the one man she had truly loved, but everything had built up her character. Circumstances had made her stronger, but also eager to please and sometimes it had made her seem like a pushover.

But one thing was certain. Donna knew she could never hurt a man who would show himself to her in such a raw, emotional state.

Which meant another thing. She would be good for Owen, if he would have her.

Lewis staggered down Davy Road in the direction of Graham Street. At least he hoped he was going the right way towards home. It was nearing midnight. He'd been struggling to focus on anything since leaving The Butcher's Arms ten minutes ago.

The night air was warm again, the area quiet; the odd light was on here and there as he passed, but most houses were in darkness. Windows were open everywhere, hoping to create a cool enough atmosphere for sleep.

If Lewis had been a bit more sober he would have stayed out a while longer. Walking around the streets during the early hours of the morning was often peaceful, giving him space to clear his head. Right now though, all he wanted to do was lay his head down and sleep. Why did he think he could drown his sorrows? It never worked, plus he was wasting what little benefits he received. It just made him feel twice as bad the next morning – usually accompanied by the headache from hell.

Up ahead, he heard noises. He stared into the darkness, trying to focus. Finally, he saw the shapes of two people coming towards him. Their laughter was loud, but their banter seemed friendly. Lewis dug his hands in his pockets and stuck out his elbows as they drew nearer.

Two boys in their late teens edged either side of him as they passed him on the pavement. The stocky one had his hands shoved into the pockets of his jeans too, shoulders hunched forward. He had more hair on his chin than his head and reminded Lewis of an upside down Mr Potato Head toy. The other youth was the same height but slight in weight. His hair was flattened down except at the front where a fringe had been gelled in a point towards the sky.

'All right, mate?' the thin one nodded at him.

'I'm not your fucking mate,' Lewis spat back.

'What did you say?'

'Are you deaf?' Lewis turned to face them and took his hands out of his pockets, trying not to shuffle on his feet. 'I said I'm not your–'

'Yeah, I heard you. What's your problem?'

'You're my fucking problem,' Lewis slurred.

The stocky lad moved towards him. 'I'd watch your mouth if I were you, old man.'

Lewis lashed out at him. Even in his drunken state, his hands moved quickly, but they missed their target completely.

A fist caught him on the side of his face. The other youth stepped forward to grab him too. Lewis managed to catch him full in the face before he was rushed by both of them and grabbed around his chest. He lost his footing and the bigger male fell to the ground on top of him.

Lewis felt another punch to the side of his head, swiftly followed by another to his mouth. As his own fists flailed around in the dark, theirs did more damage, and he tasted blood.

Finally, Lewis managed to push them off.

'I'd watch your back if I were you,' the skinny lad said, spitting on the floor at Lewis's feet after he had stood up.

Lewis lifted his head from the floor and dropped it back again as a rush of nausea came over him.

'Stupid fuckers.' He pushed himself to his feet and held onto the side of a car to support himself. 'You hear me, you stupid FUCKERS!'

When he didn't retaliate again, the two boys went on their way.

Once more, Lewis staggered off in the direction he thought was home. He knew it would take him longer to get back now; already he could feel the ache across his eyes. He'd hoped he wouldn't get another shiner. He'd never get a job interview looking like a hooligan.

Lewis swore out loud. A few months ago, he wouldn't have let two teenagers get the better of him. Was he losing his head completely?

Maybe that housing officer, that Josie Mellor, was right. Perhaps he did need to see someone about his anger, see if he could get it under control. Surely he shouldn't be feeling this way after so long out of the army?

An image of Nathan flashed into his mind and he quickly dismissed it.

What would his friend think of him if he could see him now? He'd be ashamed, wouldn't he?

Chapter Twenty-Two

Keera sighed with relief when Derek drove past The Candy Club ten minutes later and the lights were off. Everything looked fine. At least Steve didn't seem to have gone back to Ramona, something else Keera had worried about on her walk home. She hadn't even been able to warn her friend as she'd had no phone.

'There's the alleyway.' She pointed ahead to a gap in between two buildings. 'He took me down there.'

She noticed Derek bristle as he parked up. He removed his seatbelt. 'I'll go and look for it. I won't be a minute.'

'I'll come, too.'

'No, I'd rather—'

But Keera was out of the door before he could say anything further. Derek retrieved a torch from the boot of the car, and they crossed over the road. He headed into the alleyway, Keera following close behind. A feeling of déjà vu overcame her and she retched. What a bastard Steve Wilson was, thinking he could threaten her and get his own way.

'Do you know where it's likely to be?' Derek whispered loudly as he walked on ahead. 'It's so dark down here, I can hardly see what I'm treading in.'

'Yuck.' Keera lifted up a foot at the thought. 'I can remember going past those bins.'

After a few moments, shapes became a little clearer as they bumbled around. Keera had almost given up when a minute later, she squealed.

'I've found it,' she cried, lifting it up in the air. She unzipped it quickly and looked inside. 'Everything is still here! My phone, my purse, my keys! Thank God for that – at least I won't get a bollocking for waking my mum up to get in now!'

'Great stuff.' Derek put a hand on the small of her back and gently pushed her out of the alleyway. 'But I think we'd better get out of here, before we get caught and we *haven't* been doing anything, if you know what I mean.'

Keera sniggered as he followed her.

'Thanks, Derek,' she said as they hit the pavement again. 'You've saved my skin.'

'I can't have you getting into trouble or worse, losing your job now, can I?'

'It wouldn't be the end of the world. I've had better ones.' She glanced at him with embarrassment. 'Oh, I didn't mean that I wasn't grateful for it. I am, really. It's just that my family don't know what I do. They think I work in a nightclub, and that's why I work late.'

'Ah. But you're one of the good girls, Keera – aren't you?'

'Yes, I bloody well am!' she snapped. 'I've told you before, I don't do extras.'

'I know!' Derek held up his hands. 'I didn't mean anything by it.'

'Sorry.' The smell of food from the takeaway made Keera's stomach rumble. 'Do you fancy getting something to eat?' she asked, feeling embarrassed at her outburst. 'The kebab shop is a great place, really clean too. My treat for you saving my life.'

'That's a bit dramatic.'

'It's only an offer of a kebab.' She grinned. 'What do you say?'

'Okay. I'll wait here.' Derek got back into his cab.

'Don't you dare put that meter on!' she joked.

There were several people waiting for food at the kebab house, so Keera gave their order and went to sit on a plastic chair while it was prepared. Through the window, she could see Derek's car, just about make out his shape in the driver's seat. She clasped her hands together, still a little shaky after what had happened.

What a diamond he was, taking her back to find her bag. She wouldn't have got any sleep thinking about what could happen if Steve found it.

Yet, despite being rescued by Derek, which she would be eternally grateful for, she couldn't help worrying about what might have happened if Steve wasn't as drunk as he was. Or if her aim to his balls had been off its mark. Or if he'd been stronger than her regardless. He would have raped her, she was sure of it, because she had put up a fight.

She closed her eyes but all she could see was him pushing his tongue into her mouth.

'Two kebabs!'

'That's me.' Keera took the order and ran back to the taxi.

'There was a massive queue,' she said, as she climbed into the passenger seat again. She handed a paper parcel to Derek.

'Thanks.' He turned to face her. 'Are you sure you're okay? Don't you think you should report the incident to the police?'

Keera shook her head. 'I would if it didn't mean involving The Candy Club.'

'It doesn't have to. You weren't at work when it happened.'

'I know, but—' Keera wondered if she should confide in Derek, then realised she couldn't see any harm in it. 'He's Ramona's brother and she owes him five hundred pounds. He could cause a lot more trouble if I grassed on him.'

Derek gnawed on his bottom lip. 'Well, if I see him in there, I'll give him what for.'

'You don't know what he looks like.' Keera laughed. 'Thanks, anyway.' She unwrapped her food. 'I'm ready for this. I'm starving.'

They sat in silence for a few moments while they tucked into their food.

'I'll give you a lift back once we've eaten,' said Derek eventually.

'You are an angel, has anyone ever told you that?' Keera smiled. 'It's nice to have you around. I live in Trudy Place, number twenty-two. You can drop me off at the end of the street, if you like.'

'I think you've had enough trauma for one evening.' He turned towards her more. 'I want to see you going inside your house, if you don't mind.'

'Sure.' Keera shrugged. 'I'm not complaining. My feet are aching so much.'

They both watched as three young men walked past, loud but happy.

'How do you usually get home?' asked Derek once it was quiet again.

'I catch the ten past twelve bus.'

'I don't like to think of you coming out at midnight and catching the bus every night.' Derek wiped his mouth with a napkin. 'Would you be okay if I picked you up on the evenings that you work late?'

'I can't afford a taxi every night.' Keera shook her head. 'But thanks for the offer.'

'I don't want paying. How about I drive past the bus stop if I'm free, and if you're there I'll take you home?'

'But you might miss another fare.'

'It doesn't matter. I'm always knocking off around that time, anyway. I don't want any money from you, either.'

'But it's how you make your living!' Despite his kind offer, Keera still didn't want to take advantage of his good nature.

'There will definitely be no strings attached, if that's what you're thinking,' he added. 'I just want to see that you're home safe and well.'

Keera smiled. 'You're far too nice to me, Mr P.' After a moment's thought, she nodded. 'Okay, you have a deal. If I'm there, I'm there. If I'm not, go without me. I'll feel better about it if I catch the bus every now and then. But I'll be very happy to cadge a lift when you're free.'

'That's sorted then.' Derek smiled. 'You have an unofficial chauffeur.'

Keera smiled back. It seemed that she had an unofficial guardian angel as well. She'd been so relieved when she'd seen that it was Derek who had stopped. Her feet were so raw in places after her long walk. Imagine if she hadn't been able to run if she'd needed to.

Still, a nightmare had turned out to be her knight in shining armour moment, even if it was in the shape of a forty-eight-year-old man.

In a way, it was like having a father figure – Keera had hated her own father when he'd abandoned them all those years ago now, and still hated him for what he'd put her mum through. The day he'd moved out and left them to it had been good riddance.

But Derek was lovely. He'd made her feel so warm and safe tonight, and that was always a good thing in her books.

Donna lay in bed, her mind going over every single detail of the evening. Owen had left about an hour ago, and they'd arranged to meet again in a few days. The night was muggy and she pushed aside the duvet to let air to her naked skin.

Idly, she ran her fingers up and down and across her stomach just the way Owen had. Her stomach flipped every time she remembered what he had done with his mouth, his hands, his tongue. He was like a drug and she couldn't wait for her next fix.

She closed her eyes to relive it all, scrunching up her toes at the memory of the waves crashing over her body as Owen brought her to the brink of no return. She knew she was infatuated by lust, but it had awakened within her and she wanted to remember it forever.

A few moments later, she heard the front door open and close.

'Is that you, Keera?' she shouted, jumping under the covers.

'Yeah, it's me, Mum.' A few seconds later, Keera popped her head around the bedroom door.

'You're late,' said Donna. 'Everything okay?'

'Fine. I had a drink with a few of the regulars. How's Sam doing?'

'He's his usual moaning self.' She looked at Keera properly. 'You look bushed, hard night?'

'You could say that.'

'Go and get some sleep. Things always seem better in the morning.'

Keera looked embarrassed. 'I'm sorry that I haven't had time to help out much. But I need the shifts so that I can save some money to—'

'I can manage.' Donna sat up in bed, keeping the duvet covering her body. She smiled at Keera.

Keera eyed her warily. 'What have you been up to? You seem all smiley and in a good mood.'

'Oh, it's nothing.' Donna waved her away.

'If I didn't know better, I'd say you'd—' She paused and when Donna didn't speak, she grinned. 'I'm right, aren't I? You've met someone.'

'I might have.'

'Come on, spill.'

'There is no way I'm telling my daughter about my date! Besides, it's early days yet. That's why I haven't said anything to anyone.'

'Are you seeing him again?'

Donna nodded.

'Well, I hope it works out, Mum. No one deserves to be happier than you.' Keera yawned. 'I'm off to bed. Night.'

'Night, love.'

Donna tried to settle to sleep again. Even though she thought that Keera looked tired, one thing she would never worry too much about was her daughter. She could always rely on her not to bring trouble to her door.

Donna felt sad that Ibiza hadn't worked out for her and Marley, but from what Keera had told her about the attack on her friend, she was glad to have her home again, too. Keera would get by. She wasn't like Sam, determined to scrounge off the social for as long as he could. Donna hated it but she couldn't do anything about it. She'd long ago given up on telling him what to do.

The one thing she *would* like to worry about was a grandchild. She wished that the two of them would find decent partners to settle down with. It would be lovely to have some new life around her, even if that meant being a gran in her forties. And maybe with a toyboy granddad.

Donna laughed to herself before turning out the light.

Chapter Twenty-Three

As Megan was finishing her shift on Monday morning, she went into ward seventeen on the pretence of forgetting her cloths. She'd missed Sam over the weekend and having found out he was being discharged that day, she wanted to catch him to say goodbye. It had been nice having him around for the few days that she had got to know him. It had made her job that little bit more interesting.

Megan caught him packing his bag, blushing when he treated her to a smile.

'So, you're off then?' she stated the obvious when she couldn't think of anything else to say.

'I sure am.' Sam's smile widened. 'I need to come back next week to have my stitches removed, and then it's lots of physio.' He held up a bag of sweets. 'Do you want these?'

Megan shook her head. 'No, thanks.'

'Because you're sweet enough? Is that what I should be saying?'

She grinned at him. 'I'll take that as a compliment.'

'It is.' Sam sat down on the bed and beckoned her closer. 'Megan, can I ask you something?'

'Sure.'

He patted the bed next to where he was sitting but she shook her head.

'I might get into trouble if someone sees me sitting next to you.'

'Why?'

Why indeed, she cursed herself. The truth was that someone

might say she shouldn't get too close to the patients but if she said that, then Sam might know she liked him.

'They'd think I was skiving,' she replied, relieved at getting herself out of a hole.

'Oh, right.' Sam paused for a brief moment. 'Could I see you again?' He sniggered. 'Well, when I say again, I mean in proper surroundings? Take you out for a drink, maybe, or something to eat?'

It was what she had waited to hear, but still her heart sank. She couldn't see Sam unless she showed him the real Megan – but she knew that would be too painful after what had happened the last time she'd done it. But despite her misgivings, she really did want to see him again.

Why was life always so complicated?

'I'll think about it,' she said finally.

'No witty putdown?' Sam held his hand to his chest and feigned his heart stopping. 'I'm shocked.'

'Sometimes I get stuck for words too,' she admitted.

'Could I have your phone number then, and I'll text you?'

Megan shook her head. 'I shouldn't really.'

Sam wrote on the newspaper, ripped off the corner and handed it to her. 'Here's mine. I'll be waiting to hear from you.'

With a heavy heart, Megan took a sneaky peek at Sam as he stood up again. She drank in his features, the shape of his body, the gleam in his eyes, the smile she wished he reserved only for her.

Megan fixed his image firmly in her mind, because she doubted she would use his number. It was easier that way, rather than say no to him now. The closer they became, the harder it would be to face the rejection. This way, if he texted or called, she could ignore it. Her secret would be safe.

'Right, then,' Sam said, hauling his bag on to his good arm. 'I'll be off. See you soon, yeah?'

Megan nodded. 'Soon.'

Sam gave her arm a quick squeeze before moving past her. She turned to watch him until he was out of her sight. Perhaps she shouldn't automatically shut down the possibility that they might get on well enough for her to reveal the truth?

Regretting her indecision, she sighed loudly. The world had just become that little bit dreary again.

Sam let himself into his flat with great difficulty. Using his left hand to put a key into the lock seemed so alien. The bag on his right arm slid down and knocked his injured hand. 'Shit,' he exclaimed.

Behind him, Donna sighed.

'Here, let me do it.' She reached for his key.

Sam snatched it away. 'I can manage.' A few seconds later, the door was open.

'It smells like someone has died in here.' Donna covered her mouth with her hand. 'And I cleaned up at the weekend. What is that flatmate of yours doing?'

Sam ignored her as he went through into the living room. The flat was tiny for the two of them but at least there were two bedrooms so he didn't have to sleep on the settee. Brendon Carver's girlfriend had lived there until a few months ago, when she'd left him for some other bloke. Sam had seen an opportunity and badgered Brendon to let him stay for a few days. He'd been there ever since and had no intentions of leaving. Despite what his mum thought, Sam knew he could cope. He wasn't going to move back in with her.

Donna had opened a window in the kitchen and was now putting food into his fridge. 'You should have seen the state of this before I cleaned it, too,' she exclaimed as she popped eggs out of the box and into the shelving. 'Scummy, the pair of you. Do you want a cup of tea?'

Sam shook his head. 'I'm tired, I just need to get some kip. Those wards are so bloody noisy.'

Donna nodded. 'You get some rest and I'll sit here until—'

'I don't need a babysitter!'

'I know but ...'

'Mum, just go, will you? I'll be fine.'

Donna turned to him abruptly and closed the fridge door with a slam. 'I'm only trying to help. You'll need to learn to do so much with your left hand until your right is better. And you can't get that bandaging wet, so you'll have to wear—'

'Mum!'

Donna raised her hands in surrender. 'Fine.'

Alone at last, Sam sighed with relief and lay down on the settee. Feet up, he wondered what he should do first. He wasn't tired in the slightest, but he had wanted to get away from his mum's fussing.

He needed some money. He was broke before he'd had his accident and he hadn't been able to sign on, so his benefits would have been stopped until he'd shown proof that he'd been in hospital.

Sam held up his injured hand and stared at it, his fingertips poking out from the bandaging. He couldn't wait to start his physio and join his mates again. But until then he could go for a swift half at The Butcher's Arms. He could hold a pint with his left hand.

Or he could think about a certain woman who had invaded his thoughts since he'd met her last week. Megan.

Not that she would go out with the likes of him. She must know of his reputation and if she didn't she'd only have to mention his name and someone would tell her. His dodgy lifestyle would always haunt him.

Shame, because he really did fancy the arse off her.

Chapter Twenty-Four

On Wednesday morning, Donna had planned to pop in to see Sam before going to see her mum, but he hadn't been in. He'd been out of hospital for two days now and had told her he was doing fine with his hand, but she'd wanted to make sure that he was telling the truth. Knowing Sam, if he wasn't taking good care of his injury, it would become infected and take longer to heal. And she didn't trust his flatmate, that layabout Brendan, to help him out. Brendan had let her in, though, and by the time she left she'd done a load of washing and cleaned up the messy kitchen.

Rushing in to Poplar Court for a quick visit with Mary before her shift started at Shop&Save, Donna was shocked with what greeted her.

'I want to leave this place right now!' Mary yelled the minute she walked into the living room.

'Whatever's the matter, Mum?' Donna rushed over to her. She couldn't remember seeing Mary so distressed since her father had died.

Mary grabbed Donna's hand and squeezed with enough force to cause her to grimace. 'You have to get me out of here. They're going to kill me if you don't!'

Donna gently eased her hand away. 'Mum, no one is going to kill you. It's nice here. There are lots of people to keep you company. Come on, let's take you down to the lounge.'

Mary needed a frame to walk, and it took more time that she had to spare to get her along the corridor and into the lift, but finally Donna managed to get the two of them downstairs.

The lounge was an airy room, with lots of windows that ensured light flooded through and kept it bright. There were about twenty blue armchairs dotted around, and several coffee tables. The afternoon sun was moving round to the final half of the room, its beam resting on the empty seats as everyone sat in the shade.

Donna glanced around. A man slept with his mouth wide open. One woman was knitting, another pushing dominos round and round a tray she had on her knee. It was the reason why Donna didn't come down to the lounge that often. It upset her to see all these individuals virtually going backwards rather than forwards, regressing in their minds. She felt sad that the terrible realisation was that only death would set them free. She shuddered, trying not think of when she would lose her mum.

Her eyes brimmed with tears as she looked at Mary who was lowering herself into a chair, getting ready for the jolt when her knees would give way and she would fall back.

Donna took hold of her arm to ease it, but Mary gasped.

'Ow!' she cried out.

'What's the matter, Mum? Is it your arm again?' Donna pulled Mary's sleeve up to inspect it.

'I have another one,' Mary whispered.

'Another what?' Donna could hardly hear herself speak over the sound of the television that a resident had turned up to full volume.

'Another bruise!'

'Did you fall?' Donna raised her voice a little to be heard.

Mary shook her head. 'I never.'

'Where is this one?'

Mary pointed to her shin.

'Are you sure? Let me look.'

'No, I can't show you now, can I?' Mary looked around the room, as if seeing who was listening. 'But it's there. I promised not to tell who did it, though.'

Donna rolled her eyes. It was like looking after a naughty toddler. Was Mary saying something she should take note of, or was she talking gobbledegook? It was hard to tell.

'Tea, anyone?' A woman shouted as she wheeled a trolley into the middle of the room. It was Laura, one of the care assistants.

She smiled at Laura. 'Lovely day, isn't it?'

'It is indeed.' Laura beamed. 'And we need to keep the old dears hydrated. Would you like a drink, too?'

Donna shook her head; she would rather die than drink lukewarm, milky tea.

'Would you like a cuppa, Mary?' Laura patted Mary's forearm.

Donna couldn't help but notice that she didn't pull it away from Laura.

Mary nodded her head.

'You look peaky, Mary,' Laura said as she passed her a beaker with a straw. 'How's your leg?'

'Oh, she *has* hurt her leg?' Donna frowned. 'I never can tell.'

'Denise found her on the floor in her room,' Laura explained. Denise was the warden of Poplar Court. 'Said that Mary had rolled out of bed again.' She smiled at Mary. 'We don't want any damage to that hip, now do we?'

'Denise hasn't told me,' said Donna.

'I expect she will soon. She's a busy lady.'

'We're all busy,' Donna retorted. She stood up. 'I have to go now, Mum. Shall I leave you here for now?'

'Yes, I think it's safe, if she's not around,' Mary muttered, a look of panic across her face.

Unable to drop the nagging doubts in her mind, Donna went to see if she could speak to Denise before she left. While she waited for her to finish her phone call, she sat in the corridor outside her office, feeling like a schoolgirl about to get a ticking off from the headmaster. There was no one else about so she studied a leaflet about Dementia.

Minutes later, the door opened and Denise Barker came out of the room. Donna saw her feet first. Denise wore black, flat, unfashionable shoes that Donna wouldn't even want her mum wearing. She looked up to see an ill-fitting trouser suit, a face void of make-up and greying hair tied up in a bun.

'Sorry to keep you waiting,' Denise spoke with an authority that suggested nothing of the sort. 'Do come in.'

Donna followed Denise into her office and sat down across from her at an old wooden desk that was too big for the space. A tired two-seater settee was squashed into the corner over by the window, the sill above it filled with pots of plants, causing Donna to feel claustrophobic.

'Is everything all right with Mary?' Denise asked.

'I'm not sure.' Donna paused. 'I'm just getting a little worried about her. During the last few visits, over the past month, Mum has been asking to leave.'

'Oh?' Denise sat forward in her chair.

'I suppose it could be her mind,' Donna went on, 'but ever since she's been here, she's been fine. And now, all of a sudden, she's saying things about hating the place and wanting to go back home.'

'I can't say I've noticed any vast change in her.' Denise steepled her hands together and frowned. 'I wonder if she's regressed a little and feels like she shouldn't be here again. This often happens.'

'Does it?'

'Yes.' Denise nodded profusely. 'She sees you coming, she sees you going and then something in her brain connects that you're leaving her here. Maybe she wants to shock you into taking her back home again. But really, she's fine.'

Donna visibly relaxed. 'I've never seen her so agitated. It's as if she doesn't want to be left alone. She seems really scared.'

Hmm… remind me, who is her main carer?' Denise reached for a file on her desk.

'Megan Cooper.'

'I can have a word with Megan, if you like? See if there's anything she knows of that has upset Mary?'

'Thanks.' Donna smiled, not letting on that she had already asked her.

'She's such a lovely girl. We're very lucky to have her.' Denise glanced up at the clock and closed the file. 'Well, if there isn't anything else…'

But Donna hadn't finished yet. 'Look, I really don't want to get anyone into trouble, but if Mum is being treated badly by someone, I—'

Denise's eyes rested on hers. 'Just what exactly do you mean by that, Mrs Adams?'

'I mean exactly what I said, *Mrs Barker*,' Donna replied, her tone just as sharp as Denise's. 'If Mum is trying to tell me something and I'm not believing her because—'

'There's no one here ill-treating Mary. She falls, because of her age as well as the condition. I'm sure there is nothing to worry about but I will keep my eye on her over the next few days.'

Donna left the office, not at all convinced that things were as cut and dried as Denise was suggesting. Nor did she like the tone she had used with her. This wasn't the first bruise, and Donna worried that it wouldn't be the last.

But was it guilt that was making her jump to conclusions, maybe because she couldn't care for Mary herself?

If it weren't for Mary constantly asking to leave, she might have been satisfied after talking to Denise. But if someone was abusing her mum, she needed to find out who.

She needed to talk to Sam.

Chapter Twenty-Five

Donna jolted awake. She glanced at the clock on the wall. It was ten past ten: she hadn't even realised she had fallen asleep on the settee that evening. No wonder, though, as she'd completed a double shift at Shop&Save, followed by a visit to see Mum and then a quick stop off to make sure that Sam was still coping. Although Donna was surprised, Sam seemed to be doing quite well, all things considered. But still she worried about him.

Her mobile phone was ringing. That was what must have woken her up. She picked it up, smiling when she saw it was Owen. They hadn't met for a while as he'd been away for a few days on business. Already she couldn't believe how much she was missing him.

She pressed answer and turned to lie on her back. 'Hello, you.'

'Hello, gorgeous. How are you doing?'

'Fine – you?'

'Good, but I'm missing you.'

'You're not parked up outside, are you?' Donna held her breath in anticipation, hoping that he was going to surprise her.

'Sadly not,' he replied. 'I won't be home until tomorrow.'

'Shame – I have the house to myself again.'

'Shame indeed.'

A pause.

'Do you want to Skype so I can see you?' he asked.

'God, no. I look terrible without any make-up at this time of night.'

'It's not your make-up I'm interesting in seeing.'

'Don't be a pervert!'

'Don't tell me that you haven't been thinking about what we did last week?'

'Oh, no, it's never crossed my mind,' she teased. 'Not when I was at work grinning like a Cheshire cat, even after I'd been sitting behind the till for hours bored out of my brain. Nor when I was walking back from work and saw two teenagers necking and my insides fizzed.'

'Your insides fizzed?'

She laughed now, embarrassed again. 'Yes, they fizzed!'

'Can't wait to see that.'

'Can't wait to show you.'

'Show me now.'

She frowned. 'Pardon?'

'Let me listen to you down the phone while I talk dirty to you.'

She sat up and ran a hand through her hair. 'Noooo, I can't do that.'

'Haven't you ever wanted to?'

'I've wanted to do a lot of things but I don't think I'd ever–'

'Try it – you might enjoy it. And let's face it, there's only you in the room if you don't.'

'I...' Donna paused. What was it she kept saying to herself about living a little and having a bit of fun?

'Okay.' The air in the room was hot, yet her skin broke out in goosebumps at the thought of what she was about to do.

'You ready?' he asked.

'What do you mean?'

'I mean, can you get to the most appropriate places?'

'Oh, then I'm ready.' She almost squeaked with embarrassed laughter.

'Okay, here goes.'

'What will you be doing while you're, er, talking dirty?'

'I'll be doing the same thing as you. Are you comfortable yet?'

'Yes.'

'Are you wet?'

'Yes.' She was glad he couldn't see her blushing.

'I'm going to tell you what I'd like to be doing to you right now. First, close your eyes.'

Donna closed her eyes. 'Done.'

'Now imagine me kneeling down between your legs. I'm looking at you while I run my fingers up your body. Up and over your stomach, slowly, slowly, towards your chest. Up through the gap in those fantastic tits of yours.'

Donna giggled.

'Stop laughing!' His voice was light.

'Sorry.'

'Up over your neck and into your mouth. Then I move my hand lower.'

Donna laughed again.

'Stop laughing!'

'I'm sorry. I can't concentrate. Besides, I think I'd rather wait until I can have the real thing.'

'Shame.' He didn't seem annoyed. 'Because I was just getting started.'

Even the thought of him touching himself was enough to send the equivalent of electrical pulses through her entire body. She pressed the phone to her ear to concentrate.

'My mouth slides down your body to find a nipple,' he continued. 'I bite it – not too hard. You arch your back in response. You like that, I see. I move to the other one, do the same to that. Your nipples are hard, you horny bitch. I can't wait to taste more. I can't wait to taste all of you.'

Donna squirmed. Honestly, she knew some women found this kind of thing a turn-on but she didn't like it at all.

'Still not feeling it?' he asked after a moment's silence.

'Sorry.'

'Ah, well. There's always the next time we meet. Are you free tomorrow?'

'Yes, I think I am.' Although Mary wasn't far from her mind, now that Sam was out of hospital she could relax a little.

'Good,' replied Owen. 'Hold that thought.'

Lewis sat up with a start. Disoriented, he switched on the bedside lamp and glanced at his watch. It was only one a.m. With a sigh, he pulled back the covers and sat on the side of the bed. His skin felt clammy to the touch, a trickle of sweat running down the middle of his back. But it wasn't the heat of the summer night that had woken him. It was another nightmare. Shots fired, man down, man DOWN. The words ran through his mind over and over again.

As his breathing calmed, he ran a hand over his hair. Would the memories ever become just that? Would he ever have happy recollections of his time in the army – unlike the nightmares that seemed to plague his waking life as well as his nights?

Recollections of things he would rather forget always seemed to take preference over carefree times – out on a mission with his friends, having a laugh under the baking sun of an evening, friendly banter with the women, messing around with the guys. He'd always been sad when a mission had come to an end, but relieved that most of the people he cared about had survived it. That was, until Nathan had been killed.

He moved to the window, pulled back the curtain and looked down on the quiet street. The Mitchell Estate had always been his home but after being away for so long, he didn't fit in here. He didn't belong.

If it weren't for Amy, he wasn't sure he would have come back to his mum's. Now she'd made it clear that things were over between them, Lewis wondered if he'd be better off finding another city to live in. Somewhere he could start afresh, leave his past behind and get on with his future.

Being apart from Amy frustrated him, because all he wanted was for her to understand what he was going through. For anyone to understand, really. But then, he knew it was up to him to talk about what had happened, and he wouldn't do that. He wanted to block it all out. So was it any wonder she didn't know how to act around him?

He didn't want to begin again somewhere else. He wanted his life here to work. But he needed to put in the effort too, something he certainly wasn't doing.

Below on the driveway, he could see the Land Rover parked on the small space that had been created for it to squeeze onto. The vehicle was eleven years old now, but his mum wouldn't swap it for something smaller and more convenient and economical, as it was one of the last things of his dad's that she had held on to.

Laura was tiny compared to Lewis, so she looked silly behind the wheel, but she couldn't half knock up a speed in the old tub. A few times, Lewis had found himself holding onto the door handle as she'd taken a corner a little faster than he would have liked. Laura loved that she felt safe in it, laughed when she realised she had spooked the hulk of a man sitting next to her.

Until the sudden death of his father, his parents had lived comfortably in this house for years. They had stayed together too, making his family background very different to most of his so-called friends who had lived on the estate. Many of them had come from broken homes.

He'd bumped into a few of them here and there since he'd been home. Most were either married or shacked up with partners; most didn't have either a job or ambition. Some of their women had been willing to give them a few kids so they could scam the system into letting them stay at home as a family instead of working to earn their keep.

The state was a stupid thing, Lewis scoffed. He was getting to know that more from bitter experience too, in and out of the army.

Hands resting on the wooden frame in the middle of the window, Lewis fought back irritation. He banged his forehead on the glass, and again.

When was his life going to get on track?

Donna was bursting with happiness when she went into work the night after she'd met up with Owen again.

Sarah rolled her eyes the minute she saw her. 'Come on, then,' she said, 'out with the sordid details.'

'What?' Donna looked all innocent.

'You've had sex again, haven't you?' Sarah whispered to her.

'I have.' Donna grinned.

Sarah pointed at her. 'Your smile could light up the M6!'

'Well, put the kettle on and make me a nice cuppa and I might just tell you some of the details.'

'Only some?' Sarah tutted as she walked away. 'I want to know *everything*!'

Donna popped on her overall. She was bursting to tell someone about Owen and she had no one else to confide in.

Owen had picked her up the previous evening as planned, after she had collapsed into fits of laughter over the phone sex conversation. He'd taken her to a pub a few miles away, and on the way back he'd pulled over into a lay-by. She'd laughed again as she said she was too old to be taken in the back seat of a car.

But Owen had other ideas. He'd grabbed her hand and they'd gone into the woods. He'd bent her over behind a tree. She'd felt so naughty, having never had sex outside before. What had she been missing all her life?

'No way!' Sarah's eyes were wide when she'd confided in her.

Donna nodded. 'I can't believe I had the courage. Me, outside, where anyone could see us!'

'You have definitely got it bad.' Sarah shook her head. 'I can't believe all that's happened to you in the space of a couple of weeks. I know you deserve your happiness, Don, but wow. I would kill to have sex right now. Me and Craig haven't had a bit of rumpy-pumpy in months.'

'Rumpy-pumpy?' Donna burst into loud laughter. 'I haven't heard it called that in a long time!'

'You know what I mean.' Sarah waved her comment away. 'I love him but I'm not in love with him anymore.'

'Poppycock. You and Craig have everything I want. You get on so well.'

'I know, but the sex has gone stale.'

'Being together twenty years will do that to you,' Donna sympathised. 'Although with me and Joe, it was about six! But don't you think that it's staying power and commitment that are more important than sex?'

'Says the woman who's had fifty-seven orgasms.'

Donna blushed. 'You can get the sparkle back if you want to.'

'I doubt it. Like you said, we've been together for twenty years. A lot has happened during that time, like spare tyres, love handles and about four stone in extra weight between us.'

'Well, I'm no expert!'

'Yes, but you're getting some at least.'

'It's all about making an effort, I suppose.'

'But most of the time, we're both done in at the end of the day. Sex is the last thing on our minds when we're trying to stop from falling asleep on the sofa about eight o'clock.'

Donna paused for a moment. 'Well, you could read erotica.'

Sarah turned her head pretty sharpish.

'Like *Fifty Shades*? I loved that trilogy.'

'I'm reading *You Complete Me*. Very, very, sexy. Owen bought me the paperback.'

'Ohmigod.' Sarah quickly served a young boy who had come to the till with a packet of crisps. 'Wait, actually, he *sounds* like a God!' As soon as the boy had gone, she reached under the counter for her Kindle and switched it on. 'What was that story called?'

Donna smiled. '*You Complete Me.* It's in the top one hundred. I reckon it'll be a guaranteed bestseller. It's going to spread by word of mouth like wildfire. It's so hot!'

'No wonder women are reading erotica on Kindle these days.' Sarah clicked away on her Paperwhite. 'We can't get any in real life so imaginary has to do. Ah, here it is. Wow, it's got sixty-eight five star reviews!'

'Oh, I must add one. That'll make it sixty-nine!' Donna laughed and then felt her skin reddening again.

Sarah laughed. 'Power to the women!'

While two girls dilly-dallied in front of her over which chocolate bar to choose, Donna reached for her phone, checked her messages but there were no new ones from Owen. Feeling brave, and a little horny, she sent him a saucy text and got back to work.

God, she couldn't believe how much he was under her skin already. She was definitely in lust with him, totally under his spell. Last night had been amazing. She'd never thought it was possible to feel this high on emotion.

Truth be told, she never wanted this thing with Owen to end.

Chapter Twenty-Six

After receiving more complaints about Lewis Prophett, Josie hadn't wanted to call at either his wife's or his mother's homes. She knew they were only doing their best, and that it was Lewis who had the problem. So, instead, she asked Lewis to come in to see her.

She raced down the corridor towards the interview room, a manila folder and notepad tucked underneath her arm. She'd only just got there in time after running her last women in crisis session at The Workshop. Everyone had heard rumours that the money was being cut but Josie hadn't wanted to confirm anything until she absolutely had to. Now though, she was wondering if there was anywhere the members of the group could continue to meet without her. They were making real progress, and it would be a shame if the support network they'd created was going to end.

Lewis was sitting at the table when she passed the glass-petitioned wall. She smiled at him as she entered the room.

'I'm sorry I'm a bit late. Thanks for coming in.'

'It didn't feel like I had any choice,' Lewis replied, his tone sullen.

Josie sighed. Not a good start. She pulled out a chair and sat across the table from him.

'I've had another report of your anti-social behaviour over the weekend. It's becoming quite the broken record at the moment.'

'People should mind their own business.' Lewis folded his arms.

'People are trying to do just that but you're interrupting their peace, it seems.'

'Can you prove it's me?'

'Can you prove it's not?' Josie put down her pen and sighed. 'Lewis, I'm as surprised as you are to see you sitting in my office. I've no wish to tell a grown man off, but I've had several complaints about you now – mostly about the noise you make when you come home in the early hours – so it's my duty as a housing officer to let you know that you're in breach of tenancy rules.'

'I'm not the tenant.'

Josie raised her eyebrows.

Lewis sighed and sat forward. 'I'll try and stay quiet, yeah. I don't want to get Mum into any trouble.'

'Well, as you rightly say, it *is* her tenancy. It would be a shame to ruin her good record with a few silly antics.' She paused. 'Your mum told me you've recently lost your job.'

'It was a temporary contract. It didn't get renewed.'

'Any reason for that?'

Lewis shook his head. 'I was covering someone's sick leave.'

There was a silence and Josie scribbled down some notes to fill it. Then she looked up.

'Lewis, I—'

He seemed to be in a bit of a trance, holding his head in his hands.

'In the night, people don't hear you scream,' he told her.

'Excuse me?' Josie replied, unsure if he had said the words without thinking.

'But what happens when the screams are constantly inside your head during the day as well?'

Josie put her pen down. 'Are you hearing voices, Lewis?'

'No.'

'Just noises?'

'No, just screaming.'

'People screaming or engine noise?' Josie probed.

'The sounds of the army. The engines firing up, people shouting.'

'So you're still having flashbacks?'

He nodded.

'Of anything in particular?'

Lewis shrugged.

A few seconds went by before Josie closed the file, realising he'd clammed up again. 'We can try and understand if you'll let us,' she told him. 'Me, your mum, Amy. But our hands are tied if you won't make the first move.'

'What can I do?'

'Go and see someone.'

'All they'll make me do is go over everything. It doesn't help.' Lewis ran a hand over his head. 'I don't want to talk about it.'

'How long have you been back here now?' Josie continued.

'Nearly two years.'

'And how often have you talked about what's bothering you through those two years?'

Lewis looked down.

'So you're trying to forget it?'

'Trying.' He raised his eyes to hers.

'But it's not getting easier at all?'

'No.'

Josie wanted to reach across the table and touch his hand, but she didn't. 'Then *talk* to someone about it,' she said.

'No one will understand.' Lewis looked away now.

'How do you know?'

He froze completely then and refused to say anything more. After a few moments, Josie showed him out of the room and followed him into the reception area. She grabbed a leaflet from a rack at the side of the door.

'Take this. It has lots of details of where you can get help. Please don't discard it. Have a read and see what they can do for you. You need to talk to someone.'

Lewis almost snatched the leaflet from her hand. 'I *need* to get on with my life without everyone telling me what to do.'

Josie watched him storm out of the building with a worried expression. Lewis seemed to be unravelling fast, and there didn't seem to be anything anyone could do about it.

For her next visit to Poplar Court, Donna was accompanied by Sam. When she'd last gone to visit him, she'd mentioned the bruise she had seen on Mary's arm, plus her mum's accusations. Until then, she hadn't realised how worried she was, even though she was still convinced some things might have been caused by Mary's dementia. Once she'd confided in him, he'd taken it upon himself to ring a friend and had borrowed a mini surveillance camera. Donna had been far from pleased. However, by the end of the phone call, Sam had persuaded her to let him set it up discreetly for a few days.

If it gave her peace of mind, then it was worth it, surely?

Mary was asleep in the armchair when they arrived. Not wishing to wake her, Donna glanced around the room.

'Where do you think the best place would be to hide it?' she asked, watching as Sam removed the equipment from his bag.

'I need a plug nearby, plus somewhere that covers Nan's chair, I think?' Sam cursed as he struggled to get into the bag with one hand.

Donna took it from him and held it open while he accessed it.

'I feel like a one-armed bandit,' he moaned.

Donna watched Sam, but she didn't like the feeling that swept over her as he set up the camera.

'Are you sure we should be doing this?' she asked. 'Putting a camera up anywhere is dodgy, but somewhere it shouldn't be? Do you think we're taking too much of a risk?'

'What do you mean?'

'What if we get caught and they decide Nan has to leave? It's against the law to film people without their permission, isn't it?'

'If anyone's hurting Nan, the camera will be the last thing on their minds. They'll have me to deal with, as well as the police.'

Sam placed the camera on a shelf in the side unit, slipping the wire behind it. As he reached for the plug, there was a knock on the door.

'I hope that's Megan!' Donna felt her skin flush at the thought of it being anyone else. She sighed with relief when she answered the door and was right.

'Morning, Donna.' Megan stepped into the hallway. 'How are you? Everything okay, I hope?'

'Yes, everything's fine,' she said. 'I'm on a late shift this afternoon so thought I'd pop in early.'

Sam's head appeared around the door, giving Donna a quick thumbs up before his eyes fell on Megan.

'Hiya!' His smile widened as they both joined him in the living room. 'How're you doing?'

'I'm good, thanks.' Megan smiled back. 'How are you? How's the hand?'

Sam shrugged. 'Oh, it's not hurting much now at all.'

Donna eyed them both, watching as Megan's face reddened and Sam appeared to be all bashful.

'Still liking the hot weather?' said Sam.

'Yes. Can't believe it's been sunny for so long.'

'You look lovely with a tan.'

'Thanks.'

Donna was glad to see Mary open her eyes. She moved across to her, thankful that she wouldn't feel so much of a gooseberry now.

'How are you, Mum?' she said.

'I'm fine,' Mary snapped. 'What do you want?'

'Oh, don't be like that.'

'Hi, Mary.' Megan gave her a wave.

'You can sod off as well.'

Megan smiled. 'I'm going, but I'll be back later when your visitors have gone.'

Donna breathed a sigh of relief after Megan had left.

'That was close,' said Sam. 'Good job it was Megan.'

'She's nice, isn't she?'

Sam nodded. 'Yeah. I want her to come out with me for a drink but she isn't having any of it.'

'Pity,' Donna commiserated. 'I think she'd do you the world of good.'

'How?'

'Well, she'd take care of you so that I don't have to worry about you all the time.'

'You don't have to worry about me, Mum. I'm capable of looking after myself.'

'Really? Then how did you manage to nearly chop your hand off?'

Sam smirked as he positioned the wire underneath a frilly drawer run and beside a photo frame.

Donna moved to the other side of the room, looking to see if she could spot it at different angles.

'Do you think anyone will see it?' asked Sam.

'I hope not.' Donna banished her guilt as he switched it on. She stood in front of Mary and rested her hand on the side of her face, pleased when it wasn't batted away.

'I won't let anyone hurt you, Mum,' she said. 'I promise.'

Chapter Twenty-Seven

After bumping into Sam at Poplar Court earlier in the day, Megan hadn't been able to stop thinking about him. She picked up her phone again, quickly scrolling through the messages that had gone back and forth between them since.

Great to see you today. Why not come out for a drink with me?

I'm really busy.

You can't be busy all the time.

I am, sorry.

I won't take no for an answer.

You'll have to.

It hadn't been the first time they'd exchanged messages. Despite not giving Sam her number when he was in the hospital, she'd given in and sent him a text asking how he was.

She'd lost count of how many times they had swapped messages since, returning most of them, enjoying their flirty banter. He'd asked to meet her twice but she'd said she was busy on both nights. She would have been too, if you could count staying in to watch *Coronation Street* being busy.

It had been an hour until the next message had come in.

Are you giving me the brush off or are you playing hard to get?

Megan had snorted when she'd read that one. As if she would do that.

She had pondered so long on how to reply that in the end, another hour passed. Sam had sent her more messages.

I have a check-up next week. I'd really like someone to hold my hand, my good hand! I don't suppose …

Megan paused. Surely seeing him again wouldn't do any harm? She really wanted to.

What time?

11.10. You can sit and wait with me, if you like?

I finish my shift at 11.00, so I'll come and find you.

Perfect.

If I can't find you, I'm off though.

Megan sent the last message as more of a back-up plan. It could still give her time to slip away without him seeing her. She could say that she'd had to work over or something.

His reply straight back made her smile.

Always drive a hard bargain, don't you?

She tapped the phone on her chin, then looked up as her mum shouted over to her.

'I've been trying to catch your eye for ages,' Patricia said. 'What's keeping your attention on that phone?'

'Oh, it's just a silly YouTube video,' said Megan guiltily.

'Well, I just wanted to let you know that *Coronation Street* is due to start.'

'Okay.' Megan put down her phone and stood up. 'Would you like a cup of tea?'

Patricia smiled. 'And a piece of that cake you brought in with you this afternoon?'

Megan walked to the door and then hotfooted back for her phone. Sliding it into the back pocket of her denim shorts, she went into the kitchen and put on the kettle.

Once tea bags were in the mugs and the cake had been cut, she checked her phone again while she waited for the kettle to boil. She tapped on the last message she'd received. Sam had attached two photos to it. He'd taken a couple of selfies, sticking his tongue out on one of them and grinning manically on the other.

Every time Megan saw the one with a grin, the image seemed so clear it was as if he was standing right in front of her. She held the phone up and imagined Sam there. What would she say to him? Would he like her mum?

She decided that she *would* pop in and see him next week. After all, it wouldn't do any harm to be friends. She could cope with that as long as she got to see that smile for real.

When the tea was made, she took everything through on a tray and sat down again. The theme tune of the popular soap burst from the television.

'Ooh, good, just in time,' said Patricia. 'I wonder what David Platt will be up to today.'

As she immersed herself into other people's lives, Meg tried to forget about her own. Sam's smile in particular. But it kept flashing up in front of her eyes. Even if she couldn't show him her skin, he was well and truly under hers.

Sam was in the flat with Brendan. The weather still being exceptionally hot, he'd spent the afternoon in the pub with some of his mates after leaving his nan's flat. It was the only thing he was capable of at the moment until his hand had healed a little more.

He'd got lucky, though. He'd managed to figure out Scott Johnstone's whereabouts. Apparently, he was living with some woman in Marilyn Avenue. Sam had left a message with the guy who'd told him, asking Scott to get in touch. He needed to get straight with him, make sure he knew that he wasn't going to come after him for what he was owed. He'd heard on the grapevine that Scott was going to shut him up. Right now, he was in too vulnerable a place to make a noise.

The windows were wide open, the television blaring out. As they sat together continuing to drink, there was a bang at the door. Sam and Brendan looked at each other. When Sam refused to budge, with an exaggerated sigh, Brendan went to answer the door.

He heard a kerfuffle but didn't have time to move before he saw Scott appear in the living room. Still sitting down, he was at a disadvantage and couldn't stand up in time before he felt a fist smash into his face. He put up his arm to defend himself, sheer terror coming over him as he knew he wasn't able to fight back.

Scott grabbed Sam's injured hand and squeezed hard on it.

The pain brought stars to Sam's eyes and he writhed on the settee.

'I hear you've been bad-mouthing me, Harvey,' Scott said.

Sam thought back to that afternoon. Had someone heard him moaning about not getting his fair share after the robbery, when he was acting all big in front of everyone?

Still holding onto his hand, Scott dragged him to his feet.

'Put the cops on to me and you're for it, Harvey, do you hear?' Scott's face came within an inch of his nose. 'I've just got out and I sure as hell ain't going back inside because of a shit like you.'

Behind him, Sam could see Brendan, his skin ashen, seeming to shrink into the wall.

'I haven't said anything,' he lied.

Scott punched him in the stomach, then in the face a few more times. Sam felt like he was going to pass out after the last one caught him on the side of his temple. He coughed, blood coming from a split lip as he struggled to catch his breath.

'You wanted your cut?' Scott threw a few notes onto the floor at Sam's feet.

Sam could do nothing but groan.

'You keep away from me now, do you fucking hear?'

When Sam didn't respond, Scott kicked him in the stomach again. Breathless, he writhed around the floor.

'And keep your mouth shut.' Scott turned to glare at Brendan who lowered his eyes. 'Both of you.'

Once Scott had gone, Sam dragged himself up to sitting, resting his back on the settee. Already he could feel his face swelling, but he was more concerned with the damage that might have been caused to his hand. He winced as he tried to breathe. He'd have to get his ribs checked out if they weren't any better in the morning.

'What the fuck was all that about?' Brendan spoke in a high-pitched tone.

'Just a spot of bother,' Sam said, through shallow breaths.

'Are you okay?'

Sam held up his good hand.

Brendan helped him to his feet, then began to pace the room. 'He's a fucking lunatic! What did you say about him?'

'I was just after where he lived.' Sam wasn't going to tell Brendan that he had been mouthing off about Scott. The last thing he wanted was more trouble when he couldn't defend himself.

'If he comes here again, you'll have to move out.' Brendan was still pacing. 'I don't want his sort on my doorstep. I can't cope with that kind of thing.'

Sam wanted to respond, to tell Brendan that he'd stay here as long as he liked. But, right now, he needed somewhere to lay low so it would be best to let this die down. He'd get round Brendan later. He might be the only friend he had right now.

One of his so-called mates must have grassed him up. With no one to watch his back, Sam realised he was on his own. And things would probably get worse once word got round that Scott had given him a beating. There was no honour amongst thieves as far as he was concerned.

Knowing his hand was going to take months to heal, he couldn't go back to what he used to do anyway. And, until it was better, he was in danger of being attacked again unless he kept his nose clean.

Maybe this was his chance to start afresh, keep away from the idiots he'd hung around with and go on the straight and narrow. Besides, he was tired of having no money, of others being wary of him, or looking down their noses at him.

Other people turned their lives around – surely he could?

And if he didn't, he was going to live in fear. Someone would always be out to get him. Did he really want to live his life looking over his shoulder all the time?

Chapter Twenty-Eight

Lewis knocked on Amy's front door. It still seemed strange not to let himself in with his key, but he couldn't do that. He didn't live here anymore, and it didn't seem right.

As he waited on the doorstep, he felt his hands shaking and pushed them into his pockets. He hadn't had a drink in three days and, although the nightmares had continued, he'd wanted to stay sober.

He'd known that Amy might not want to talk to him but he had to try to see her. After chatting to Josie, and then having another conversation with Daniel, he wanted to talk to Amy now.

Actually, he just wanted to see Amy and this seemed a perfect excuse to visit. He'd called ahead after he'd cocked up on his last visit.

'You look tired,' she said as she let him in. He followed her through to the kitchen, checking out how amazing she looked in shorts and a bright orange vest. Lewis couldn't really recall a time when Amy had ever looked anything less than amazing, though.

'I'm not sleeping well,' he told her.

'Me either, because of the heat, but I expect you'll be used to these temperatures.' She smiled. 'Tea or lemonade?'

'Lemonade, please.' Lewis smiled back, thankful that she was making him feel welcome. Again, he felt like a stranger in a house where he had once belonged. He glanced around the homely kitchen, photos of him on the side of the fridge, just like at his mum's. This time the father and son were him and Daniel.

'Is Dan home?' he asked.

'Yes, he's—' Amy jumped as there was a thump on the wall.

Dan's head popped up outside the kitchen window and he waved at Lewis. He held up his football and beckoned him outside.

Lewis raised his hand, stretching out his fingers. 'Five minutes,' he shouted.

Dan was off again before Amy had handed Lewis his drink. He took a sip of the cold liquid.

'I – can we talk?' he said, all of a sudden feeling like he was stuck for words.

'As long as you don't snap my head off like the last time.'

Lewis looked abashed. He pointed to the table and they sat down. Taking a deep breath, he told her about his meeting with Josie and how he was thinking of getting help.

'Why are you telling me this?' she asked him afterwards.

'Because I need something to work towards, aim for, you know? I was hoping you'd say that if I change then you'd let me come home.'

Amy had been sitting forward but sat back in her chair now. 'I'm not sure I can promise you that – and it's really unfair of you to ask.'

'But if you …'

'It sounds like blackmail!' She stood up and moved to the sink. Keeping her back to him, she continued. 'You know it won't ever be the same between us. Even if you get help, I can't be there for you as a wife.' She turned back to him then. 'But I can be there as a friend.'

Lewis swallowed. Why had he expected anything more? But it was something he could work at. He was determined to save his marriage, so it would have to do for now.

'Stay for tea?' Amy spoke into the silence. 'Dan would like it.'

'Would you like it?'

Amy paused. 'Yes, I would. You know I would. But it doesn't mean anything.'

'It doesn't mean that I'll stop trying either.'

They shared a strained smile.

Lewis knocked back his drink and went out into the garden. 'Right, you,' he said, running at Dan and manoeuvring the ball off him, 'let's see who's best. Father or son.'

As Lewis switched off, chasing Dan around the garden after he'd regained the ball, he heard himself laughing. He couldn't remember the last time he had laughed. He hoped it would continue. Because it felt good.

He glanced at the kitchen window to see Amy watching them. He smiled again, and she smiled back. God, he missed her.

Maybe it was too late for him and Amy to start again, but he wasn't giving up on his family yet.

Keera hadn't long been at work that night when Steve Wilson showed his ugly face. She'd been helping Ramona out with her computer after the screen had gone blank, and was on all fours beneath the counter, checking that all the cables were still plugged in. He didn't see her as he came bursting through the door.

'You got my money?' he said to Ramona.

'No, not yet.' Keera could hear the tremble in Ramona's voice. 'I said I'd get it to you by the end of the month and … stop, you can't come—'

Steve reached over the counter and grabbed a handful of Ramona's hair. 'I said you needed to get it to me by last weekend. I have people after me for money too, so I need that cash.'

'I haven't got it!' Ramona tried to free herself as he pulled her nearer. He drew up his hand just as Keera crawled out from beneath the desk. She grabbed the stapler from behind the counter and brought it down on Steve's knuckles.

Steve let go of Ramona and clasped his hand. 'You mad fucking bitch!' he screamed.

'She hasn't got the money.' Keera folded her arms and stood up to him. She felt better that she was behind the counter, glancing to her right to see that the baseball bat was still there if he tried to jump over.

As he came at them again, she grabbed for it, raising it high above her head. 'Come any closer and I will use it!'

Steve stood in front of them both, catching his breath for a moment. Keera could smell the alcohol fumes from where she was standing. She glanced at Ramona, cowering by her side.

The door opened behind them. Estelle came through first, followed by the new girl, Sophie. Behind them was one of their regular clients.

'Everything okay here?' Trevor Price asked, coming to stand in front of the women.

'Mind your own business.' Steve glanced at him fleetingly.

'But these women are my friends.'

'Your friends?' Steve sneered as he looked around the room. 'You're old enough to be their father.'

'Steve!' cried Ramona.

Trevor shook his head. 'Your sort aren't welcome if you're out to hurt any of them, so I suggest you sling your hook.'

'I don't fucking think so.'

'Oh, I do fucking think so.'

'Why, you …' Steve launched himself across the room, a fist drawn back in the air.

Trevor punched him in the side of his face.

Steve staggered but stayed on his feet. With a roar, he charged at Trevor again and pushed him back against the wall, but Trevor stood his ground and rammed his fist into Steve's stomach.

'Stop!' Ramona cried, coming from behind the reception. 'No more, please.'

Trevor relented and pushed Steve to the floor. He wiped one palm across the other as if ridding himself of their filth.

Keera grinned. 'Way to go, Trev. I didn't know you had it in you.'

'Only when it's called for,' replied Trevor. 'I can't stand people who use violence as a means of getting their own way but I do believe in dishing it out to those people when necessary.' He looked at all four women in turn. 'I used to be a street fighter … got paid good money for it too, but like most things, I became too old.' He pointed to his nose. 'And this got broken one too many times for my liking.'

Trevor held out his hand, offering to help Steve up from the floor, but Steve slapped it away. However, once Steve had got to his feet of his own volition, Trevor grabbed the lapels of his jacket and pulled him near.

Come round here again causing hassle, and I will have you seen to,' he told him quietly. 'These girls deserve to be treated with respect, you got that?'

Steve said nothing. Keera couldn't believe how much of a coward he was when challenged.

'You got that?' Trevor repeated, pulling Steve closer.

'Yeah, I got it.' Steve pushed Trevor's hands down. He turned to Ramona, first letting his eyes rest menacingly on Keera. 'I still want my money.'

Trevor pushed him towards the door. 'I'll see you out. Goodnight, ladies, and be careful.'

'Goodnight.' They chanted in unison.

When he had gone, all four women started to talk at once.

'Ohmigod, did you see that!' said Sonia.

'I can't believe he was a street fighter.' Estelle shook her head. 'I mean, I know he keeps himself fit but…'

'Wow, he's our hero,' said Keera. 'I never would have thought.'

'He's done me more harm than good,' Ramona pouted, going back behind the reception. 'Steve won't give up. He'll come back when the likes of Trevor isn't around and he'll probably cause more damage then. He's a lunatic, especially when he's been drinking.'

'You shouldn't put up with him,' said Estelle.

'I owe him money, babe.' Ramona blushed. 'It's my fault.'

'Don't you have any family who can bail you out?'

'Are you kidding? They're as scared of him as I am!'

Keera put her arms around Ramona and gave her a hug. 'I can chip in with some money if it helps,' she offered.

Ramona started to cry. 'But if I give him money, he always wants more. I'm not even sure if I owe him anything now or if he's trying it on. I just know that the debt is never paid off.' She looked at them with watery eyes. 'My own frigging brother.'

'It's not your fault that he's a lunatic,' Keera admonished. 'If he comes again, I'll find something else to batter him with. He'll get fed up sooner or later.'

'He'll never get fed up.' Ramona shook her head before bursting into tears again. 'I don't think I'll ever get rid of him.'

Keera threw her a sympathetic look. Although she tried to

comfort her friend, she was concerned about seeing Steve again. She'd thought he'd grass her up to Sam when she'd kneed him in the balls to get away from him. Now, she had given him more ammunition to get her back.

Surely he would say something soon.

Chapter Twenty-Nine

Donna was starving as she got ready for her next date with Owen. She was glad he was picking her up at half past seven or she swore she would die of hunger, used to eating much earlier in the evening. In another summer dress, although the weather threatened to bring a storm, she gave herself the once-over in the long hall mirror. She grinned as she twirled around, noticing that her arms and legs were quite toned because of all the manual work she did in the shop. Tangerine orange painted toenails peeped out of her strappy sandals, but nothing was as bright as her smile.

Half an hour later, she was standing by the window looking out onto the street. So far, there had been no sign of Owen. She'd texted him a couple of times with no reply and then she'd rung to find his phone was switched off.

What the hell was going on? Was he lying ill at home, unable to reach anyone? Had he been involved in an accident on the way here or something? A shiver of fear swept over Donna. God, she hoped not.

It was nearing eight thirty when her calls were finally answered.

'Owen!' She cried. 'Are you okay?'

'I'm fine, thanks.'

'I've been trying to contact you for the last hour I thought you might be ill or had an acc—'

'I said I'm fine.'

'Oh!' He seemed really irritated with her. 'What's up?'

'I'm just a little confused.'

'About what?'

'When we last met, you said you weren't after a relationship. I thought you didn't want to see me again.'

Donna cast her mind back to the conversation he was referring to and then she understood. They had been talking about how they hadn't been seeing each other for long but how they felt as if they had been together forever. It was lust talk, she knew. People were always giddy to see each other at the start of a relationship.

'When we chatted, I thought you meant that I was coming on too heavy,' she explained, 'and that you wanted to see how things went before we committed to anything. So I said what I thought you wanted to hear, I suppose.'

'You did?'

'Yes. I'm happy to take things as they come as I— I really like you and I don't want things to be spoiled.'

'I thought you wanted some no-strings attached fun.'

Donna's heart lurched. 'If that's the impression I gave you, then I'm sorry. That's not what I'm after at all.'

'I assumed …'

'You assumed I was after you spending some money on me and then I would dump you?'

'Well, I—'

'I'm not like that at all.'

A pause.

'I've made a fool out of myself, haven't I?' said Owen.

'No!'

'It's just that when we met, everything seemed too good to be true.'

'For me, too.'

Another pause. Oh, please don't say she'd blown it, Donna thought to herself.

'So would you like to see me again?' he asked.

'Of course!' Donna had to stop herself from shouting down the phone.

'Thank God for that!'

Donna giggled.

'How about I make up for tonight and take you somewhere special?'

'You don't need to do that.'

'I know, but I'd like to. Could you get away this weekend or next, just for a night?'

Donna sighed. 'I'm not sure. My mum isn't too good at the moment. Keera will probably be working so I can't ask her to look in on her, either. And I know Sam isn't doing too bad on his own but I'm concerned that he—'

'Stop!' Owen interrupted. 'Listen to yourself for a moment. You should be able to have a life outside of your family. You deserve a little fun, don't you?'

'Well, yes, but I worry that—'

'You worry too much.'

It was exactly what Sam had implied earlier. Maybe they were both right. Donna couldn't help herself. Her family meant everything to her, but she could have some fun too. And she did deserve to be pampered, didn't she?

'Okay,' she said.

'Fantastic. I'll book somewhere nice, not too far away, so we can spend a lot of time at the hotel, if you catch my drift.'

'I'm looking forward to it already.'

As she disconnected the call, Donna grinned. Despite the disappointment about not seeing him that evening, plus the guilt after she had said yes to a night away, she was looking forward to spending more time with Owen. She could get to know what had caused him to be so guarded.

A full night together. She couldn't wait.

After checking in on Mary, Donna arrived at work the next morning just in the nick of time. She ran past Sarah, giving her a wave, and went into the staff room.

'How was your date?' Sarah shouted through the door to her.

'It didn't happen. Owen had to work late.' For some reason, Donna didn't want to tell Sarah about the misunderstanding. 'But he's making it up to me,' she added. 'We're going away for a night this weekend.'

'Wow, he's a quick mover.'

Donna froze in the doorway. 'Do you think?'

'Oh, don't mind me, I'm just envious.' Sarah batted away her comment. 'Where is he taking you?'

'He won't say.' Donna raised her eyebrows. 'It's a surprise.'

'Oh, how romantic.' Sarah sighed. 'You're such a lucky cow.'

'I wish!' Donna thought back to the situation with her mum at Poplar Court. 'I worry, though. What happens if Mum needs me – or Sam?'

'Don't panic so much. How's Sam doing, by the way?'

'Okay, I think. I haven't seen him in a couple of days but I've spoken to him on the phone.' Donna rushed to take her place behind the counter where Sarah had a mug of tea waiting for her. She took a quick sip, her shoulders dipping in appreciation. 'Thanks, I needed that.'

Sarah swiped a newspaper across the scanner for a customer. 'Eighty pence, ta.' She took a coin from the man, rang it through the till and handed him the change.

'And it seems he's taken a liking to someone he met when he was in hospital,' Donna continued.

'Oh?' Sarah turned to her. 'A patient?'

'No, someone who works on the wards. She's a cleaner. Nice girl – wears far too much make-up for her pretty face, though.'

Once the rush of customers had gone, Sarah lifted a box of crisps high onto the counter and began to fill the shelf below. 'So, tell me again about this night away.'

'Not much else to say, really. I just wish it wasn't this weekend.' Donna paused. 'I daren't even mention to Sam or Keera that I'm going away with someone they haven't met yet. I feel really deceitful.'

'They'll be fine. Neither of them are children anymore.'

'I wish I could remember that!' Donna shook her head. 'Well, I don't ever have to worry about Keera, but Sam – honestly, he's always on my mind.'

Sarah stopped what she was doing. 'What are you really scared of?'

'I'm not scared.'

'Yes, you are.'

Donna smiled. Sarah had her sussed out. Although her family took her for granted, she knew she was a carer first and foremost and would always be there for them, even it meant little time for herself. But really she knew that she was coming up with every excuse possible not to go away for the night with Owen because she was terrified of blowing it.

She shrugged. 'I'm just not sure I'm ready for another man in my life right now,' she shared.

'You need to start thinking of yourself for a change,' Sarah admonished. 'Go and have a bit of fun. It's only one night. You'll be back before you know it.'

Donna nodded. It was the first time in years that she had been able to do something like this.

Sarah was right. Despite everything, it would be good for her to get away from it all, even just for one night.

Lewis couldn't sleep so he'd taken himself out for a walk. At two a.m., the estate was at its quietest. He wished his head were the same. He still couldn't get rid of the noises. During the last nightmare that had woken him, he could almost smell burnt flesh, see body parts that had been ripped from his colleagues scattered across the ground. He was almost afraid to sleep because everything seemed so real.

Lewis missed the army, the camaraderie, the sense of purpose and order in his life, but how much had they cared when he had left? "I'm signing off now. Okay, off you go, bye bye." They'd trained him to be a soldier, a killer, but they didn't then train him to be a civilian again.

Why couldn't they have given him a little bit back? Rehabilitated him for six months at least? No wonder he didn't want anyone near him. He didn't want anyone other than Amy to see what he was going through, even though he'd often scared his wife when he'd woken screaming, lashing out at her until he'd realised where he was, that he was safe.

Vincent Square was quiet as he crossed it, a lone cat his only companion as it trotted a few feet behind him. He wished he could tell someone what had happened to his friend, Nathan, why he'd been killed, but every time he thought about it, he became angry. The guilt was still so raw. It shouldn't have happened. As well as

Nathan, he had seen some of the best people he'd ever meet in his life put in the ground too. *He'd* put people in the ground. That was bound to change him.

The cat left him alone but dodged in and out of parked cars as he doubled back and walked the length of Davy Road. For as far as he could see, there were no upstairs lights on in the houses he passed. Was he the only person who couldn't sleep? It was still warm; there were windows open everywhere, but no one as mad as him walking the streets rather than going to sleep for fear of waking in a panic.

He shoved his hands in his pockets, his footsteps heavy. Amy said he needed to leave it all behind, look towards a brighter future. But he couldn't forget the things he had seen, couldn't rid himself of the disgust he felt over some of the things he'd done. Taking a life, no matter if that person was going to kill you if you didn't act in self-defence – no one could get over that.

A dog started to bark as he kicked a brick along the pavement. He wished he'd gone to the pub now, drunk until he was unable to stand, so that he could fall asleep that way. Lewis wanted blackness, so that the nightmares wouldn't return.

He wanted to forget everything. Because if he didn't, he was going to explode.

Chapter Thirty

Ever since Sam had fitted the camera in Mary's room, Donna had checked the feed whenever she'd visited her at Poplar Court. But all she'd seen so far was Megan and several workers coming in to check on Mary, helping her with her needs. The camera had captured nothing out of the ordinary.

However, when she let herself into the flat on Friday morning, Megan was waiting for her.

'I've found your camera,' she whispered angrily as they went through into the kitchen.

Donna paled as she closed the door behind them. She thought about lying and saying that it wasn't hers, but decided to come clean and find out what Megan knew first.

'Have you looked at it?' she asked.

'No.' Megan shook her head.

'Have you wiped it clean?'

'Of course not!'

'Good.'

'But why is it there?'

'I wanted to be sure that Mum isn't being abused.' Donna watched Megan's eyes widen.

'I could never hurt her!' Megan whispered loudly. 'But I could get into trouble if I don't report what I've seen.'

Donna folded her arms. 'Surely she can't get all those bruises by falling? And if she did fall, why wasn't I ever informed?'

Megan paused. 'I think you're right to do it, though. I've had my suspicions for a while.'

Donna stared at Megan. 'Go on.'

'Mary was much happier when she first came here. I know dementia has different stages - I learned about them when I was at college - but I'd like to think after a year working here that I can gauge when things are wrong, or different, or if someone's condition is worsening. But Mary; well, she seemed to be happy one minute and then very quickly began to withdraw.'

'You've been keeping an eye on her?' Donna said incredulously.

Megan nodded. 'Unofficially.'

'And you never said anything?' Donna's tone was harsh.

'I'd lose my job if it came out,' Megan replied. 'That's why I've been in her room a lot lately. I wanted to see what was causing her so much distress.'

Donna stared at the young woman, still unsure whether to believe her or not. 'I need to look at the camera first.'

Megan put her hand in the pocket of her overall and pulled it out.

'You removed it?' Donna frowned.

'I didn't want anyone else to spot it. You'll have to hide it better now.'

Donna took it from her and pressed the rewind button.

'Will you let me know if you see anything, please?' asked Megan, not moving from in front of her. 'Mary means the world to me. I promise I won't tell anyone that I found the camera.'

But Donna wasn't listening anymore. She was too shocked at what she saw on the screen.

'What is it?' Megan stepped forward.

'That bitch.'

Donna turned the screen round to Megan. It had captured Mary sitting in her chair. A woman came into view, shouting at her to turn the television off. When Mary didn't do as she'd asked, the woman swiped up the remote control and smacked it down on Mary's arm.

Mary's cry of pain brought tears to Donna's eyes. Megan's hand covered her mouth.

They both watched the footage as the woman stood over Mary and continued to shout into her face. She then grabbed Mary by the hands and hoisted her to her feet, pulling her up way too fast.

As she yelled at her once more, she pushed Mary back into the chair.

Mary yelping in fear was the last straw for Donna.

'I'll bloody kill her,' cried Donna, racing to the door. 'No one assaults my mum and gets away with it.'

Donna marched along the corridor to the warden's office. She knocked on the door and walked right in, not waiting to be asked.

Denise was sitting at her desk. She looked up with a mix of curiosity and annoyance.

'Mrs Adams, you can't come barging into my office without—'

Donna moved around the side of her desk and slapped Denise hard across the face. 'You bitch!' she seethed, as a batch of files and papers dropped to the floor. 'It was you. You attacked my mother.'

'I haven't—'

'You won't get away with this. You're nothing but a bully.'

'I don't know what you're talking about.' Denise put a hand to her cheek where there was already a red patch showing.

'Oh, I think you do.' Donna watched her squirm in her chair. 'You touch my mother again and I swear to God, I'll harm you in just the same way.'

'I haven't done anything to Mary!'

Megan came rushing in behind her.

'Call the police. I want her arrested.' Denise caught Megan's eye. 'She's gone mad!'

'I don't think you want to do that.' Donna took a step nearer.

'I'll have you charged with assault for this.' Denise picked up the phone receiver.

'Go ahead,' said Donna. 'I shall be calling the police myself soon. I'm sure they'll be interested in the video evidence I have.'

'Video?' Denise faltered.

Donna nodded. 'I fitted a camera.'

'But you can't do that! It's a breach of my rights.'

'What about my mum's rights? You should be looking after her. But I saw you pull her out of the chair by her hair. I saw …' Donna stopped as the screams she'd heard on the video ran through her mind again. 'She was screaming because of it, and then you pushed her back into the chair again. I saw you hit her with the TV remote control.'

Denise said nothing.

Behind Donna, Megan shook her head. 'It was you that caused the bruises on her body. How could you do that to someone so frail?'

'I—'

Donna turned back to Megan. 'Call the police. I think they'll be interested in what I have to show them.'

'It's not easy, you know,' Denise spoke, her voice brittle and accusatory. 'It's hard work looking after so many residents with so many special needs. Once in a while, I lose my temper, that's all. It won't happen again, I swear.'

'You're right about that,' said Donna. 'Call the police, Megan.' She turned to leave.

'Wait, I can explain!' Denise put a hand on Donna's forearm.

'Oh, you're going to hit me now?' Donna recoiled.

'No!' Denise put her hand down at once. 'I …'

'Of course you wouldn't hit me, because I can hit back, can't I? And I will, if I have to.' Donna shook her head. 'You're nothing but a bully and I hope you get what you deserve. I shall certainly be reporting you.'

'It was awful, Sarah.' Donna wiped at her eyes as they sat in the back room of Shop&Save later that same day. 'The bloody warden, of all people. How could she do that to Mum?'

'It's unbelievable,' Sarah sympathised. 'What happened when the police came?'

'The cow was arrested. I thought I might get dragged down to the station after I had slapped her, but Megan backed me up and said Denise was lying.'

'Good for her. It wasn't your fault you were so upset. I'd have slapped her too.'

I hope she gets what she deserves.'

'Do you know if she abused any of the other residents?'

Donna shrugged. 'I'm not sure, but if she did, she won't be doing it again. Surely she can't come back to work there after what she's done?'

'I'm so sorry.' Sarah passed her a mug of tea. 'And after Mary seemed so settled.'

'I know.' Donna sighed. 'And, selfishly, I'll have to cancel my night away now.'

Sarah shook her head. 'You can't do that.'

'I have to. I can't leave Mum on her own after what's happened.'

'I expect she'll be safer now that Denise is out of the way. They'll have to bring in another warden, and Mary will be their first priority.'

'I suppose.' Donna still wasn't convinced. 'I can't go.'

You can go – and you will,' Sarah insisted, folding her arms. 'I've told you before that you need time to yourself. Keera will help out, surely?'

'I doubt it.' Donna huffed at that idea. 'She'll be working. Besides, I've hardly seen anything of her over the past few weeks. She treats the place like a hotel.'

'That's a bit unfair. Most teenagers are like that.'

'Well, she's never been one for hanging around the house. I'd love to see more of her now and then.'

'But you and Keera have always been like that, passing ships in the night.'

'I know, but—'

'If you ask her, she'll stop by.'

'She'll cause a fuss, more like.'

'Most kids do that when they're having to do something that they don't want to. Your Keera is a lovely girl. You should be proud of her.'

'I am proud of her!' Donna felt as if she was being told off. 'But she's just too independent and I wonder at times if she's –'

'– Too much like her mother?'

Donna grinned at Sarah's intuitiveness. 'Piss off, you cow,' she said, her tone light-hearted.

Sarah grinned too. 'If Keera won't help, then *I'll* check up on Mary,' she added. 'And while you're there with Owen, you can switch off completely knowing that everything is fine here.'

Donna pondered. She should go, really, especially after Owen had booked a hotel. And *she* wanted a little attention – was that too much to ask?

But doubts still crowded her mind. What if Mary needed her? Or Sam? What if Keera wasn't able to pop in on Mary?

'It's only one night,' said Sarah.

Donna nodded. 'If Mum is all right when I visit her on Saturday morning before I leave, I will go.'

'Good, and then you can tell me all about it once you get back!'

Donna smirked. 'I knew there was a method in your madness.'

'Yes, I want to live vicariously through you!' Sarah turned to look in the shop. 'Jeez, that bloody Darren is so slow. There's a queue a mile long. Best get back to it.'

Donna got up too. But she couldn't shake off the guilt. She tried to convince herself that everything would be fine.

She didn't need to worry about everyone!

Chapter Thirty-One

The hotel that Owen had booked was only forty minutes' drive away from Stockleigh. They turned off a country lane and onto a sweeping driveway. Donna's face lit up as they parked on a gravel car park to the side of the main building.

'We're staying here?' She almost squeaked, taking in the elegant three-storey building that resembled the country manors she had only seen in magazines. Gardens stretched as far as the eye could see, and a lake to her right had a tiny jetty, two rowing boats bobbing idly about.

She turned to Owen and repeated herself. 'We're staying *here*?'

'We are.'

She leaned over and planted a kiss on his cheek before opening the car door. The heat from outside burst in like backdraft from a fire. She hadn't realised how much of a luxury it was to have air conditioning inside the vehicle. Quickly, she flicked down the visor and checked her reflection in the mirror. No rogue flakes of mascara - check. Lipstick still intact - check. The wanton look she'd found recently - check.

Owen killed the engine. 'Looks great, doesn't it?'

'It looks like it costs a fortune! Are you sure ...'

'You deserve something special after all you've been through recently.'

She smiled as Owen retrieved their bags from the boot and took her hand. 'Come on, not a minute to lose. I can't wait to get you alone.'

Once inside the main building, Donna forced back the giggles she feared would erupt as she glanced around. It was so posh that she wondered if she needed to take her shoes off at the door. Tiled flooring stretched across a vast area, leather armchairs dotted around occasional tables covered in flowers, thick cream curtains hung at white-framed sash windows. The view was incredible and Donna pictured the two of them looking at it later as they shared an aperitif.

Owen ushered her towards a walnut bow-shaped reception desk. After they had checked in, they took the lift to their room. Once the doors were closed, Owen dropped his bag and pressed her up against its wall. He kissed her, taking her by surprise with its force but she wrapped her arms around his neck. Wait until Sarah heard about this, she thought, happily.

Donna did take her shoes off as they stepped out into the corridor once the lift doors had opened again.

'I want to feel this carpet between my toes,' she told Owen as he watched in amazement. 'It's so plush!'

'I hope you'll feel the same about it when you're lying on it.'

Donna blushed as a maid from the room they were passing came out of the room. She must have overheard him.

'Afternoon,' Owen greeted her as they walked past. The woman smiled.

They laughed as they continued. Donna could feel the heat from his hand resting in the small of her back. She giggled as he opened the door to their room.

Once inside, Owen took her bag from her hand and led her to the bed. 'I think it's time you and I got reacquainted.' He pushed her backwards and straddled her in one swift move.

'Hmm-hmm.'

'I've brought along some things.'

She froze. 'What kind of things? Because I'm not into any kinky sex, if that's what you mean.'

'Really?' He raised his eyebrows. 'From what I've seen of you lately, I think you'd like it.'

'No, not really.'

'You won't know until you try – why not open your mind to it?'

His mouth dipped to her neck and she groaned as his hand

slid inside her top. She gnawed at her lip, arching her back as he caressed her with the tips of his fingers.

'So?' he whispered.

'So?' she whispered back.

'Let's have a bit of fun this weekend.'

As his fingers went to work again, curiosity got the better of her. 'What have you brought with you?'

'Remember that scene in *You Complete Me* last week?'

Donna remembered. At Owen's insistence, he had read some of it to her. Again, she had been embarrassed more than turned on. She grimaced.

'The one where she was tied to the bed and blindfolded?' she asked. 'I'm not sure I'd like that.'

'You'll never know until you try.' Owen's hand had come out of her top now. He pressed a finger to her lips. 'And we can have a safe word too. It's all about trust.' His eyes bore down on hers. 'You do trust me?'

Donna nodded.

He kissed her gently on the tip of her nose. 'Let's run you a bath and pour some wine and get this party started.'

'Sounds good to me, as long as you're sharing both with me?'

'Sure. I have to check a few emails and then I'll come in to you.'

'Don't be too long.'

Donna grinned as she stepped inside the bathroom. It was as large as her living room at home, with white tiles, a white suite and chrome accessories. The only dash of colour came from a huge pile of deep purple towels. The shower cubicle was big enough for two - she hoped they'd get time to test it out - and the bath in the corner of the room, sitting on chrome claw feet, seemed as big as a cruise liner.

It took an age to fill it, but after a few minutes she immersed herself into the hot water, bubbles covering the surface, and sighed. Then she laughed again, picking up her wine glass.

Relaxing back, she closed her eyes and felt the stress and worries of the last few weeks being washed away as she soaked in the bubbles, the smell of lavender invading her senses. She hated her bathroom in Trudy Place, with its unstoppable patches of mildew appearing the minute her back was turned, its ancient aubergine-coloured suite and ghastly tiles with greying grout. She'd long ago given up lounging in the bath there.

A few minutes later, she surveyed her surroundings again with a grin. In anticipation, if a little nervous, she hoisted herself out of the water and reached for a towel. If Owen wouldn't come to her …

Almost immediately, he was by her side. 'Need any help getting dry, madam?' he smirked.

He took the towel from her and rubbed it gently over her shoulders, down her arm and hand, drying each finger individually. Then the same with the other arm, while staring at her with intent. It was so erotic as he stooped down to dry her feet and then moved the towel up her leg to her thigh, slowly, slowly.

At the top, he stopped to kiss her stomach before moving down the other leg. Then he stood up and dried the top half of her body, taking longer than necessary over her breasts. The friction of the material against her skin made her gasp. He took her hand and led her to the bed.

She noticed a black gift bag placed on the covers.

'For you.' He smiled, handing it to her.

Donna opened it to reveal sexy black underwear. Blushing a little, she smiled. 'Shall I put it on?'

'Let me.'

Owen helped her to slip on the bra, closing the metal clasp at the front. The knickers had ties at either side but he placed them on the floor for her to step into.

'Lie on your back,' he told her afterwards.

Donna scrambled across the bed. 'Like this?' She laughed as she spread herself out like a starfish.

'Exactly like that.'

'But you're fully dressed,' she said.

'I won't be for long.'

Owen reached down to the side of the bed and pulled out two white nylon scarves. 'Ta da!'

Donna laughed again. 'You look like a magician.'

He took her left hand and lightly tied it to the corner post on the headrest. He straddled her body, taking her right hand and pushing it over her head. Then he tied that to the opposite corner of the headrest. This time, he pulled the scarf tight.

'Ouch, that hurts,' she said.

He moved back to the other side of the bed but he didn't reply. Instead, he pulled two more scarves from the bag and tied her feet to either side of the base of the bed.

'I'm going to blindfold you now,' he smiled, 'so that you lose all your senses.'

'No, I don't think I—'

'And then, you can do the same to me. Deal?'

'Okay, but if I—'

He placed the tip of a finger on her nose. 'Close your eyes.'

She did as he said, wishing that she could just go with the flow and enjoy herself. She'd said she wanted a little excitement in her life but now she had the chance, she was scared again.

Get a grip, Donna, she told herself.

When she felt something touch her lips, she opened her eyes again. Owen pushed the scarf into her mouth. Her cry was muffled as he lifted her head and tied it at the back, pulling tightly on it to see that it was secure.

'I had thought of blindfolding you,' he said, stepping off the bed, 'but I didn't want you to miss the fun.'

Owen removed his clothes, and she felt his weight as he straddled her again. His eyes were dark pools as he leaned forward, closer and closer to her face.

'Donna, Donna, Donna, you stupid gullible bitch.' He grabbed her chin and squeezed it. 'Never trust anyone who asks if you trust them.'

Owen drew back his hand and slapped her hard across the face.

Chapter Thirty-Two

It was just before midnight and Keera was waiting outside The Candy Club. Derek didn't work on Saturdays as a rule but he'd been asked to help out as one of the other drivers had phoned in sick. He'd offered to give her a lift home, which she was glad about.

She'd just about had enough of men for one evening. Firstly, she'd had to massage smelly Martin Smith, then a man who wouldn't stop talking about his wife. She was sure he was going to burst into tears if he mentioned her name again. Thankfully, the last client had fallen asleep after a few minutes so she'd had a bit of peace and quiet before she finished her shift.

She looked down the road, feeling vulnerable after her recent run-ins with Steve, but there was no one near her. Steve hadn't shown his face for a few days. She wondered if he'd had enough after being threatened by Trevor Prince.

Her thoughts turned to her mum. She'd been slightly envious, but excited for her too, as she'd told her she was going away for a night with the new fella. She'd asked to meet him but Mum had said all in good time.

Keera sighed loudly. Her mum seemed to be having more of a social life than her at the moment. She was happy for her and if she was honest, Keera wasn't too bothered about going out. She'd had a couple of good nights at The Butcher's Arms, yet on both occasions she'd felt lonely without Marley. However, Marley had sent her a message again earlier to ask if she could come and stay with her for a couple of nights, so Keera was looking forward to that. She couldn't wait to see her friend, have a laugh like they used to.

A minute or so later, a car approached and stopped right in front of her. Keera stepped towards it and opened the passenger door.

'Good evening, Derek.' She slid into the passenger seat.

'Good evening, Miss Keera,' Derek replied playfully. 'Did you have a good shift?' he asked as he set off again.

'It wasn't too bad, thanks.' She fastened the seatbelt and settled further into the seat with a sigh.

Relishing the fact that Derek would take her home safely, she marvelled at their relationship and how it had strengthened over the past few weeks. Since she'd been attacked, he'd been waiting for her at the bus stop to take her home most evenings and Keera had found herself looking forward to seeing him. It felt good to have someone looking out for her, and it was perfect being taken home in a taxi as no one would think anything of it. If anyone saw them, she didn't need to explain their friendship. She could say that the nightclub had arranged it for her – or that she'd arranged it herself. But so far it had worked out well.

Even their working relationship had been fine. Keera had been worried since they had become so friendly that all other things would cease. As much as it was a job at The Candy Club, she did enjoy her time with Derek. For a while, it made the job less sleazy. She knew what he liked now and took pride in giving him pleasure, running her hands down his back and over tattoos on his shoulders.

Keera glanced at him as he drove, feeling a little guilty. She'd decided not to tell Derek about Steve coming in and having a go at them again last week. Although Steve had threatened what he'd do on his return, she didn't believe him. His sort were usually all mouth. Estelle had said that if he came back, she would call management and they could deal with him. Keera had agreed that it was the best option but didn't want to upset Ramona any more than was necessary.

'How's your friend doing?' Derek smiled when he caught her eye. 'Marley?'

'She's good, thanks. In fact she might be coming to stay with me soon for a couple of days. Would you like to meet her?'

'What do you think?'

'I think maybe I want to keep you all to myself.' She giggled. 'Marley's going to study again – can you believe that? She's gone from a beach bum to a study freak.' Just as quickly, she stopped. 'I think the attack changed her in more ways than one.'

'Do you wish you'd studied more, Kee?'

The way he shortened her name made her smile. 'Sometimes,' she admitted. 'But there's nothing to do around here. That's why I'm going to Manchester as soon as I can afford to.'

'Shame. I'll miss you, though.'

'Ah, there will be other girls.' She grinned, realising how ridiculous the conversation might sound to someone who didn't know them. From the outside, they must seem an odd couple.

'I won't miss you just because of your massaging skills!' he cried.

'I don't think I have a lot of anything else to offer.'

'You do but you don't realise it yet.' Derek slowed down as the traffic lights turned to red. 'You're young and have your whole life ahead of you.'

'Don't go all philosophical on me, now, Mr P,' she admonished.

'It's true. Whereas I will always have a massage parlour, I suppose.'

Keera pondered for a moment before blurting out what was on her mind. 'Do you find it hard coming to The Candy Club? Because if you do, I could come to see you at home.'

They were on the estate now, heading up Davy Road. Derek indicated suddenly and pulled the car into the kerb.

Keera's brow furrowed as he turned towards her. 'Sorry, have I overstepped the mark?'

'Of course not.' It was his turn to pause. 'You don't think I've been giving you a lift home so that I could ask you that, do you?'

'No! I just thought I'd offer. I know the stigma attached to one of those places.'

Derek shrugged. 'I don't have to go. It's my choice. But I know this really good masseuse and …'

Keera playfully slapped the hand he had resting on the side of her seat.

'Do you fancy a coffee at mine before you go home?'

'At your house?' Derek balked. 'What about your mum? I don't think she'd be too pleased.'

'She's away for the night. Some fancy fella she's been seeing.'

Derek shook his head. 'Better not. The neighbours might talk. I don't want to get you into any bother.'

'Well, what are your neighbours like?'

'Sorry?'

'We could have coffee at yours. Where do you live? I mean, I know you're on the estate but I don't know where.'

'Are you sure?'

'Yes, it's just coffee. Not a secret code for I want to shag you. You're my friend, Derek.'

He paused for a nanosecond before starting the engine again. 'Okay, coffee and then I'll take you home.'

Donna woke with a jolt. The room that she had been so in awe of when she'd first arrived at the hotel was in darkness except for the glow of a bedside light. The curtains had been drawn and despite the heat of the room, she felt a shiver caress her bare skin.

She tried to get up from the bed but she couldn't move. How the hell she had managed to fall asleep was beyond her comprehension, but maybe it was her mind's way of getting her through the trauma.

Looking to her right, she could see that her hands were still tied to the post of the headboard. Tears fell again and she struggled to cry against the scarf that was still in her mouth. She tried to control the panic for fear of suffocation. She had to stay calm or she would never get out of this room alive. Never see her family again.

Tentatively, she lifted her head from the pillow and looked around. Over on the wall in front of her, the television had been left on, the volume loud enough not to draw attention. Below the image on the screen, the familiar yellow ticker tape of *Sky News* alerted her to the latest breaking news. She didn't want to know that three people had been killed in a crash on the motorway. She narrowed her eyes and concentrated on the small digits of the time: It was 12.30.

She'd been tied up for over six hours.

She turned her head to the left to see if the room was completely empty. The door to the bathroom was ajar, the light off.

She was alone.

But she was far from safe.

Tears trickled down her face and onto the pillow. This was all her fault. She'd often thought that women who went on one-night stands were carefree, did it for the danger element as well as the sex. But she'd been envious too. She'd wanted a bit of fun with a man she hardly knew and look what had happened.

She closed her eyes but images came rushing at her. After that first slap, there hadn't been any more to the face. Owen didn't want anyone to see the marks. So instead, he'd punched her in the ribs, scratched at her stomach until her skin was bleeding and bitten her shoulder until she had writhed enough to knock him off balance.

How could she have been so stupid - so trusting? She'd screamed when he'd attacked her – oh, how she'd screamed – but with no one to hear her muffled cries he'd been free to ram himself into her over and over.

When she thought he'd finished and he'd rested his weight on her, she'd laid quietly, fighting to hold back her tears, and hoping he would untie her so she could think of getting out of the room. But he'd waited for a while until he was able to do it again.

The final time he'd pushed himself into her, he'd punched her thighs open as she'd desperately tried to keep him out. Another punch to the side of her ribs and she'd given in.

She couldn't believe how Owen had changed into a monster. Up until now, the way he'd treated her since they'd met had been beyond her wildest dreams. He'd been attentive to her needs, reeling her into his web of lies to gain her trust, make her feel safe; wanted even. He'd given no indication that he would attack her, and in such a brutal way. Donna had thought he was too good to be true. She cursed herself now – she wouldn't be that lucky. She was never that lucky.

She was just fucking gullible.

In desperation, she began to scream again, kick out, pull at the scarves that bound her to the bed. Exhausted after a few seconds, she stopped. She knew it was pointless. No one would hear her.

Instead she tried to concentrate on listening, dreading the moment that Owen would return. Every door that opened and closed, every shout. It was Saturday evening, and most people were enjoying themselves.

She wondered where he was. Had he left her here so that she would be found in the morning by the maid? At least then her ordeal would be over. But her bladder was full. She needed to pee, and pretty soon she wouldn't be able to hold it in. She couldn't go yet. She just couldn't.

It was almost one a.m. when she heard the door open. Owen switched on the main light, causing her to squint as her eyes adjusted to its harsh brightness after so long in the dim room.

'Hello, my little pumpkin,' he smiled. 'I hope I haven't been too long. It was someone's thirtieth birthday bash and they ended up asking me to join their party. Well, it seemed rude not to. The food was divine. It's a shame you missed it.'

It had been hours since she'd eaten, but Donna felt herself retching at the thought of it. She watched as Owen pulled his T-shirt over his head and stared at her. Then he slid the belt from the loops on his jeans, never once taking his eyes from hers.

He dropped the belt to the floor. Behind the scarf, Donna screamed as he walked towards her and sat down on the side of the bed. She winced as he ran a hand from the bottom of her stomach and up to her chest, the scratches he'd made earlier sore beneath his touch. As his fingers rested around her neck, she closed her eyes.

He was going to kill her. Ohmigod, what had she done?

Owen laughed as he moved his hand up her arm towards her wrist. 'Relax. I did say you'd be safe with me. I'm going to untie you. You promise to stay quiet if I do?'

Donna nodded vehemently.

He untied the scarves at her arms and then her legs. Although she was free to kick out, her body went limp and she felt more vulnerable than ever. She was naked too. He knew she wouldn't run, the bastard.

When he removed the final scarf from her mouth, his eyes bore down on her, daring her to defy them. She wanted to curl up in a ball and move as far away from him as possible. But she said the first thing she could think of to get away from him.

'Owen,' she said. 'I have to pee.'

'Okay.' He pulled her off the bed, steadying her, gripping her arm as her legs were weak after lying still for so long. She tried to loosen his grip, but it tightened.

'I'll come with you.'

He led her to the bathroom, switched the light on and stood by the open door.

'Can you leave me for a moment, please?' she asked.

'I'm staying right here.' He folded his arms.

Donna lowered her eyes. Her last piece of dignity was being taken from her.

She relieved herself as he watched, feeling his eyes on her, seeing his lips curl up in a half smile.

'You sound like a horse,' he laughed as urine poured out of her.

'Well, I've been a bit tied up.' The sarcasm came out before she had time to think.

But Owen just laughed as she wiped herself and flushed the toilet.

'I need to freshen up,' she said.

He took hold of her hand. 'No need for that. I'm tired, come to bed.'

As his grip tightened on her again, Donna realised that the only way she would get out of this room in the morning was to go along with what he had in mind. Holding in her tears, she got back into bed, curling up into a foetal position, despite every part of her aching.

Owen removed the rest of his clothes, climbed in behind her and wrapped his whole body around hers. Ordinarily, she would have relished the thought of his closeness but now it terrified her. If she could wait until he was asleep, maybe she could creep out of the room.

'Donna.'

She stiffened at the sound of his voice.

'If you're thinking of telling anyone about this, and you make out that we weren't two consenting adults having fun, then I'll go after Keera next.'

Chapter Thirty-Three

Keera couldn't believe Derek only lived three streets away from her on the Mitchell Estate. Christopher Avenue was just about on the cusp of the nastier bits. It could hardly be called living on the 'hell, and it was a walk in the park compared to some streets on the estate. But at least neither of them lived on Stanley Avenue, the worst street of the whole place.

Derek's house was the end of a block of four terraced houses. Even in the dark as she walked up the path behind him, she could see how tidy the garden area was, noticed that the hedges had been cut back.

'So how come you haven't met anyone recently, Kee?' Derek asked as he poured hot water into two mugs. He turned to her with a smile. 'A lovely girl like you should have a man she can depend on.'

'I do.' She stared at him. 'I have you.'

'You know what I mean. I'm far too old for you.'

'Age is but a number, don't they say?'

He looked at her again. She kept her face straight for a few seconds before bursting into laughter. 'I'm winding you up!'

Derek pretended to bat the comment away with his hand. 'But don't you have interests and hobbies?'

'You disappoint me, Derek. I thought you'd be up for dancing around the room with me, singing One Direction songs at the top of your voice.'

'One who?' He passed her a mug with a grin. 'Seriously, what do you really want to do with your life? Besides go to Manchester to be with Marley.'

Keera sighed loudly as she took it from him. 'There isn't much I can do. That's why we headed out to get some sun rather than mope around here.'

Derek sat down at the small pine table and Keera followed suit. 'Now that Marley is going to college in September, maybe you could do that too?' he suggested. 'Have you ever wanted to study?'

'Not really.' She shook her head. 'I was always one of the thick-os at school.'

'I find that hard to believe.'

'I didn't like school. Come four o'clock, you wouldn't see me for dust as I ran out of the gates.'

'Perhaps you just messed around, like most kids?' Derek eyed her. 'I think a lot of teenagers leave school with regrets that they didn't knuckle down when they should have, but it doesn't mean that they can't try again later. I went back to college and studied law.'

Keera was just about to take a sip from her mug but she stopped midway, eyes wide. 'Did you?'

Derek nodded. 'I was going to be some hotshot lawyer, but my mum was taken ill. My dad died shortly afterwards and there was only me that could take care of her. My parents meant the world to me so I gave up a chance of a career to look after her.'

'Wow, that's so kind of you.' Keera took a sip of her drink before continuing this time. 'Not a lot of people would do that. I know I couldn't. My nan lives in sheltered accommodation because my mum doesn't have the expertise to look after her. Nan needs someone there all the time now, to keep an eye on her, make sure she's safe. She kept on wandering off when she lived by herself. I think she was lucky to be brought home each time she went missing. Anything could have happened to her.'

'Dementia?' Derek queried.

'Yes.'

'That's such a cruel condition.'

Keera nodded. 'She hardly remembers me, so I don't visit often now.'

'Oh, you should,' Derek encouraged. 'She might never recognise you again, but just imagine if you went one day and she did. How good would that be? I bet all you feel now is guilt about not going to see her.'

'I guess.' Keera loved these philosophical talks with Derek. 'I reckon you'd like my mum. I'd introduce you but she's just got herself a fella.'

'Oh? What's he like?'

Keera shrugged. 'Haven't met him yet. It's early days, she says. I'm not so sure she's in love or anything.' She checked the time on her watch. 'Going back to our original chat, would you like me to come to your house instead of visiting me at The Candy Bar?'

'No, I think I'd prefer to keep that part of things the same, if you don't mind?'

She shook her head. 'Would you like a massage before I go?'

Derek sighed. 'There is nothing I would like better.'

Keera put down her mug.

'But … I'm going to decline.'

'Oh?'

'I'm knackered. I gave chase to two fare dodgers earlier and I think I pulled my groin.'

'You old timer!' Keera covered her mouth with her hand as she yawned. 'You should be careful what you get up to. It's a jungle out there.'

'Talking of which …' Derek opened a drawer and took out an envelope. He passed it to Keera. 'I've been thinking whether or not to give you this for ages. Now that you're here, it seems only right.'

Keera took it from him. Inside the envelope were a bundle of notes. She looked at Derek in confusion.

'Five hundred pounds,' said Derek. 'I thought Ramona could get Steve off her back.'

'But … but I can't let you do that.' Keera tried not to blush because she hadn't told Derek that Steve was still hanging around outside The Candy Club, even though he wasn't necessarily threatening Ramona.

'Where do I say it's come from?' she asked.

'Tell them you've borrowed it from your mum or something. Or you raided your piggy bank.'

'That's a lot more pennies than I'd ever have!'

'Maybe, but no one need know.' Derek paused. 'I want to help. I don't like bullies, I don't like the thought of him coming back to hurt her – or you – so, well,' he shrugged, 'it's only money.'

Keera looked at the notes in her hand. Was Derek for real? She couldn't take his money. It wasn't fair to get him to bail Ramona out. But if she took the money, Ramona's problems and her own could be over.

'Take it with you,' Derek urged as they stood in silence. 'Sleep on it and decide what to do in the morning.'

Keera looked at the money again. 'Are you sure?'

'I'm sure.' Derek looked at the clock. 'I should take you home.'

'No need.' Keera stuffed the envelope into her bag. 'I'm only minutes away.'

'And it will take me a minute to get you back there safely.'

'It's only–'

The look he gave her made Keera realise that he wasn't going to take no for an answer. She found that she quite liked it.

Donna waited for ages before she dared to move. Owen was snoring gently behind her, his body still pressed close to hers, his arm slung territorially over her middle. She felt her legs cramping and stretched a little, hoping that it would make him move. It did the trick and he rolled away, turning his back to her. She lay in the silence, waiting to see if he would settle, or turn to her again.

Her whole body ached where he had assaulted her, yet she didn't dare to move in case Owen woke up. The clock illuminated on the television said it was half past two. She had to try to get away.

Every thirty seconds or so, she lifted the duvet a little more from her and inched across towards the edge of the bed. She tried to recall where her bag was. Her shoes, she remembered, were under the dressing table.

Several times, she urged herself to sit up but found that she was too scared. Finally, she realised it was now or never. As quietly as she could, she stood up.

Owen didn't move.

It took every bit of willpower that she possessed not to rush towards the door, but if she were to get away, she would have to creep around and not wake him. She needed to stay quiet enough to get out of the room, without the chance of him dragging her back and attacking her all over again.

In the dark, she located her bag and grabbed her shoes. Then she tiptoed to the door. Without taking time to dress, she undid the lock and held her breath. Still he didn't stir.

Donna opened the door as quietly as she could, wincing as the hinges creaked. Outside, the corridor was empty but she wouldn't have cared if there had been anyone there at all. Even naked, she just wanted to get away.

When there was still no noise behind her, she stepped outside the room and inched the door shut. Knowing that it would make a loud clunk when it closed, she left it ajar a little. Then she flew as fast as she could down the corridor, trying not to think of how excited she'd been earlier to run along the carpet in her bare feet.

She looked behind but Owen wasn't following her. At the nearest fire exit, she pushed open the door and ran down two flights of stairs, clutching her clothes and shoes. It was only then that she stopped to dress, trying desperately to breathe between her sobs, the tears falling so fast she could hardly wipe them away.

Once she was dressed again, she held onto her ribs as she walked down the final flight of stairs.

It was quiet in the lobby, with only a security guard sitting at the reception. The clickety-clack of her heels echoed across the tiles, making him look up before she got to the desk.

'Could you call me a taxi, please?' she asked, trying to keep the tremble from her voice. She put a hand to her cheek to cover the bruising she suspected might be there.

'Sure, madam. It will take a while to get here, though.'

She nodded. 'Could you ask them to hurry, please?'

'Yes, of course.'

Donna waited while he made the call, all the time keeping an eye on the lift and the door to the stairs. Any moment now, she expected Owen to appear.

'They'll be about twenty minutes.'

She looked up. 'Thanks.' A tear escaped and she brushed it away quickly.

'Are you all right?' The security guard stood up. 'Can I get you some help?'

'No, I'll be fine.' Donna shook her head. 'I just need to get home.'

'Can I get you a coffee?'

'No! Could you… would you stay here with me until the taxi gets here?'

'Of course, madam.'

Donna relaxed a little, knowing that she wouldn't be alone. All the while she waited, she tried not to think about what had happened, sitting on her hands as they began to shake. She kept her eyes glued on the lift. If Owen came into view, she would run behind the reception desk and beg the security guard to keep him away. God, what had she been thinking to put her trust into someone she hadn't known for long?

The taxi finally arrived. Donna thanked the security guard and rushed out to the car, sliding into the back seat, closing the door quickly.

'I need to go to Stockleigh, please.'

'It will cost you, love,' the driver told her. 'It's a fair way to— '

'I don't care. Please, just take me home.'

Donna wrapped her arms around her body as she began to shake. She rested her head on the window, looking out on the darkness as she put distance between her and Owen. For now, she was safe.

She didn't want to think of what would happen when Owen woke up and found her gone. All she wanted was to get back to The Mitchell Estate.

Chapter Thirty-Four

When Donna awoke the next morning, for a few glorious seconds, she lay contented. Then as the horror that had unfolded the night before came rushing back to her, she sat up in bed with a jolt. Wincing at the pain in her side, she looked around. Then she relaxed a little when she realised she was safe at home.

She pulled herself up to sitting and drew back the duvet. Lifting up her nightdress, she recoiled at the mess she saw. There was a bruise the size of a tennis ball just below her ribs on the right side, and several deep, bloody scratches over her chest and stomach. Her legs too had bruises on them, her vagina felt bruised too. It hurt every time she moved.

Covering herself up again, Donna burst into tears. What a bastard Owen was to trick her like that. To play on her good nature, and the fact that she was struggling to cope; knowing that her life had centred around helping others rather than having any fun herself. He'd found her at her lowest point and used it to get at her – to do that to her.

She shuddered as she thought back to the night before, squeezing her eyes tightly shut as an image of him thrusting into her over and over again played on repeat. How could everything have gone so wrong? She had just wanted a bit of love in her life, someone to share the lonely times with. A bit of levity amongst the drudgery of her daily routine. Now all she would be left with was hideous memories of the attack. In time, she might be able to block those out, but Owen had gone too far when he had threatened her daughter. She couldn't let him get to Keera.

She jumped as her mobile phone burst into life and reached for it, only to see Owen's name flashing across the screen. Quickly, she cut the call. She didn't want to speak to him yet. But it rang again and again.

For fear of waking Keera, she switched it onto silent but still it kept ringing, vibrating as the screen lit up. Finally after a couple of minutes, it stopped.

Carefully, Donna pulled herself up again, swinging her legs slowly to the floor. Pain shot through her body, and she wondered if she'd need to go to A&E for an X-ray on her ribs. Everything ached too, like she had the flu and wasn't capable of supporting her own weight.

Was she still in shock? After all, it had been less than twenty-four hours since she had been attacked.

Rape.

The word flashed across her mind. She'd been raped, hadn't she? Tears ran down her cheeks. There was no doubt in her mind, yet she could never tell anyone what had happened. She had seen what Owen was capable of; but the power to keep her daughter safe was in her hands. She couldn't risk him going after Keera.

When she'd got home last night, Keera had been in bed. When Keera had shouted out to her, asking her why she was home so early, Donna had popped her head around her bedroom door and made up a story, saying that she hadn't been feeling well so had come home rather than stay out overnight.

Even so late, she'd showered, crying as she had scrubbed at her skin. When it was red raw, Donna had climbed into bed and cried again.

No, she wouldn't tell anyone what had happened. The bruising on her cheek would go, the scratches on her body would heal. No one would know any different from the outside. But inside, the scars would stay with her forever.

Her phone started lighting up again, vibrating across the carpet. She toyed with declining the call once more, but knew if she didn't, Owen would only continue to phone, and she'd have to speak to him at some point. Would it be better to get it over and done with?

She answered the call. 'What do you want?'

'That's a charming way to speak to the love of your life.'

Donna clutched her free hand to her ribs. 'There's a very fine line between love and hate.'

She heard him laugh again. 'How are you feeling?'

Donna gasped. 'How the hell do you think I'm feeling? You attacked me, you bastard.'

'I did nothing of the sort.'

'You attacked me!'

'You enjoyed it.'

'I did not!'

'Well, I can't remember you saying the code word to stop.'

'How the hell could I speak when you shoved a scarf in my mouth!'

Another laugh. 'Oh, yes, silly me.'

Whereas Owen's laughter yesterday had made her smile, it now chilled her to the core.

'I don't want you to call again,' she told him.

'Fine by me. I've done what I set out to do.'

'You heartless -'

'Now, now, let's not get all moody. You had a bit of fun, and you didn't like it rough. But I won't leave you alone until you agree not to mention this to anyone, you got that?'

Donna disconnected the phone and began to cry again. Owen had her over a barrel. She couldn't let him get away with what he'd done, but she couldn't risk him getting to Keera either.

There was a knock on the bedroom door. 'Are you okay, Mum? '

'Yes, I'm fine, love. I feel a lot better now.'

The door handle went down.

'I'd love a cup of tea if you're offering?' she shouted, hoping that Keera would leave her alone until she was dressed.

'Okay. I'll bring you one up.'

'Thanks.'

As soon as she heard footsteps treading down the stairs, Donna pulled herself out of bed and across to the wardrobe. In the full-length mirror, she lifted up her nightdress again to see the damage that Owen had wreaked.

Through her tears, she took photos of her injuries before covering them up again. She might not want anyone to see them, but she was certainly going to record them for herself.

Chapter Thirty-Five

Monday morning and Josie was at her desk when her phone rang. She reached for it, recognising the number. She'd left a message with one of the advice officers she knew at the Citizen's Advice Bureau.

'Den! Thanks for getting back to me. I need a bit more information about Post Traumatic Stress Disorder, and I've been told you're the man,' she said.

'Sure, how much do you know already?'

'Well, not a lot really. Only what the media has reported, or what I've Googled. I'd like to know more about the symptoms.'

'Well, someone with PTSD might experience feelings of isolation, irritability and guilt, angry outbursts, sleeping problems and difficulty concentrating. This state of mind is known as hyperarousal.'

Josie sighed. 'What a horrible thing to suffer.'

'Then there's re-experiencing.'

'Re-experiencing?' Josie reached for a notepad and pen.

'It's when a person involuntarily and vividly re-lives the traumatic event in the form of flashbacks, nightmares, repetitive and distressing images or sensations, physical sensations – such as pain, sweating, nausea or trembling. Some people have constant negative thoughts about their experience, repeatedly asking themselves questions that prevent them from coming to terms with the event. For example, they may wonder if they could have done anything to stop it, which can lead to feelings of guilt or shame.

'Then there's the mental health problems – depression, anxiety or phobias, self-harming or destructive behavior, such as drug or alcohol misuse. Physical symptoms can be headaches, dizziness, chest pains and stomach aches. Need I go on?'

Josie thought back to some of the things Lewis had shared with her. 'And it can happen long after the event, am I right?' she asked.

'Yes, it can occur weeks, months or even years later. Although, it's not clear exactly why some people develop the condition and others don't. In most cases, the symptoms develop during the first month after a traumatic event. However, in a minority of cases, there may be a delay of months or even years before symptoms start to appear. Each case is different. Has he been diagnosed?'

'No,' said Josie.

'Shame. If he was, he'd be entitled to a disablement pension.' There was a pause on the line. 'Ask him to call in and see me and I can point him in the right direction, if you like?'

'I will, thanks,' said Josie, 'although that might be an issue in itself. He doesn't want to talk about things.'

'Maybe not to you or I, but perhaps someone else who is suffering with PTSD. If we ask him to get help too often, he'll think we're preaching. If he meets other sufferers, he might open up.'

'I'll see what I can do.'

Josie wrote down a few more details after she had finished the call. She really hoped that she could persuade Lewis to meet up with Den. Maybe if Lewis talked to someone else going through the experience, he might open up.

Maybe he wouldn't but it was definitely worth a shot.

Mission impossible? She hoped not.

Lunchtime and Lewis was sitting in the park. He'd just had a kick about with Dan and a few of his mates. Sweat was pouring from him but he didn't want to remove his T-shirt while he was so close to a group of young children.

The boys had gone about ten minutes ago, but Lewis had found he didn't want to leave. Despite having a laugh with Dan, he knew he'd only end up in the pub if he did.

He'd had a miserable weekend, feeling utterly depressed after being turned down for another job. The woman at the job centre had told him there had been twenty-three people ahead of him already. Twenty-three! What hope had he got of getting an interview for that? He didn't even want the job anyway. Who'd want to stand at a bench sorting out screws into different boxes?

He glanced around the park. There were lots of people around, mainly mums and small children, a few groups of older kids.

'Hey,' a voice shouted. 'Lewis Prophett?'

Lewis turned his head slightly to see a man around his age. The man was a lot shorter than him, made worse by the fact that his paunch was bursting out of his shirt. His skin had seen better days and his thin, greying hair needed a cut. When he smiled, he revealed far less than straight white teeth.

Lewis peered at him through narrowed eyes. Although his face looked vaguely familiar, even after searching his memory he couldn't remember his name.

'Nick Steadman.' The man held up a hand to wave slightly. 'You must remember me. You were in my class at school.'

Lewis nodded as he finally recognised the man's name.

Without asking if it was all right to join him, Nick sat down next to Lewis. He pointed to a boy of about seven who was on the swings. 'That's my lad, there. Drake. Which one is yours?'

'Mine's just left with his mates. Been playing footie with him,' said Lewis.

There was an awkward silence.

'It must be years since I last saw you,' said Nick.

'I've been around.' Lewis stared into the distance.

'I heard you went in the army. I could never do that. I have enough taking orders from the wife all day and night. Nag, nag, nag.' He sniggered. 'How about you – are you married?'

'Yeah, but we're not together.'

'How long were you away?'

'Twelve years.'

Nick's eyes widened. 'Did you have to stay in that long?'

Lewis shook his head. 'I got out two years ago.' When Nick still looked confused, he explained, 'I wanted to do something with my life. And it was better than hanging around here.'

Two girls came running past them, screaming as one chased the other.

Nick looked at Lewis again. 'So what are you doing now?'

'I'm in between jobs.'

'Same here.' Nick laughed. 'Have been for near on five years now. As long as the government keep paying me to stay at home, that's where I'll stay too.'

'Rip off Britain.'

'What?'

'Can't believe you're a scrounger.' Lewis shook his head.

Nick's brow furrowed. 'You don't know me, or my circumstances.'

'But you're not working?'

Nick shuffled around on the bench. 'I'm not getting out of bed to earn six pounds an hour.'

'The same old excuse. Haven't you ever heard of working your way up from the bottom?' Lewis smirked. 'You're a waste of time. I've killed more people than you've had hot dinners.'

'You think that's something to brag about? Only cowards hide behind a uniform.'

'I'm not a fucking coward.' Lewis bristled. 'Tell me, what have you done with your life?'

Nick didn't answer.

'And how much of the world have you seen?'

'I've been to Spain on my holidays a few times.' Nick's chest puffed up. 'And I've been to Rome on a stag do.'

Lewis laughed. 'Whoop-de-do.'

'Are you mocking me?' Nick glared at him now.

Lewis shrugged. 'I'm just telling it like it is.'

'So how many countries have you visited, then?'

'Nine.'

Nick whistled. 'Not bad, I suppose.'

'Beats living around this dump.'

'This place isn't so bad. Especially if you have the right woman. Which you obviously never had. So I can beat you on that score.'

'I did have the right woman.'

Lewis stood up. He didn't want to listen anymore.

'See you around,' Nick shouted.

But Lewis ignored him as he walked away. Once outside the

park, he thought he'd go to see Amy but he chickened out at the last minute. He needed to make more of an effort, but not when he was so angry.

As he made his way back home, he wondered which one out of him and Nick Steadman was the bigger fool. Nick was a scrounger but he had a family who he could go home to, one that didn't resent him. Lewis had fought for his country and lost everything because of it – his wife, the chance to form a close relationship with his son, their beautiful home. He'd tried to better himself by joining the army but he'd still ended up back on the estate.

Was it any wonder he was angry and drinking to block out his miserable existence? Surely he deserved a place in life again, a chance to make things better?

As he walked past a young woman with a baby in a pushchair, unexpected tears filled his eyes. He'd missed out on so much of Dan's life as he'd grown up, yet here he was at thirty-two, still young enough to have more children.

Maybe that was it. If he and Amy got back together and had another baby, things might work out this time. But Lewis knew that if it was down to him, then there was no going back. He should look forward but it was hard without Amy.

God, he missed his wife.

Why did Nick have everything when he hadn't worked to achieve it? Lewis should have been going home to Amy, not living at his mum's place.

And if he couldn't patch things up with his wife, where would he find another woman who would understand his mood swings, help him through the bad times enough to see a hint of the good every now and then? Since Nathan had died, he'd hardly slept through a night. What effect would that have on a new relationship? It would be a shambles.

Lewis thrust his hands in his pockets, imagining how life would be if he was back with Amy and he could bond with Daniel again. He wished he shared the same simplistic outlook on life that his son did as a teenager. To Dan, everything could be worked at, or worked out.

If only.

Chapter Thirty-Six

Megan finished her shift and went into the staff changing room to freshen up. After making sure everything was still covered underneath her make-up, she added a little more lipstick and sprayed perfume liberally over herself. Smelling of disinfectant would not be sexy.

She checked her reflection one more time, and sighed. Was all this worry for nothing? If Sam did see her face, would he think less of her? Should she throw caution to the wind and see what his reaction would be?

'No, Megan Cooper. You're not ready for that yet,' she chastised herself. She couldn't risk him trampling all over her feelings.

She made her way over to the outpatients department, through the maze of corridors. There were people everywhere, following various coloured lines marked on the floors that showed the way to different areas of the hospital.

When she'd first started to work there, Megan had found herself in the wrong places for weeks until she'd found her way around. Most of the staff laughed about the made-up story of someone dying here because they'd been trying to get out for so long, and whose ghostly apparition wandered around the corridors at night. Although Megan knew it wasn't true, it still gave her the creeps if she'd ever had to do a late shift and found herself alone in a corridor.

Sam was nowhere to be seen when she arrived at the waiting area, but before she could ask at the nursing station for his whereabouts, she heard him.

'If you don't want me to swear, don't be so bloody rough.'

Megan giggled as she walked over to the cubicle the noise was coming from. 'Need any help in here?' she popped her head around the curtain.

'Megan!' cried Sam. 'Tell him to go easy, he's bloody killing me!'

Megan pulled the curtain aside enough to let herself in before closing it again. 'Hi, Stu,' she said to the nurse who was tending to Sam. 'Is he being a baby?'

'Do you know this guy?' Stu raised his eyes for a moment to give her a pitiful expression.

'Yes, we met on ward twelve.'

'Lucky you,' he muttered before turning to Sam with a grin. 'Right, the dressing is a little stuck, I'm afraid, so I'll have to pull it back to remove it. It'll sting but it'll be over in about a minute.'

Megan moved to Sam's side, noticing that his top lip was split and scabbing over. She looked closer and saw the yellowy-black tinge of a bruise underneath his right eye.

'What have you been up to?' she asked, pointing to his face.

'Had a fight with a wall.' Sam reached for her hand and she gave it a quick squeeze.

'If it hurts too much, don't squeeze me back,' she warned.

'Tell him a joke,' said Stu. 'Take his mind off things.'

Megan frowned, trying to think of one.

Sam wriggled again as Stu pulled off the dressing. 'Argh!'

'Nearly there, Sam.' Stu pried a little more off. 'If you can't think of a joke, Megan, sing a song.'

'No way!' Megan shook her head. 'I'd have you all running from the building. My singing is pathetic. I can't put you through that.'

'One last bit, Sam.'

'Argh!'

'All done.' Stu gently wiped a sterile cloth across Sam's hand before inspecting it. 'It's looking really good. I just need you to pop down for an X-ray before you go, to make sure everything is still in place after the operation, and then we can make you some appointments.'

'Appointments?' Sam queried.

'For more physio. The tendon is a little shorter now so you'll need to go slow with it as it heals. Stretch and release. The physiotherapist will get you doing some different exercises to strengthen it up again.'

Once out of the cubicle, Megan and Sam went round to the X-ray room. They sat down on the row of empty seats outside.

Megan glanced at Sam, his colour fading as he stared at his hand. She wanted to ask him about the fight but could see tears glistening in his eyes.

'Are you okay?' she asked.

'Look at it,' he whispered, turning his hand slowly from left to right to inspect the damage up close.

Megan glanced down. The skin on Sam's hand was wrinkled and dry, reminding her of a waxwork dummy. He had a three-inch scar but it looked to be healing well, and the scab on his index finger that had been stuck to the dressing didn't seem to be infected.

'They've made a great job of stitching the wound,' she told him.

'I look like a freak,' he hissed.

'That's only because it's been covered up with a bandage for a while. New skin needs to form as the old falls off.' She nudged him playfully. 'I'll be calling you lizard man as soon as it starts to peel away.'

But Sam didn't smile. He didn't even look at Megan, unable to take his eyes from his hand. She wished she could think of something to say that would make him feel better.

They sat in silence, the noise of the hospital around them. When Sam eventually looked up at her, there was sheer panic in his eyes.

'I'm going to be scarred for life, aren't I?' he said. 'I have an ugly scar plus a dent where I used to have a knuckle. I can't even bend my fingers properly to form a fist!'

'Good. You won't be able to get into any more fights. Not that it seems to have stopped you.'

He frowned. 'Something needed sorting out.'

'And was it?'

'You should see the other guy.'

'That's not funny, Sam.'

There was a pause. 'Look, I get into trouble now and then. It's what I do.'

'It's what you *choose* to do.'

Another pause as Sam continued to look at his hand.

'At least you didn't lose your finger, like the surgeon originally thought you might have to,' Megan soothed, realising she was judging him. 'It'll improve in time.'

'So that's okay then?' Sam glared at her. 'How would you know how I'm feeling?'

Sometimes Megan wanted to shake people who didn't understand what it was like to live with scarring every single day of their lives. Annoyed by his attitude, she waited for a lady to walk past them before speaking again.

'It isn't the end of the world because you've had an accident. You're on the mend now.'

'I know but—'

'Stop feeling sorry for yourself.' She pointed along the corridor where there were scores of patients waiting to be seen. 'Look at all these patients. They're hurting too, but you don't seen them whining.'

'Whining?' Sam recoiled. 'You'd feel sorry for yourself if you were scarred.'

'I am scarred!' Megan blurted out without thinking. She looked at the floor as several people turned her way.

Sam's brow furrowed. 'What do you mean?'

'Nothing.' Megan cursed inwardly. 'Forget it. It doesn't matter.'

'No, tell me.'

'I—' Megan's stomach lurched as she struggled with her thoughts. Maybe it would be better all round to walk away now, rather than allow herself to get any closer to Sam and risk the chance of getting hurt. But she needed to know if he would be repulsed if he saw her face without make-up. Had she been stressing too much, making a meal of it over the years, so much so that it was like having an elephant in the room?

Would it matter if he were shocked?

All of a sudden, she realised that it would.

'Let me show you something.' She reached inside her handbag and pulled out her purse.

'Samuel Harvey!' A door opened in front of them.

Sam stood up. 'I won't be long. Will you wait for me?'

Megan nodded. She watched as he disappeared into the cubicle.

Running a hand through her hair, her right knee jigging up and down, she knew she wasn't ready to show him the photo.

She stood up and walked down the corridor, out of the building and away from Sam.

Chapter Thirty-Seven

Donna decided to call in to see Mary before her shift at Shop&Save started at lunchtime. Having been awake most of the night, she'd been out of the house far earlier than usual.

Driving was painful, but at least she could concentrate on something else for a little while. She'd give anything not to keep replaying what had happened to her on a loop inside her head. All she wanted to do was forget Owen, but the more time went on, the angrier she became about what he had done.

'Hi, Mum, how are you?' Donna asked as she let herself into the flat.

Although her hair was untidy, Mary was up and dressed and sitting in her chair. But she wasn't talkative today. No matter how Donna tried to coax her into speaking, she wouldn't respond at all.

She sighed. The silent visits were much worse than the ones where Mary was vocal. Dementia was such a volatile condition.

Donna moved to the window, looking across the fields. Everything outside looked so calm and peaceful. He eyes filled with tears as her thoughts returned to Owen again. How could he have charmed her – and then abused her in that way? Had she missed the warning signs, being so enamoured with him? Had she just not been able to see what he was capable of? Or was he a manipulative, scheming, psychopath?

The phone call from him yesterday had made his words seem more of a threat. She couldn't believe it when he'd said that she had been mistaken in thinking that it was an assault, that it was supposed to be a bit of fun. Well, she might be gullible but she wasn't stupid. That wasn't fun for anyone but him.

Donna went to sit nearer to her mum, desperate for someone to talk to as she perched on the arm of the chair. She couldn't burden Keera with what had happened, and even if she could tell Sam, he'd want to find out where Owen lived and get his revenge. He could injure himself more in the heat of the moment, and harm his hand irreparably. Worse, he could try to use a weapon and end up in real trouble.

Donna couldn't even confide in Sarah, she felt too ashamed. She was dreading going into work, having to face her wanting to know everything about the night away. Her ribs were sore too, her face piled with make-up to hide the bruise inflicted by Owen's hand.

No, she couldn't face it today. She'd have to ring in sick. Then, tomorrow, somehow, she'd have to pretend that everything was fine.

'Oh, Mum, I've been so stupid,' she sniffed. 'I let someone get under my skin and he took advantage of me. He turned out to be a horrible man.'

Mary didn't take her eyes from the television but Donna continued to talk anyway. She told her about Owen, about the attack and the phone call where he was denying all knowledge of hurting her.

Knowing that she wouldn't get any response from Mary made it easier to offload. Mary couldn't tell her she'd been stupid, couldn't tell her that she'd been lucky to get away when she had, or tell her that she had been gullible, foolish – pathetic to even think that someone like Owen would fall for her.

She looked down as she felt Mary's hand on her arm.

'Don't cry, Donna,' she said.

Donna's tears spilled over. Having her mum back for a little time was a bonus, even though Mary knew she was upset but wouldn't understand why. It felt comforting that she had reached out to her when she had needed it most.

A few seconds later, Mary was watching the television again. Donna took out her phone and reread the message that Owen had sent to her after he'd called.

Remember – I can see your every move.

She didn't believe that for a moment, but the idea of him watching her, following her, was enough to make her shiver. She hovered over the delete button, wishing she could erase him from her mind with the click of a button. But even though it hurt like hell to see his name displayed on her phone, something inside Donna made her think she should keep the message.

Chapter Thirty-Eight

It was all that Donna could do to drag herself into work later that week, but she knew Sarah would be short-staffed if she didn't turn up, and besides, she needed the money. Getting docked pay would cause her enough problems with the time she'd been away so far.

'Jeez, you look terrible,' Sarah said as soon as she saw her. 'Are you sure you're all right to work?'

Donna had told Sarah that she had slipped down the stairs, hurting her back and pulling her stomach as she had reached for the bannister to steady herself.

'I – I think so,' she fibbed. 'I'm still in agony, if I'm honest, but I'll be fine.' She couldn't look Sarah in the eye, instead rubbing at the small of her back and praying that the bruise on the side of her face had been concealed enough with make-up.

'You'll tell me anything, won't you?' Sarah exclaimed.

Donna froze until she saw Sarah's warm smile and realised she was teasing her.

'You've been swinging off the chandelier with Owen this weekend, haven't you?'

Donna managed a smile. 'I wish.'

'If you need to leave, let me know. I'll get that idle cow, Maxine, to cover for your shift for a change.'

'I'll be fine. Working will take my mind off it.'

'Well, you go easy, then. And later, I'll make a cup of tea and you can tell me all about your night away. I'm dying to hear how it went!'

Donna was halfway through her shift before she managed to take a break. She couldn't believe that she'd got through the morning without bursting into tears. Her nerves were in shreds. Every time someone came into the shop, she expected it to be Owen. She wasn't sure how she would feel when she saw him again. More to the point, if he did come into Shop&Save, how would she explain to Sarah why she didn't want to see him?

'Special delivery for you, Don,' Sarah opened the door to the stockroom and shouted through to her.

Donna pushed herself up gently and made her way carefully back through to the shop floor, where Sarah was holding a huge bouquet of flowers.

'These just came for you.' She pressed her nose to them and inhaled their scent before grinning. 'I wonder what you did to deserve these, you dirty mare.'

'You wouldn't believe me if I told you.'

Donna still held onto her tears. She couldn't let Sarah see how upset she was or else she'd start to see through her act. She took the flowers, barely looking at them.

'You and your kinky toyboy.' Sarah grinned. 'I still want to know all the details when you're up to talking about it.'

It took Donna all the strength she had to smile, hoping to fool Sarah that even though she was in agony, she was still happy.

Sarah touched her arm. 'We can manage without you if—'

'Honestly, I'm fine,' Donna fibbed. 'I'd rather keep busy.' She looked down at the flowers as she tried to hold it together. 'I'll just put these in water until I finish.'

Once she was on her own again, panic welled up inside her. With a sense of trepidation, she removed the small envelope attached to the cellophane. She didn't want to read the greeting but equally she needed to know what it said. Hands trembling, she opened it and read the message on the card.

No one needs to know our little secret.

Donna ripped the card up into tiny pieces and shoved it into the nearest bin. *Our little secret*? How could he say that? Here she was, keeping it to herself because she was ashamed she'd got herself into that predicament, scared that he might attack her daughter, and there *he* was lording it up as if it were some sort of game.

Donna gasped with realisation, pain shooting through her chest as she did so. Had Owen done this before? Was she not the first to play right into his hands?

She covered her mouth with her hand as she retched. Throwing the flowers to the ground, she rushed to the toilet, barely getting there in time to be sick.

Afterwards, she closed the door, put the lid down on the toilet and sat, resting her head against the cold tiles. She shouldn't have come into work today. She should have stayed in the safety of her own home. Those flowers weren't a kind gesture. They were to show Donna that he was watching her.

A few minutes later, still feeling nauseous, she texted Sarah and asked her to come through to the back. She didn't want to be seen in the shop in this state.

'Oh, Donna,' Sarah said as soon as she saw her. 'You're as white as a piece of chalk.'

'I'm going to go back home,' Donna told her. 'I still don't feel right.'

'You should have stayed off for the whole week.'

'I can't afford to.'

'I know it's a cliché, but your health is far more important than money, even if the bills won't get paid.' Sarah paused. 'Maybe you've pulled a muscle and it's making you feel sick all the time. I'm sure it will wear off soon. Leave your car here and I'll get Maxine to hold the fort while I take you home. Come on.' She held out a hand.

'No!' Donna lowered her voice. 'I'm fine driving myself home, thanks.'

Sarah didn't look convinced. 'Well, if you're sure?'

Maxine popped her head around the door. 'Sarah, do we have any salted crisps out here?'

'I'd better get back,' Sarah sighed. 'You know what it's like if I'm missing for more than thirty bloody seconds. You stay here, catch your breath and go home when you're ready. I'll give you a ring later, yeah? See how you are.'

Donna nodded.

Sarah brought Donna her bag and she waited until she was serving behind the till again. Then she pushed open the back door and left, leaving the flowers behind.

When Donna arrived home, she let herself into the house, praying that Keera would be out so that she wouldn't have to explain anything. But as she looked out of the kitchen window, she could see her daughter in the back garden. The sky was a vivid blue, not a cloud in sight, and Keera was lying on a lounger in her shorts and vest, grabbing a few rays of sun. Even though she felt so miserable, Donna smiled. It seemed that everyone she spoke to as they came into the shop was getting fed up of the heat, people complaining that they wanted rain, that it was too hot, too muggy. But Keera loved sitting in it.

She went out into the garden to her, taking her a glass of orange juice.

'Thought you might like this,' said Donna, handing the drink to Keera.

Keera looked up at Donna, and took the glass. 'Thanks. I thought you weren't finishing until five. Are you still feeling off?'

'I was fine until this morning.' Donna's smile was faint but she couldn't meet Keera's eyes as she lied again. 'I slipped and fell down a few stairs. It's a bit sore right now, but nothing to worry about.'

'God, you are in the wars. I'm glad they sent you home. Why don't you take off your uniform and come and sit in the garden with me? Can you do that – is it more painful to stand or sit?'

'I think I'm going to lie down a little.' Donna rubbed at the bottom of her back. 'Have you been to see Nan today?'

A guilty look crossed Keera's face. 'No, not yet. I will go on my way to work, though. I promise.'

'You sure? Because I know she needs some fresh bread and milk, but I'd really struggle to drive and—'

'I'm sure,' Keera nodded. 'I can use the car?'

'If you want to fill it up with petrol. I'm nearly on empty.'

Donna went back into the house and went upstairs, pulling herself up a step at a time by holding onto the bannister. She couldn't believe how much she still ached. Some of the bruising was fading, and she knew she hadn't broken any ribs as the pain there had subsided a little too.

At least Keera hadn't asked her about Owen lately. She'd mentioned it on Sunday and yesterday, but seemed to be pacified when Donna had changed the subject.

In her room, she pulled off her uniform and lay on the bed in just a t-shirt, closing her eyes. After a few minutes, there was a knock on the door. Keera pushed it open.

'I thought you might like some tea.' She stopped. 'Ohmigod, that bruise looks so sore! How did—'

'It's nothing.' Donna pulled the duvet around her. 'Really, I'll be okay.'

But Keera didn't want to leave.

'What's wrong, Mum?' she asked, her tone gentle. 'You're not your usual cheery self.'

Donna groaned. 'Give me a break. I can't be bloody cheery all the time!'

'Okay, okay.' Keera put up a hand. 'No need to snap. I'm only concerned.'

'I'm sorry, love. I'm a bit cranky, that's all. I'll be fine with a couple of hours' sleep.'

'Do you need any painkillers?'

'I've just taken some, thanks.'

'Well, if you're sure.'

'I'm sure.'

Keera left the room but Donna knew she hadn't fooled her. She hoped she could keep her pain to herself for a little while longer. Maybe things could get back to normal soon.

And then she needed to decide if she was brave enough to do anything about Owen.

Chapter Thirty-Nine

Lewis woke up and grimaced when he turned over in his bed. His ribs were hurting and he couldn't open his right eye properly. He touched the lid gingerly, feeling the swelling and wincing at the pain.

He pulled both hands from beneath the duvet. Shit: his knuckles were swollen and red too. Well, it seemed as if he'd given as good as he got.

He wondered whether to stay in bed until his mum had gone to work or whether to get up and face the music. Either way, she would be none too happy when she clocked the mess he was in. Last night, Lewis had found himself back in the pub. After another couple of hours, the booze had got the better of him completely. As he'd headed for the door, he'd turned sharply when he heard a gang of men laughing.

'What the fuck's up with you lot?' he said.

The laughing stopped. 'What the fuck's it got to do with you?' a voice shouted back.

'I can't hear myself thinking.'

A young stocky lad sniggered. 'You don't look as though you could understand yourself, you're that plastered.' He pointed to Lewis's trousers where there were a few drops of water. 'And you can't hold yourself either. Look, you've pissed your pants!'

Lewis groaned as he remembered swinging his fists around, missing everyone he could see as they stepped out of his way. That was when a fist had come back at him, catching him on the chin.

He'd lost his balance, falling to his knees. One of the group had taken the opportunity to give him a kick to his stomach before the landlord had come over and broken it up.

As he was ushered to the door, Lewis hadn't had the strength to retaliate but he could recall what Bob had said to him. "'I'm sick of you, coming in here getting drunk and taking your troubles out on my regulars. One of these days, I'll leave them to you.'"

He'd nearly been home when he heard footsteps behind him. Two of them had been on him so quickly that he hadn't even had time to turn. Luckily, someone shouting at them, telling them to stop or they would call the police, had disturbed them enough to slow their punches. They hadn't injured him as much as they could have done, but he had still come off worse.

There was a knock on the door.

'I'm asleep,' Lewis muttered, hoping his mum would go away.

'It's just after nine,' she told him. 'I thought you might like a mug of tea before I leave for work.'

'Come in.' He watched as her shoulders dropped when she noticed his face.

'What's happened? Are you okay?'

'Yeah, I'm fine. I just got into a spot of bother.'

Laura's eyes narrowed as she put down the mug on the bedside table. 'You mean you got into a fight?'

'Yes, but it wasn't my fault.'

'Oh, Lewis! Not again!' Laura reached a hand to look at his eye but he knocked it away.

'You don't have to baby me,' he snapped.

'Yes, I do, because you're acting like a child.' She threw her hands in the air. 'Going out and getting drunk every night, picking fights. That's what I'd expect off a teenager – not a grown man.'

Before Lewis could answer back, there was a knock at the door. Laura glared at him before going to answer it. Lewis turned over to face the wall. He'd get up when she had gone out.

'Lewis, there's someone here for you,' she shouted up a minute later.

Lewis groaned, grabbed some clothes and hastily got dressed. Who would be calling for him?

Downstairs in the kitchen was Josie Mellor. Laura stood behind her, face like thunder.

'What the hell do you want?' he muttered.

'I had a complaint about a commotion in the street last night. I thought I'd come to see if you were involved.' Josie raised her eyebrows as she saw his swollen eye. 'You've been fighting again.'

'Ten out of ten for observation.' Lewis would have clapped his hands sarcastically if they weren't hurting so much. 'You should see the other guy.'

'Less of your cheek, Lewis,' admonished Laura.

'I fell.' Lewis blinked as best he could. 'Happy now?'

'Not really.' Josie shook her head. 'I think your mum is right, Lewis. I'm really concerned—'

'Who are you to question me?' Lewis cut in. 'You're not the police.'

'Just be glad that I'm not or else you'd be locked up by now.'

'Why?'

'I've had reports that you attacked some poor lad in the street last night and his friend tried to stop you and—'

'Are you out of your mind?' Lewis exclaimed. 'They jumped me!'

When both women said nothing, he shook his head. 'It's my life. I can do what I want.'

'Up to a certain point, I agree …'

'Look, get out of my face, will you!'

'You need to stop with the anti-social behaviour,' said Josie.

'*I'll* be in trouble, Lewis, if you don't watch what you're doing.' Laura prodded her chest with a finger.

Lewis glared at his mum. How dare she insinuate this was his fault?

'I was jumped on last night!' he cried. 'Don't you care about that?'

'People would be civil to you if you were civil to them,' said Josie.

Lewis shrugged. 'People change.'

'For the better, mostly,' said Josie.

'Are you always so fucking irritable?' Lewis asked her.

'Lewis!' Laura shook her head in disgust.

'Your family are worried about you,' said Josie. 'They can see you spiralling out of control. Why won't you tell someone what happened? What's changed you?'

'*Everything* changed me, can't you see that?' he shouted. 'The whole fucking time I was in the army changed me.'

'Language!'

Lewis pushed his foot into his boot and laced it up quickly. 'I can't be who you want me to be anymore. I left that Lewis behind in Afghanistan.'

'Nonsense,' said Josie. 'I think you just need time to find yourself again.'

Lewis shook his head. 'I hope I *never* find myself again. The truth is far more painful than the nightmares.'

'But—'

'Just leave me alone!' Lewis pushed past his mum, flew up the stairs and into his bedroom, slamming the door shut behind him. What was with everyone wanting to help him? Didn't they realise he could look after himself?

He cursed loudly. Slamming doors and running away from arguments? Now he really was acting like a teenager.

Maybe it would be better for everyone if he moved out – even more so if he moved on. The Mitchell Estate had nothing to offer him.

At home that evening, Megan had seen to her mum, all the time keeping up appearances. She laughed at *Coronation Street* when she was supposed to. Patricia watched *Benefits Street* too, and she found herself getting involved in the story of a couple who had no money and nowhere to live but they were so much in love that they were determined to survive.

Before she'd come into the house, she'd switched her phone on silent. Sam had rung her several times throughout today and yesterday but she'd let the calls go to voicemail. She'd listened to his messages, trying not to cry at the sound of his voice. His concern seemed genuine. He was worried about her, wanting to know why she hadn't waited for him.

The texts had come then.

Where did you go yesterday?

I thought you wanted to show me something.

Can I see you tomorrow?

Tell me what I've done wrong.

At ten o'clock, she stretched her arms in the air and yawned. 'Think I'll head upstairs now, Mum. Do you need anything before I do?'

Patricia shook her head. 'No, I'm fine, love, thanks.'

Megan was at the door before she spoke again.

'Are you okay? You seem a little quiet. There's nothing bothering you, is there?'

Megan put a smile on her face before turning back to her. 'No, Mum, I'm fine.' She faked a yawn. 'I'm just a little tired.'

'Well, if you're sure … I know you work so hard but you do need to have a bit of down time too.'

Megan nodded. 'Night, Mum.'

In her bedroom, Megan threw herself face down onto her bed. At last her tears could fall freely and she sobbed into her pillow.

She hadn't been able to stop thinking about Sam all day. Why had she said she would show him? And then why had she run out on him? It had only made things worse.

Her phone beeped a few minutes later. She picked it up and read another message from him.

I know you like me. I like you too.

A few seconds later, another message.

What is it that you're trying to hide?

Megan sat up and wiped at her eyes. Staring back at her from the mirror on her dressing table was a mess. Crying had made her birthmark more visible now that her whole face was red and blotchy. She wiped off her make-up and took a long look at herself.

Why couldn't she accept that she wasn't perfect? She might be about to ruin something that could be good. And she was judging him again, wasn't she?

The right thing to do was to show Sam, let him make up his own mind. If he couldn't deal with her imperfection, then he wasn't worthy of her.

But as much as she was giving herself a pep talk, she knew she wouldn't be able to do it. She couldn't stand the thought of him being repulsed by her.

She read his last message again, part of it sticking out in her mind.

Why won't you let me get close to you?

It was laughable really, because she had already let Sam get too close. More to the point, she'd let herself get too close to Sam.

Megan switched off her phone and dragged herself into bed. If he rang her or sent another message that night, she knew she would cave in and reply. Better not to be tempted.

Chapter Forty

Although her alarm went off at seven a.m., Megan had been awake for ages. The room was stifling and having a window open meant a noisy dawn chorus from the birds outside in the tree. She reached over for her phone. She'd switched it back on in the early hours after she'd awoken yet again, although it was on silent.

There had been several more messages from Sam, each one asking her to get in touch. She could barely see as her eyes had puffed up so much, but she read them all again.

Finally, feeling exhausted, she got up, took a shower and dressed in her hospital uniform. Her face was so red and swollen from crying that it made her birthmark seem more prominent. She rubbed on far too much concealer to try and compensate, hoping it wouldn't slide off her face again in the heat.

She was halfway through applying the rest of her make-up when her phone vibrated. Sam's name flashed up on the screen. This time, she decided to answer it.

'Megan! You're alive!'

Despite herself, Megan found a smile. Even though she hadn't returned any of his calls and messages, he was trying to put her at ease.

'I am,' she replied, for want of something better to say.

'Good, because I'm beginning to lose my patience. What the hell's wrong with you?'

'Why do you care?'

'Meg, stop talking bollocks.'

'I'm not!'

'If you don't want to see me, then tell me but stop stringing me along.'

Megan drew in a breath. 'Is that what you think I'm doing?'

'Well, isn't it? One minute you're chatting to me, and the next you're ignoring me. Do you have a husband I don't know about?'

'No!'

'Well, what's with all the bloody secrecy then?'

Megan sighed. 'You're persistent, I'll give you that much.'

'Hey, you're highly honoured. I am *never* up at this time in the morning. This is stupid o'clock.'

Megan closed her eyes. Should she trust him with her secret? Could he see past the birthmark on her face and maybe love her for what she was?

'What do you see when you look at me?' she asked, her tone blunt.

'I see someone who doesn't want to get involved with a scrote like me.'

'But, that's not it—'

'I know what people think about me. I saw it on your face when the police came to see me, and when you were questioning me about the bruises on my face. You think I'm a troublemaker and no good.'

'You couldn't be further from the truth if you tried.'

'What do you mean?'

'It's just that – I'm not what you need.'

'You're not making sense!'

Megan's tears began to flow again. 'I have to go,' she said before he could tell she was crying.

'Don't you dare hang up!'

She disconnected the call. Staring at herself in the mirror again, she wiped at her eyes. If she didn't stop crying, she'd have to start her make-up again.

'Are you okay, love?'

Megan turned to see her mum standing in the doorway. She was holding onto the frame.

'Sure I am, Mum.' She wiped away her tears quickly. 'Are you going for a shower? Why didn't you say? I'd have come down to give you a hand with the stairs.'

'I'm not in too much pain this morning.' Patricia pointed to Megan's bed. 'Help me sit down on there a minute, would you?'

Megan did as she said. She went to sit at her dressing table again but Patricia pulled her down to sit next to her.

'What's the matter?' she asked, running a hand over her daughter's hair. 'I know you well enough to see that something is eating at you. Has someone hurt you?'

'No.'

'There is something, though … or am I right in thinking there is *someone*?'

Megan nodded.

'A boyfriend?'

She shook her head this time.

'But you want him to be?'

Megan raised her shoulder and dropped them again with a huge sigh. 'Oh, Mum, I think I've made a big mistake.'

She told her mum what had happened with Sam, even though she was unsure how she would react. She'd never felt able to talk to her much about her birthmark before, knowing Patricia might get upset too. But instead, she listened, never once trying to tell Megan that it didn't matter, that she was pretty anyway.

'When you were young,' said Patricia when Megan had finally stopped talking, 'I remember saying that you were special because you had a birthmark. I've often thought that I shouldn't have said that. You weren't special because of that, you were special because of who you are.' Patricia pointed to her chest. 'For what's inside there.'

'This isn't your fault,' Megan objected.

'Maybe – I don't know.' Patricia's shoulders dropped. 'But what I do know is the older you've become, the more conscious of it you seem. I've seen it change you and, well, I don't think it should. I know that's easy for me to say because I don't have to live with it every day.' She placed a hand on her thigh. 'But I do have to put up with these things and I would much rather be able to go out and live my life.'

Megan felt herself blushing.

'We're all born with something that won't make us happy. And look at you. You're beautiful, you're young and so full of life. You deserve to find happiness and be loved by someone.'

'I can't let him see me like this.' Megan pointed to her face. 'What happens if he doesn't like me afterwards?'

'Then he's not worth bothering with. Love should be unconditional.'

Megan smiled through teary eyes as her mum beckoned her closer.

'You are beautiful, even though I'm biased because you are my daughter.' Patricia cupped Megan's chin in her hands and looked her in the eye. 'But just remember one thing, Megan. Beauty is only skin deep.'

Donna walked downstairs to a pile of letters on the carpet. Wincing at the pain, she bent down to scoop them up and took them through to the kitchen. There was a catalogue for Keera, bills, a flyer addressed to her and a plain white envelope. As she opened the envelope and read through the letter, her hand covered her mouth. It was from the hotel that Owen had taken her to.

She reached for her phone. It was answered after a few rings.

'Ah, Donna. I hope you liked the flowers – I see you didn't bring them home with you.'

'I don't want your flowers,' she snapped. 'You gave the hotel my address and then left without paying? They've sent me an invoice!'

'You didn't think I was going to pay, did you?' His laugh was cruel. 'Get real. You're a slut and deserve to be treated like one. I don't pay for sex.'

'But it's nearly four hundred pounds! I don't have that kind of money.' Donna closed the kitchen door in case she woke Keera.

'You shouldn't have such expensive taste.'

She pulled out a chair at the table. 'I can't afford to pay this. You need to tell them you can.'

'I can, but I won't.'

'Then I'll go to the police and tell them what you did to me.'

'We had sex. Granted it was a little rougher than the first few times, but you did agree to my terms.'

'I did not agree!'

'You said you trusted me.'

'You – you raped me.'

'It was consensual.'

'It was NOT FUCKING CONSENSUAL!' By this stage, she didn't care if Keera heard her, she was so angry.

'Now you're behaving like a spoilt child. What did you expect when you gave yourself to me so freely? You're nothing but a whore.'

'I am not a—'

'So you didn't like the fact that I bought you an erotic novel? And what about sex outside in the open – you remember, in the woods? I thought you were up for a little fun. You certainly gave me the impression you were game for anything.'

I didn't,' she sobbed. 'I really didn't.'

There was silence down the line before he spoke again.

'Just remember – no police. And if you dare so much as mention the word rape, I swear to God I will get you for it.'

'Leave me alone!' she sobbed.

Donna disconnected the phone and dropped her head into her arms. She'd have to ring the hotel and explain. Wait, they would have his credit card details, surely? He would have needed them to confirm the booking.

Twenty minutes later, she admitted defeat after she'd called the hotel and they had told her that although the card had been fine on the day they had booked in, when they went to settle the bill after Owen had left without paying, the card had been no longer valid. He must have cancelled it, or reported it stolen after he had given them the details. They had no other address and the telephone number he'd given them was unobtainable.

Despite her protestations, they'd told her if she didn't pay then they would pass it onto the small claims court.

She wouldn't pay it. They couldn't make her, surely? Let them lock her up, she didn't care.

Donna stared ahead, wondering if there was anything she could do, if there was some small way she could make him pay instead. But she was beat.

Owen had her exactly where he wanted her.

Chapter Forty-One

In The Butcher's Arms, Lewis had downed one pint but was struggling with the next. For some reason, it left a bitter taste in his mouth. Since being attacked, and having a brushing down off Josie Mellor, he'd begun to think about exactly where he was heading. He'd already made up his mind that leaving the city might be his best option, but first he needed to talk to Amy one more time. He had to get her to take him back and try to fix their marriage again. With her beside him, he could make a go of his life then. He would stop drinking and be a loving husband and model dad.

Leaving his drink on the bar, he marched over to Russell Place. This time he used his key to let himself in. He found Amy in the kitchen.

'Lewis?' she frowned. 'What are you doing?'

Lewis threw his hands out wide. 'Amy Prophett, I love you!'

Amy folded her arms and stood firm.

'Where's Dan?' He looked through the garden window, hoping to see him playing football again.

'He's out with friends,' Amy told him. 'Lewis, I think—'

'Good, because you and I need to talk.' Lewis nodded vehemently. 'Talking is good.'

'No, you need to talk.' Amy shook her head. 'I – I want you to leave.'

'But I've only just got here!' He held up his hands. 'And this is my house too. I decorated this room.'

'It isn't a house since you've moved out,' said Amy. 'It's a home now, for Daniel and me. You don't live here any longer.'

'That's what I've come to see you about.' Lewis smiled. 'I'm moving back in!'

'You can't.' Amy stood firm.

'Why not?'

'Because I can't cope with you anymore.'

The room dropped into silence.

'But we belong together.' Lewis reached forward, grabbing Amy by the arm and pulling her towards him.

'No, we don't!' Amy tried to get away from him.

'Always and forever.' Lewis wasn't listening.

'Stop it, Lewis, you're hurting me!'

Lewis lessened his grip on her arm. He looked at her, seeing the fear in her eyes.

'You're scared of me?' His face crumpled.

'Yes,' Amy admitted. 'You come here to talk but it's only on your terms, and only when you want to. You don't think of anyone but yourself. And you're always so … so angry.'

Lewis groaned, storming past her as he made to leave. Just before he got to the door, Amy grabbed his hand.

'Go and see someone,' she spoke quietly. 'Please.'

Lewis pulled his hand away. 'Leave me alone.'

'But you need help – why won't you see that? There are people who can—'

'I said leave me alone!' Lewis pushed Amy from him.

Amy fell backwards, landing on the floor with a bump.

'Oh, God.' Lewis stepped forward and held out a hand. 'I didn't mean to do that.'

'Get away from me.' Amy shuffled backwards on her bottom.

'Amy—'

'GET AWAY FROM ME!'

Amy screamed so loud that Lewis covered his ears. 'I'm sorry! I didn't mean to …' He backed away, turning and heading into the living room.

What had he done?

He paced the room for a few moments before stopping in front of the fire. Resting his hands on the mantelpiece, he stared at himself in the mirror above it. The menacing look in his eye; the frown that had somehow become the norm.

He didn't recognise himself anymore. Lashing out at Amy had been the last straw. He wasn't that man – shouldn't be that man, didn't want to be that man.

He put his hands to his head on either side of his temple. Then he heard a noise, all at once realising he was roaring like an animal in pain. A hand curled into a fist. He pulled it back and knocked everything from the mantelpiece in one fell swoop.

A framed photograph of him in his army uniform crashed to the floor, the image smiling back at him now with a crack down its middle. It was exactly how he felt, like he had a split personality. Old friendly Lewis trying to find his way again. New angry Lewis who couldn't cope, and lashed out at anyone who threatened him.

He sank to the floor, and head in hands, he began to cry.

Chapter Forty-Two

Josie was getting ready to head home for the day when she received a phone call from Amy Prophett.

'I don't know what to do,' Amy said after she had told her what had happened with Lewis. 'His mum is at work so I can't call her. But I don't want him in my living room.'

'Do you think you should call the police?' Josie picked up her mobile phone, ready to locate Andy's phone number in her contacts. 'If there's an officer on the estate, I can get someone to you as quick as I can.'

'No! He doesn't need locking up.'

'But if he's turned violent, he might—'

'Please, don't call them.' Amy paused. 'Could you – could you come and talk to him?'

'Me?' Josie replied. 'You know I'm not Lewis's favourite person.'

'Please, just see if you can make him leave. I don't want to get him into trouble.'

Josie wondered if turning up would calm the situation or make it worse.

'He isn't a violent man,' said Amy. 'He's just breaking down and shutting off from a world that he doesn't feel a part of anymore. He needs help.' The line went quiet for a moment. 'I don't know what else to do.'

'Okay,' said Josie, making a split second decision. 'I'm on my way.'

Ten minutes later, Josie was shown into Amy's house.

'He isn't usually this bad,' said Amy, wiping tears away from reddened eyes.

'I know,' Josie agreed, 'but he's getting worse by the week. I've never had so many complaints before.'

Amy gnawed on her bottom lip.

'Shall I try to talk to him now?' Josie asked. 'We can't give up on him, and I know that you don't want to do that.'

Amy nodded. 'Okay.'

Josie went to the living room door and rapped authoritatively. 'Lewis, it's Josie Mellor.'

'Go away.'

'I just want to talk to you.'

'Everyone wants to talk to me!'

'Amy is really upset.'

'It's got nothing to do with you.'

Josie stalled for a moment as she thought what to say next to get a response. 'You remember when we spoke the other day about the noises in your head?' she asked. 'Well, I think I'd like to hear more about them. You can hear them now, can't you?'

'I can hear them all the fucking time.'

Josie jumped as she heard a thump behind the door. She took a step away before she realised what might have happened.

'I think he's slid down the door on the other side,' she told Amy who was beside her. She knocked again. 'Lewis, please let me in so that I can talk to you.'

'What's the point?'

'If you keep getting drunk and into fights, you do realise that sooner or later something really terrible is going to happen? You might not be able to control your anger and you'll attack someone for no reason. You might even kill them.'

'I wouldn't do that.'

'But you're trained to kill.'

'I'm trained to protect!'

Josie grimaced at her bad choice of words. She tried again. 'Lewis, can I come in for a minute? I feel really stupid talking to a door.'

The silence was unbearable but she didn't want to be the one to break it. It took a few seconds but the door finally opened. When Lewis came into view, he nodded.

'Only you,' he said, looking at Josie.

Josie went into the living room, praying she had read the situation right.

'Close the door,' Lewis demanded.

Josie shook her head. 'I can't do that.'

'You can or I won't talk.'

'No, really, I can't. I'm scared of confined spaces and, believe me, sitting in a room with a loose cannon and having no way out would freak me out far more than you.'

Lewis frowned. 'Are you trying to wind me up?'

'I'm deadly serious. I would flip.' Josie glanced around, taking in the mess. 'Even more than you have, I would say. Can I sit down?'

Lewis nodded. He sat down too, glancing anywhere but at Josie.

'You seemed to have sobered up a little?' she questioned.

'A little.'

There was a pause.

'How long ago was it when your dad died?' Josie asked, even though she knew the answer.

'Eighteen months.'

'And it was a heart attack, right?'

'You know it was.'

A silence enveloped the room again. Josie thought Lewis might talk to fill it but he didn't say anything.

'Tell me what happened,' she said. 'Tell me what you're blaming yourself for.'

Lewis's face crumpled. He looked away again.

'Lewis,' she urged.

'I can't.'

Silence dropped again.

Finally, Lewis began to talk. 'During an ambush, my friend, Nathan, took a shot in the neck. We tried to stop the bleeding but the blood was pumping out so fast.' Lewis held out his hands as if the blood was all over his palms right now. 'We couldn't – we couldn't stop it. The blood. He died. Right there in my arms.'

Josie swallowed, almost feeling his pain. 'But you all did your best to help him,' she said. 'I can't see how it was your fault.'

'Because I led them to us.' He prodded himself sharply in the chest. 'Earlier, I was messing about with some kids on the side of the road. We gave them some sweets and when we went back they— they had all been killed. Their throats had been cut because they spoke to us – to me.'

Josie's hand covered her mouth. 'Oh, Lewis.'

'They were innocent kids.' His eyes filled with tears as he relived the horror. 'Their parents were made an example of. Three kids from one family, two boys and a girl, all no older than ten.' He pointed to the floor. 'Laid out and left there for us to see.'

'That wasn't your fault either. You were in a country—'

'It was! Can't you see? They'd waited for us to come back. They knew we would stop again. When we were with the kids at the roadside, that's when they shot at us.'

Josie watched as Lewis's face contorted.

'They killed Nathan,' he whispered. 'I should have taken that bullet. It was meant for me.'

'No!'

'But I let him die.'

'Do your friends all blame themselves?'

Lewis looked at her with a frown.

'I bet they don't.' Josie moved along the settee to be a little closer to him. 'You were all just doing your job.'

It went quiet again. Lewis stood up, paced the room for a few seconds and then dropped to the floor on his knees.

Josie dropped to the floor beside him and took him in her arms as he cried. Amy opened the door and hovered in the doorway, tears pouring down her face too.

When Josie caught her eye, she stepped forward, but Josie put a hand up to stop her. Hard as it was for Amy, she didn't want to risk Lewis getting angry again until he had calmed down.

'I miss him so much,' Lewis spoke after a few minutes. He pulled away and stood up, clearly embarrassed by his outburst.

'I bet you all miss him,' Josie soothed as she stood up too.

'No, not Nathan. I miss my dad.' Lewis wiped at his cheeks. 'If I had known he would die so young, I would never have left the country.'

'We're always saying "if only."'

'But I realise how much of his life I missed while I was away. If I hadn't gone into the army, I would have seen more of him.'

Lewis shook his head. 'I don't think I can ever forgive myself for not being around more.'

'You need to remember how proud he was of you,' said Josie. 'Maybe it's time that you and your mum had a good chat about things? Laura's grieving too. You might be able to help each other.'

Lewis nodded.

Josie glanced at her watch to see it was nearing five o'clock. 'I need to go now, and I think you do, too.'

'But I need to talk to Amy.'

'Amy can see you another day. Would you like a lift back to Graham Street?'

Lewis nodded again. 'Thanks for listening – and not judging.'

'Sometimes it's easier to talk to a stranger.' Josie smiled and squeezed his hand.

Chapter Forty-Three

Megan was walking back from her shift at Poplar Court. The weather was muggy, a tad overcast. She reached for her phone and sighed. There had been no new messages from Sam since she'd hung up on him the day before. She couldn't blame him for not sending any. He'd been good enough to keep in touch with her, despite feeling that she wasn't interested in him. What was the point if he felt as if he was hitting a brick wall every time?

She couldn't help thinking that she'd made another mistake. What happened if he was fine after he saw her birthmark? Since talking to her mum, she'd soon realised that if he was grossed out by her mark, then it would show he was a shallow person. But if he wasn't…

Megan was a firm believer in giving people the benefit of the doubt. She knew Sam was a troublemaker and would probably bring her more grief than happiness but she didn't care.

She was falling for him.

So maybe he would give her a second chance? She had to let him know what was wrong with her before giving up her dreams. She couldn't deny herself happiness. Because if she lost the opportunity to be with someone who cared about her, she would never forgive herself.

After deliberating some more, she quickly typed out a message on her phone.

Sorry for hanging up on you. I was really upset.

She paused, then continued typing.

Do you think we could meet and I could explain why?

Her finger hovered over the button. Should she send the message or should she delete it? She shouldn't class Sam the same as the others – he deserved a chance. He might be totally cool with it. She *wanted* him to be totally cool with it. And if she didn't let him see for himself, then she was letting herself down too.

'Stop being so indecisive,' she scolded herself.

Holding her breath, she pressed send.

When Lewis was dropped off by Josie, he looked at the house and saw his mum standing in the window.

'Now I really do feel like a five-year-old,' he joked. 'I'm going to get told off by my mum again. Amy must have called her.'

'Not necessarily.' Josie's smile was encouraging. 'Just talk to her. Tell her what you said to me.'

He shook his head. 'I need to sort myself out first before I can tell anyone that.'

Lewis got out of the car and walked up the path. Laura was in the hall when he opened the door. He took one look at her and hung his head in shame.

'I'm sorry, Mum,' he said. 'I was selfish and I—'

'I'm lonely, too,' she broke in. 'I can't believe he's gone. It happened so quickly.'

Lewis stayed quiet, realising she needed to talk. And he needed to listen.

'Don't you think it's hard for me to put on a brave face every morning?' Laura spoke softly, her voice breaking with emotion. 'I miss your dad every single day. I miss him every time I open my eyes, every time I take a breath. I miss him when I go to bed every evening. Sometimes I don't want to get up in the morning because he won't be around. It's a terrible cliché, I know, but life goes on. Your dad wouldn't want either of us to mope around.'

Lewis tried to grasp some of what his mum was going through. They were both grieving but she was doing a much better job than he was of hiding her pain. Nathan had been taken quickly too, but so had his dad. There had been no time for his mum to say goodbye. One minute, they'd been a couple: the next the life had gone from his dad as he'd keeled over and had a heart attack.

How could he have not realised, not tried to understand how she was feeling?

Ashamed of his actions, Lewis opened his arms. 'I'm sorry, Mum,' he repeated.

Laura walked into them. Moments later, he felt her sobs against his chest, her tears soaking his T-shirt.

Lewis hugged her tightly, his own eyes welling up, too. Saying what he had to Josie had come out of the blue. Of course, he'd known he was affected by Nathan's death, but he hadn't realised it was also because he was grieving for his father, and the problem it had left him with, not having anyone to confide in.

He needed to make amends with a lot of people. With Amy, even if their relationship was unsalvageable. With Dan; he was a great lad and a son to be proud of. With his mum, hopefully too.

Then he'd go and see Nathan's parents. They'd offered to chat to him a few times but he hadn't wanted to intrude. Now he thought perhaps it might do him good to sit down and talk it through with them. He needed to shed his pain, his anger, his grief.

He needed to get on with his life.

Josie Mellor was right: Nathan would have liked that. He knew his dad would too. It was the best thing he could do for them both. He would move on with his life in their memory, make everyone proud.

'If I come and help out with the old dears at Poplar Court until I get a job, could you put up with me on a regular basis?' he asked Laura.

Laura smiled through her tears. 'Your dad would be so proud of you,' she told him.

'Dad would have kicked me up the arse, Mum.'

'Maybe so – but he would be proud of you, too.'

Lewis hugged her again. Perhaps he would never forgive himself for all those wasted years he could have spent with his dad, but he could make the following years with his family ones to remember.

Sam had had a boring day. The weather had been hot and he'd spent most of it sitting in the tiny garden behind the flats. All he could think about was Megan. He couldn't understand the pull he felt towards her. She was giving him the brush off big time, yet he didn't want to give in yet.

Something about her mannerisms was telling him not to quit. There was something she wouldn't share with him, and he needed to know what it was before he walked away. He could cope with the rejection if she just wasn't into him, and he wasn't going to chase after her. But she seemed so vulnerable, so sweet when she was with him. The last time she had seen him she'd been trying to soothe him, and the next she was gone when he came out of the room.

He thought back to that conversation. Had he said something to upset her? Okay, he'd been a grumpy bastard but that was nothing new so it probably wasn't that.

Was she too wary of his past? Did she not want to get involved because of what he had done? She knew he'd been involved in a fight, she knew he'd been in trouble before.

With spare time to mull things over and over, it had made him realise that if he wanted to find love, settle down, perhaps get married and have kids, then he needed to be a good catch. It had also made him understand he was far from that. What would any woman want with him right now?

But if he kept away from the likes of Scott Johnstone, and his so-called mates who had all but abandoned him anyway, he could perhaps go on the straight and narrow. Maybe in time he could earn some decent money the legit way. After all, he hadn't earned much as a criminal. It wasn't as if he was some Face with a huge house, flashy cars and loads of money, and people doing the dirty work for him. He was a petty thief, and had been very lucky to avoid jail.

The thought of being locked up now, especially being so vulnerable, not knowing how long it would take for his hand to get better, if he ever got the full strength back, was too much.

Yes, to get a girl like Megan, he would have to change. She wouldn't put up with him and his ways. And he realised that was far more important to him.

He was falling for her, wasn't he?

Half an hour later he checked his phone to see a message. He opened it, smiling when he saw it was from Meg.

Chapter Forty-Four

With the weather recovering after a sudden downpour earlier that morning, Megan took her break in the hospital grounds. Although it was always noisy with so many cars, staff and visitors coming and going, she found a bench on a small patch of lawn next to the helipad, and sat down. Gazing up, she closed her eyes in the sunshine and let the warmth flood over her while she waited for Sam.

Over the past few days, they'd begun to send text messages again. Their conversations veered on the friendly side now. Sam hadn't asked her to go out with him again and, although she was glad, she hoped she hadn't missed her chance altogether. Maybe if the friendship built up, she could trust him enough to take things from there.

Last night, they'd arranged to meet during her break. Sam had an outpatient's appointment that morning. Although she was nervous about seeing him again, she was excited too.

'Hi, Meg.'

Megan jumped at the sound of a voice. She hadn't heard anyone coming towards her. Shielding her eyes as she looked to see who it was, her stomach did its usual flip. Sam's smile was as warm as the sun, his blue eyes shining down on her just as brightly.

He sat down next to her. Megan moved along a little and an awkward silence fell between them.

'How are—'

'Are you—'

They spoke in unison and then laughed. Embarrassed to look at him, Megan watched as a woman expertly parked a people carrier in the tiniest of parking spaces in front of them.

'How's your hand?' Megan asked.

Sam held it up. 'It's getting better slowly. Man, those women in physio are brutal! It's aching so much now.'

Megan smiled. 'Wimp.'

Sam turned to face her, bringing his arm to rest behind her on the bench. For a moment he stared at her, then he began to speak.

'Am I wasting my time with you, Meg?' he asked. 'I can keep badgering you with texts and phone calls asking if we can meet, but I don't want you to think I'm a stalker. If you don't like me enough to go out with me, then you only need to say. I'll probably curl up and die if you don't, but …'

Megan didn't know what to say. She shook her head.

'Is that a no, you don't like me? Or a no, I'm not wasting my time with you?' He gave her shoulder a friendly poke.

Meg looked at him, took in his smile, his warmth, his genuine affection. Her mum's words rang in her ears.

You're beautiful, you're young and so full of life. You deserve to find happiness and be loved by someone.

She turned towards him slightly.

'I have a port wine birthmark,' she blurted out. 'It's purple and it's ugly. It covers most of my cheek, some of my nose, my right eyelid and forehead.'

'Where?' Sam narrowed his eyes and studied her face. 'I can't see anything.'

'That's because I cover it with make-up. Haven't you ever noticed that it's trowelled on?'

Sam leaned in closer and tilted her chin upwards.

Almost immediately, Megan felt her skin flushing. Damn, that would make things worse. She needed to look away from the intense gaze of his eyes, but she found herself drawn to them.

'I look like a freak without any make-up,' she said, her eyes brimming with tears. 'I hate looking so made up but I don't have a choice. It's that – or let everyone see this!' She pointed to her face.

'I get the birthmark,' said Sam, 'but I don't get why you let it bother you so much. Why are you so reluctant to get too close?'

'There was a boy I met when I was sixteen, Damien Broadhurst. He wasn't from our school so he hadn't known me when I was growing up. I hadn't realised back then how much my friends accepted me the way I was. I got close to him, enough to, well, you know. Afterwards, I confided in him about my birthmark. Up until then I'd covered it up with make-up, but suddenly I felt brave enough to show him. He took one look at my face and I could tell that he was revolted.'

'But that was one pathetic idiot!' Sam shook his head.

Megan quickly wiped away a tear that had fallen. 'He took a photo of me on his phone before I could stop him and he posted it everywhere. It was on Facebook and he texted it to lots of people. He'd added two words to it – baboon's arse. Some of the kids who'd known I'd got a birthmark but had forgotten about it as it had been covered up for so long, started to tease me. I became the laughing stock of the school again – and the name stuck with me.'

'But it's only a birthmark!'

Megan shrugged. 'Until then, I'd been fine letting some people see it, but after that I covered myself up all the time. I – I kept away from boyfriends, too. I have my work, and I have my mum to take care of and that's enough.'

Sam grimaced. 'You have no friends, now?' He hazarded a guess.

Megan shook her head.

'I find that hard to believe.'

'Why?'

'Kids are usually the first ones to accept people for what they are.'

'Kids maybe, but teenagers don't. They're the first to label us with names that we're stuck with for the rest of our lives. Baboon's arse was mine. So once I left school, I purposely lost touch with everyone.'

'You hid away?'

Megan shrugged.

'Why do you think you're not good enough?' Sam wanted to know. 'It's not the birthmark that bothers you, is it? It's the rejection.'

Megan looked away. Was it being rejected by her father that had made her feel too conscious of her birthmark? Was that when it had become more of an issue, and then exacerbated by Damien Broadhurst?

'And I thought I was hung up on scars.' Sam looked at her sheepishly. 'I'm feeling pretty pathetic about that now.'

Megan reached inside her bag for her purse. Inside it was a photo. She slid it out and gave it to him, holding her breath as she waited for his reaction. The silence almost killed her why he looked at her, then at the photo and then back to her again.

'Wow, I'm shocked,' he spoke at last.

'I told you it was revolting.' Megan snatched the photo away from him and stood up.

'Hey.' Sam's voice was soothing as he took hold of her hand. 'I'm shocked that you cover it up so well, that's all.'

Tears welled in Megan's eyes as she wondered whether to believe him or not.

'It's part of you, so what? It certainly doesn't turn me off at all, if that's what you're thinking. And if you are thinking that, actually, that's quite shallow to judge me without letting me know.'

'You're just saying that.' Megan looked down at him. 'Once you've gone, you'll say you'll call me and I won't hear from you again.'

'Sure you will. I'm not giving up that easily.'

'That's why I took the photo, so that I couldn't be humiliated in person,' Megan carried on as if she hadn't heard him.

'You should wear it as a badge of honour.'

'Now you're being stupid.'

'It's part of you, Meg. It's what gives you the character you have because it's made you tougher.'

'It's hard to keep it hidden all the time,' she admitted.

'You should try being me. I've acted up so much in my life that I don't know who I am anymore.' Sam sighed. 'I know you remember me from school too, and know that I've been in trouble most of my life. I've not been to prison but it's been close a few times.'

'But you grew up with friends around you, didn't you?' Megan was confused.

Sam shook his head. 'Not the ones I really needed to be with. Funny though, since meeting you I feel like I want to settle down and – my mother will have a heart attack if I admit this – but once my hand is better, I'm thinking of getting a legit job.'

Megan was taken aback.

'It's you! You're such a grafter and I can see how determined you are.' Sam looked shamefaced as he continued. 'I'm sorry that I mocked you for being a cleaner rather than a nurse, as if it's not a worthy job, because it is. But I like how you get the job done. You're happy with your lot, Meg, and that isn't a bad thing. It just makes me realise that I'm not.'

'Oh?'

'When the police called to see me at the hospital,' he raised his hand in the air, 'I'd been doing something I shouldn't, clearing away some land so that me and my so-called mates could get easier access to rob somewhere.'

'Was that Jackson's Electronics?' Megan frowned, recalling the headline in the local newspaper that. 'I read about that.'

Sam nodded. 'But when it all went wrong, eventually I realised that my mates wouldn't stick by me. I realised that I didn't care much either. One of them beat me up as I wanted my cut—'

'Two wrongs don't make a right.'

'I know that, but it made me realise that I had nothing to look forward to in my life. And then you came along and that made me realise that I enjoyed being with you, and that I wasn't about to give up until you made it absolutely clear that you didn't want to know me.'

Megan checked her watch, realised she'd had far longer for her break than she was allowed. 'I'd better be getting back.'

'Meg, I feel a bit soppy saying this,' Sam stood up, 'but I think you're gorgeous. You need to let go … and maybe trust someone again.'

'What, someone like you, you mean?'

'You make me sound like a right good catch!' Sam put his hand to her cheek, resting it gently until she stopped flinching.

Megan knew he would be able to feel the lumps beneath his touch, so she closed her eyes and breathed in the scent of him.

'I don't know what you're worried about,' he spoke at last. 'Scars – they all define us but that's what makes us individual. Unique, I suppose.'

'So, you won't be repulsed by it?'

He shook his head.

'You would be if I didn't hide it. People would stare.'

'Let them, I wouldn't care. And maybe people might not stare as much as you think. Women wear make-up anyway, so at least you can cover it up if you like. Whatever makes you happy.' He took out his mobile phone. 'Let's take a selfie.'

'No!' She put up a hand.

'Yes.' He held onto it until she put it down.

Megan looked at him and smiled. It might take her a long time to trust him but he was right there for her. Her mum had been right too. Beauty was only skin deep.

Chapter Forty Five

At home alone that evening, Donna was unable to rest. Since Owen had known she'd left the flowers at Shop&Save, she'd been constantly wondering if he would be watching her, ready to strike again when she least expected it. Even still, she tried to put it to the back of her mind, hoping against hope that he would get fed up and leave her alone.

But as she sat in the living room watching *Coronation Street*, there was a knock at her front door. It still came as a shock as she went to the front window, flicked up a slat on the venetian blind to see Owen standing there.

She jumped back as if burned, but he had seen her. In an instant, he was at the window, knocking on it.

'Let me in, Donna,' she heard him say. 'I only want to talk.'

'So you can attack me again?' she shouted. 'Go away and leave me alone.'

'I need to clear up the misunderstanding.'

His voice was so calm that something inside Donna snapped and she went into the kitchen. Before she opened the back door, she reached for her mum's old walking stick that was standing up in the corner. She grabbed her keys too and went outside, locking up behind her. Then she hid them under a plant pot. If Owen did get the better of her, he wouldn't be able to get inside the house.

Her heart pounding in her chest, Donna opened the side gate and walked along the path. As she got near to the corner of the house, she propped up the stick by the side of the wall, so that Owen wouldn't be able to see it.

He was knocking on the door again as she came into his view. Just looking at him made her want to throw up. She swallowed down bile as she faced him.

'This is private property,' she said, hoping she sounded sharp and unafraid. 'I don't want you here.'

'Relax.' Owen turned to her with a smile. 'I only wanted to see you because you're clearly ignoring my phone messages.'

'That's because I don't want anything to do with you anymore.'

'Don't be like that.' His smirk never faltered.

Somehow as Owen walked towards her, Donna managed to stay her ground. She glanced around the street quickly, not seeing anyone in particular, but noticing a few front doors and windows open due to the heat made her realise she could scream if she had to.

As he came closer still, images of Mary being pulled out of the chair by Denise came into her mind. She'd been a bully, too. Remembering, also, how angry she'd felt when Owen had threatened to harm Keera, she stood tall. What he'd done was wrong, and if she let him win, Donna knew she would be a victim forever.

'What do you really want?' she challenged as he stood in front of her.

'You, of course!' His smile was snide. 'As if. I'm still not certain that you'll keep your mouth shut about our little… get-together.'

Channelling her anger yet hiding behind a mask of fear, she pretended to look afraid to let him think he had her attention. He thought he had power over her? He shouldn't have. No one should.

Her arm reached out to her side. 'Get away from my house or I will call the police.'

A dark shadow passed across Owen's face as he drew level with her. 'You're in no position to threaten me.'

Donna's fingers clasped around the curved handle of the stick. With all her force, she brought it up in the air and hit out at him, aiming for his bicep, hoping to deaden the strength of the muscle.

'You might think you had the better of me when I was tied to a bed, but I won't be a victim for you now,' she hissed. 'You raped me and I won't let you get away with it.'

'You mad bitch!' Owen's facial expression was one of surprise.

Donna raised the stick again. Owen grabbed it, pulled it out of her hands and threw it across the garden, out of reach.

He was on her in seconds, pressing her up against the wall. Her arms flailed as she struggled.

He grabbed her chin roughly. 'You think the police will believe anything you say? I'd only have to play back the phone conversation that we had to let them doubt your word. I recorded it, you see. And you remember, the saucy fun we had the other night, the night in the woods too? I can tell them about that – then how would things look?' Spittle flew over Donna's face as he spoke. 'I'll deny anything you say. It will be your word against mine, and you'll have to look over your shoulder for the rest of your life – because I can disappear easily and quickly, but you'll never know when I might return.'

'I have photos too, of the injuries you caused,' said Donna. He was staring in her eyes as if he was going to attack her again, but she had to fight back. 'I have evidence of us at the hotel. I've spoken to the security guard who saw how upset I was.'

'That doesn't prove anything. We had a lover's tiff.' He sneered. 'Not that I would ever love anyone as desperate as you.'

A tear dripped down Donna's cheek. 'Why did you pick me?'

'You were an easy target.'

'This is my life you're messing with!' she sobbed, her bravery of a few minutes earlier deserting her completely.

'Don't worry, I might set my sights on a younger woman now I've had my fun with you. I've been keeping an eye on that daughter of yours. Quite a little minx you have there.'

'No, please.' Donna's voice cracked.

'You don't know where she's working, do you?' Owen's face lit up. 'Your little girl shops her wares at The Candy Club. It's a massage parlour, if you don't know. I wonder what she does there? Nudge nudge, wink wink.'

'No, she works at—' Donna stopped. This could be a trick. She wasn't going to tell him where Keera worked.

Owen sniggered. 'That's how much you know. She does tricks at The Candy Club. She's seeing some old fella, too. I've seen her getting into his taxi lots of times at the end of her shift.'

'You've – you've been following her?'

'A little bit.'

'You're lying.' Donna's brow furrowed, not wanting to believe what he was saying. 'She doesn't work there.'

Owen shrugged. 'Ask her, if you don't believe me. She finishes work most nights at twelve and he picks her up at the bus stop. He lives over in Christopher Avenue, halfway down. Now, if *I* can see that, I can't understand why you don't know anything about it? I reckon she's ashamed of sucking cock all night, although I don't see anything wrong with—'

'Everything okay, Donna?'

Donna had never been so thankful to see Rita Manning peering over the garden hedge.

'Everything's fine.' Owen stepped away from Donna and gave Rita a warm smile. 'We were just – getting acquainted, if you know what I mean.'

A look of realisation crossed Rita's face and she grinned. 'What are you pair like?'

Owen smiled at them both. Before she could react, he planted a kiss on Donna's cheek. 'I'll see you later.'

Donna dropped to the ground, her legs refusing to hold her body as Owen walked back down the path. She was sure she didn't take another breath before she heard his car moving away from the kerb. Relief washed over her and she burst into tears. Oh, God, he was going to keep harassing her if she didn't do something soon.

'Are you okay?' Rita was in front of her in seconds.

'I ... I ...' Donna struggled to get her words out.

'What the hell was all that about?' Rita stooped down beside her. 'Don't worry, I'm not after the gossip. But he hadn't come because he was missing you, had he?'

Donna shook her head. 'It didn't take long for me to fuck things up as usual.'

'Do you want to talk? I can come back inside with you, if you like?'

Donna shook her head. She knew deep down that Rita was really after the gossip. But Donna wouldn't tell her what had happened because she was still so ashamed. And, despite being brave enough to confront Owen, she hadn't given him the intended impression that she wasn't a victim. What might have happened if Rita hadn't come to her rescue?

With trembling hands, she let herself back into the house, locking all the doors and windows behind her. Then she tried Keera's phone but her message went to voicemail.

She sat down at the kitchen table, head in hands and sobbed. She wouldn't rest until she saw Keera. She wanted her safe at home. She couldn't stop wondering if Owen was out there watching her, ready to strike at any time.

But first she needed to talk to her.

She needed to know if what Owen had told her was true. And if it was, why was her daughter lying to her? More to the point, what the hell was Keera getting up to?

Keera was massaging Derek's back. She'd started her shift two hours ago and was already wishing he was her last client so that she could get him to take her home. She wasn't sure if she was fed up with The Candy Club and her job, or if she just wanted to spend more time chatting to Derek. Either way, the clock just wasn't ticking fast enough.

'I can't believe you get so much tension in the bottom of your back,' Keera said, pushing her knuckles into the base of his spine.

'It's sitting in the car for long periods that does it.' He groaned as she continued. 'If I didn't have regular massages, I'd be in even more agony.'

'Well, I can certainly—'

The commotion downstairs startled them both.

'What's going on?' Keera heard footsteps thundering along the corridor. She could hear Ramona yelling and another voice she recognised.

The handle went down on the door and it was pushed open, slamming into the wall with a loud bang.

Steve Wilson stood in the doorway, his eyes narrowing as he tried to focus. He took a step forward, staggering slightly.

'What the hell do you think you're playing at?' Keera snapped. 'You can't just barge in here when I'm working.'

Derek grabbed for his shirt. 'You have no right to be in here.'

'I wanted to see for myself.' Steve stepped further into the room. 'So you let him screw you but not me?'

'I've done nothing—'

Ramona had reached the room and stood behind him in the doorway.

'Steve!' She pushed past her brother to stand in front of him. 'Just go, will you?'

Steve didn't move. 'You're nothing but a slut!' he slurred, pointing a finger at Keera. 'A fifty pence whore.'

'Oi! Watch your mouth.' Derek stepped forward now.

'Keep your fucking nose out of my business,' Steve told him.

Keera glared at Steve. She had never told anyone at The Candy Club what he'd tried to do to her, but if she could use it now as leverage to get him out of the place, she would.

'Is that why you attacked me?' she said, pointing a finger back at him.

'What do you mean?' Ramona swivelled round to face Keera.

Derek's face darkened. 'It was him?'

Keera nodded, then looked at Ramona. 'He tried to force me down the side of Albert's fruit shop. He wanted me to give him a blowjob but I wouldn't. He's been watching me ever since.'

'She's lying,' Steve said to Ramona, staggering another step to the right.

But Ramona wasn't listening. 'I told you after the last time that if I caught you doing it again, I'd get the management to sort you out. You know I only have to say one word and they'll come after you. You can't keep doing this. I'll lose my job – and then where would your money come from?'

'But she's my girlfriend,' Steve slurred.

'In your dreams,' Keera snorted. 'I wouldn't touch you with a barge pole.'

Derek pulled Keera behind him and turned to Steve. 'I think you should leave before I call the police.'

'No, please don't.' Ramona grabbed her brother's arm. 'Come on, Steve. I'll make you a coffee. Get you sobered up a little.'

'Move out of my way!' Steve pushed Ramona to the side and lunged at Derek, landing a punch in his mouth.

Derek thumped Steve in the side of the head. As punches began to flail, the women tried to break them apart.

'Steve, stop!' cried Ramona, grabbing his arm.

Keera screamed too. 'Leave him alone, you bastard!'

The couch screeched across the room as Derek's back caught the edge of it, but he dodged Steve's fist this time. He grabbed Steve around the waist and managed to push him towards the door.

'I said, you need to leave!' Derek repeated.

Steve thumped him in the stomach and as Derek bent to catch his breath, Steve brought his elbow down on his back, knocking him to the floor. He drew back his boot as Derek curled up into a ball.

'Stop!' yelled Ramona, pulling on Steve's arm again.

'Leave him alone!' Keera pushed Steve, trying to knock him off balance. 'He's a client.'

'So you *do* screw clients?'

'I told you, no!'

'It's fucking sick, if you ask me.'

'No one is asking you.' Keera pushed Steve away. 'Now, get lost before I call the police.'

Steve grabbed a handful of Keera's hair and brought her face within inches of his own. 'Don't you fucking threaten me.'

'Hey!' Derek tried to sit up.

Keera wrestled with Steve, trying to release his grip on her hair, but he was too strong. He pushed her away roughly, her shoulder hitting the wall with a thud. She groaned but as she turned back, she saw he had a knife in his hand.

She screamed when he raised his hand in the air above Derek. 'Don't hurt him,' she yelled. 'Please! I love him!'

'Aww, hear that, old man? She says she loves you.' Steve bent down, glancing at Keera for a moment. 'Let's see how much you fancy him after this.' He drew the point of the blade down the side of Derek's face.

Keera screamed and ran at Steve, disregarding her own safety. 'Derek!'

Steve still had the knife in his hand. He turned quickly, waving it around.

'Do you want some of this too?' he shouted, his dilated pupils bulging from wide eyes.

'Stop it, Steve!' Ramona was sobbing now. 'You've caused enough damage.'

Derek stayed on the floor. Keera froze, unsure what to do next.

With the knife still in his hand, Steve ran from the room.

Before anyone could speak, Ramona followed after him. 'I'm not letting him get away with this any longer,' she muttered.

Through the open doorway, Keera could see Steve disappearing down the stairs.

With arms outstretched and a roar in her throat, Ramona pushed him.

Steve toppled forward, his head hitting the wall as he fell, collapsing in a heap in the hall.

'What's going on?' Estelle, who had come out of her room at last, pushed past Ramona and went downstairs. She knelt next to Steve, looking back up the stairs.

'What the hell did you do that for?' she cried.

Ramona stood there in astonishment. 'Do you know what he just did!' she yelled. 'He's just attacked a client. Derek is going to be scarred for life!'

'But if he's injured, we'll have the police around,' Estelle patted Steve's cheeks to try and wake him, 'and it'll be all our jobs on the line!'

In her room, Keera sat next to Derek. Blood poured through his fingers and down his face.

'I'm sorry,' she sobbed, reaching for a towel. 'This is all my fault.'

'No, it isn't.' Derek sat up and leant against the wall.

'I don't know where he got the idea that I was his girlfriend,' Keera went on. 'I never said anything to make him think that. As if I would go near a creep like him.'

'It's not your fault, Kee.' Derek groaned as she pressed the towel to his face.

'But—'

'Pass me my phone. I'll get someone from the rank to pick us up.'

'Here?' Keera shook her head. 'It might not look good for—'

'I'm not ashamed to say that I visit.'

Keera burst into tears. She needed to know what had happened to Steve after Ramona had pushed him down the stairs. He could have broken something. He might be paralyzed, or worse, dead. Ramona would be in real trouble then and it would all be her fault.

And what would that mean for her, and Derek?

Chapter Forty-Six

Two hours later, Derek and Keera were sitting in a cubicle in the A&E department. Steve had been so drunk that he couldn't recall anything when he finally came round and Ramona had managed to persuade him that he had fallen down the stairs of his own accord.

Keera didn't feel sorry for him after what he had done, but she did feel glad that Ramona wasn't going to get into trouble for her little bit of mad revenge. Luckily, nothing had gone too wrong – except for the attack on Derek.

Derek was waiting to be seen by a doctor. Thankfully, the blade of the knife hadn't penetrated too deeply and the wound was mostly superficial, but it would leave a visible scar for a long time as it healed and faded.

Keera took Derek's hand in her own. 'How are you feeling?'

'A lot better now that the painkillers are kicking in.' He smiled, then winced in pain. 'At least it's not too deep.'

'But you'll be left with a scar.' Keera pointed at his face. The cut measured at least three inches, running from the front of Derek's ear down to his chin.

'Not a prominent one. It will disappear in time.'

Keera knew he was trying to make her feel better. The fact that he had a scar at all was down to her. 'If that lunatic hadn't got the wrong end of the stick, this wouldn't have happened. I can't believe he thought I'd touch him after what he did to me. I'll make him pay once—'

'Kee, what you said earlier,' Derek cut in. 'You don't really love me in that sense, do you?'

Keera felt her skin redden. What *did* she think of Derek? She enjoyed his company, looked forward to being taken home by him and she had a good rapport with him. She liked how he made her laugh, and how he called her Kee. But that was all, wasn't it?

'Thinking about it now?' Keera shook her head. 'I know I said it but it's because sometimes I see how much you care about me and it's hard not to wonder if this—'

'It can't happen, you do realise that?'

'Why not?' She shrugged, embarrassed now that she had admitted it. 'Lots of people fall in love with older people. It's okay.'

'It doesn't seem healthy.'

'I don't really care as long as the two people are happy about it. That's all that should matter really.'

'If only it were that simple.' Derek winced as he moved up the bed a little. 'Christ, I was lucky he stopped when he did. That mad bastard could have stabbed me next in his frenzied state. He was definitely on something as well as drink.'

Keera reached for his hand. 'I'm so sorry.'

'There's no need to apologise. It wasn't your fault.'

'But what he said about me sleeping with you -'

'We know it isn't true. Although, I suppose to the outside world we seem like an odd couple.'

'But we're not doing anything wrong.'

'We know that, but other people will see what they want to see.'

Keera sighed. Deep down, she knew what he was trying to say, and she knew that he was right. Their relationship was odd but she loved spending time with him. She wondered – was he becoming too attached to her? Was he trying to let her down gently?

So many things rushed through her mind. Did she want to risk losing his friendship? And was she latching on to him because she missed her dad? A tear trickled down her cheek and she flicked it away furiously.

'I bet you wished you'd never met me now,' she said quietly.

Derek frowned. 'Of course I don't. I think you're lovely and I enjoy spending time with you. But—'

Behind them, the curtain opened and a man wearing a blue

hospital uniform and white clogs came towards them. 'Mr Paige,' he shook Derek's hand. 'I'm Doctor Latimer. May I call you Derek?'

Derek nodded.

The doctor turned to Keera. 'And, you're his daughter?'

Keera and Derek glanced at each other. Doctor Latimer looked perplexed as they erupted into fits of giggles.

Donna went from anger to tears that night as she waited for Keera to come home. She hadn't wanted to ring her again, for fear of alerting her to anything that would worry her, so instead she'd decided to wait up and confront her when she returned.

But that meant she had too much time to think about Owen. Once again, he had scared the life out of her. Despite Donna's pathetic attempt at a bit of bravado, she couldn't stand up to him, and he knew it. So unless she did something to stop him, he would always be in the back of her mind. Was she really prepared to live her life like that?

It was just after three a.m. when Keera finally came home. Donna was sitting on the settee, the mug of tea cupped in her hands having long since gone cold.

'Mum!' Keera jumped as she spotted her in the dim glow of the lamp. 'Is everything okay?'

'When were you going to tell me?' she said bluntly.

Keera froze. 'Tell you what?'

'Don't come the innocent with me.' Donna glared at her daughter. 'I know you're working at The Candy Club.'

'Oh.' Keera looked at the floor. 'How did you find out?'

'Is that all you can say?' Donna put down the mug and stood up.

'It was the only thing I could get when I got back from Ibiza.' Keera shrugged off her jacket and hid a yawn. 'And at least I'm working. Sam can't be bothered to get a job.'

'You think I'd be happy to find out what you were doing?'

'It's only a massage parlour.'

'I'm not that green,' Donna pouted. 'I know what goes on in those kinds of places.'

'I–'

'Is it just hand and blowjobs? Because if it is, then I can cope with that.'

'Mum!'

Keera couldn't believe it. All those times she'd tried hard not to offer extras, when she knew she could have earned some good money, and her mum didn't believe her anyway.

'Well, is it?'

'I see you've changed the subject.' Keera folded her arms.

'What do you mean?' Donna's brow furrowed.

'Sam! He can't do any wrong in your eyes, can he? He doesn't go to work and scrounges off the social, yet me,' she prodded herself in the chest, 'I pay my way but get it in the neck for holding down a job!'

'That's not a job!'

'I get a decent wage for it.'

'If you hadn't been working at The Candy Club you wouldn't have met that bloke you've been seen with.' Seeing Keera blush, she continued. 'Who is he?'

'It's nothing to do with you.' Keera flounced off into the kitchen.

'Don't give me lip!' Donna raced after her. 'Is he a punter?'

'Mum!'

'Like I said, I know what goes on in those type of places.'

'And you think I would stoop that low?'

'Some women do.' Donna folded her arms.

'Well, *I* don't and *those* type of places live on their reputations. The Candy Club is a massage parlour.'

'You expect me to fall for that?'

'You don't have to believe me.' Keera looked up through eyes filled with tears. 'But it hurts that you don't respect me enough to think that I would never do that. And it's only temporary, so that I can get some money together. I'll be moving out then, don't you worry.'

'But you've not long been back from Ibiza!' Donna cried, all at once realising the implications of her accusations.

'I didn't want to come back. I still want to get away from this estate but,' Keera paused for a moment, 'now I want to get away from you, too.'

Donna was lost for words.

'You don't care about me. All you want me to do is fetch and carry things for Nan. I work doing whatever job I can find, Sam can't be bothered to get off his arse but it's always me who ends up going to Poplar Court. I feel like I'm your skivvy.'

'That's not how it is at all!'

'That's what it feels like to me.'

Donna had tears in her eyes now. 'Keera, I don't want you to leave – unless you want to go.'

Keera wouldn't look at her.

'You're my daughter and I much prefer having you around rather than you not being here at all.'

There was a silence as they both digested what had been said.

Donna made the first move for peace. She sat down at the table and beckoned for Keera to do the same. Then she reached across the top for her hands, covering them with her own.

'Maybe I haven't given you the attention you need because I'm too busy looking after Sam and your nan, but it's only because I don't feel I have to worry about you as much.' She held up her hand as Keera began to speak. 'Of course I worry about you every time you go out of the door, pray that you come home safely every time. But I don't worry about what you're up to and whether you're going to bring trouble home – because you're a good girl. And I love you for that.'

'Even though I work in The Candy Club?' Keera gave a faint smile.

'Yes, even though you work in The Candy Club.'

'You won't mind me still working there?'

'I don't like it but like you said before, at least you are working - which is more than I can say for that layabout brother of yours, even without the dodgy hand.'

'Sam will be okay, won't he?' Keera asked. 'I mean, his hand, once he's got used to it, it will get better in time?'

Donna nodded. 'Although it will always be scarred. He seems to have found someone to help him get over it, though.'

'You mean Megan? I know her from school.'

'I think she'll be good for him. I might even stop worrying about him, too.'

'Oh come on, Mum,' Keera teased. 'You know that will never happen.'

They shared a smile this time.

'So, this bloke?' Donna probed.

But Keera brushed away her comment. 'He's only a friend.'

'Did you want him to be more than that?'

'I don't think so.' Keera shrugged. 'How about you? Didn't yours work out either?'

Donna shook her head. Now wasn't the time to tell her about Owen, but she knew it would have to be soon.

'No, love, it didn't,' she replied.

Getting into bed at last, Donna reflected on the day. So much had happened during the past few weeks that she had neglected some of the things that were important to her.

Who could really blame her for getting involved with Owen, wanting something to look forward to for once?

In a way, it was only now that she could see just how much of a perfect target she had been. Family were everything to her. She was proud of Keera and her willingness to work, stand on her own two feet.

So there was no way that she could leave things open and constantly be on her guard, worrying that Owen could attack her at any minute.

It was time to be brave.

Chapter Forty-Seven

Donna rang Sarah and asked her to call round to her house before she started her shift. It wasn't often that either one of them wasn't working at Shop&Save but Donna had checked the rota to see that they were both not due in until midday.

Over the past few days, she'd thought long and hard about what she was going to do next. One minute, she was going to forget all about Owen and hope that he never showed his face round here again. The next minute she was damning him to hell and was going to report him to the police.

Realising she wasn't strong enough to do the right thing, she'd called Sarah for moral support.

'What's wrong?' Sarah asked Donna the minute she saw her face. 'You seemed really anxious on the phone and I was—'

Sarah had stopped because Donna hadn't been able to hold in her tears.

'Something happened,' Donna spoke quietly.

'This is about Owen, isn't it?'

Donna began to cry again. Sarah manoeuvred them both to sitting on the settee and gave her friend a hug. She held onto her until the tears had subsided.

'How did you know?' Donna asked.

'You stopped talking about him.' Sarah wiped the hair from Donna's forehead. 'I didn't want to pry but it was obvious to me that he'd done something to upset you, especially when you left the flowers at work, too. Do you want to tell me about it?'

Donna nodded. Slowly, she told Sarah what had happened, what Owen had done. Then she took out her phone and showed her the photographs of her injuries.

Sarah's hand covered her mouth, her eyes brimming with tears. 'That evil bastard!' She shook her head in disbelief. 'You have to report him.'

'I can't face it.'

'But he raped you! He lured you away and held you against your will. He mustn't be allowed to do it again.'

'I know.'

'You have to go to the police.'

'And tell them what?' Donna's voice was brittle. 'How naive I was for believing all that rubbish he spun me? How stupid I was to think a woman of my age could pull a man like him? How I hopped into bed with him because I was besotted? Oh, they're clearly going to think he raped me then.'

'He did rape you!'

'It will be my word against his.'

'It won't.'

'Won't it? You know how it looks. Older woman falls for younger man who she is flattered by because he made her feel so fucking special.'

'The man is clearly a psychopath!'

'And I am clearly the most gullible woman in the whole universe for being taken in by him!'

'Of course you're not.' Sarah shook her head. 'Men like Owen know how to work their charm on women; get under their skin, use your vulnerability to their advantage. He's a predator, and we need to warn others off.' She looked at Donna again.

'I can't.'

'But what happens if he goes through with his threats? If he attacked Keera, you'd never forgive yourself.'

Donna baulked. 'That's a low trick to play,' she said quietly.

'I'm sorry but it has to be said.'

'He wouldn't go after her. She's too young – to manipulate and for his tastes.'

'He seems a sadistic bastard so he might not be bothered who he hurts, especially if he wants to get back at you.'

Donna shook her head again. But then she saw tears in Sarah's eyes.

'I'm so sorry, Donna.' Sarah was crying too. 'I was the one who told you to go! I kept on at you to do something for yourself and—'

'This isn't your fault,' Donna soothed.

'But if—'

'This isn't your fault,' Donna repeated. 'I'm not having anyone blame themselves, only me. I was the stupid one. And I need to find the courage to report him. That's why I asked you to call round. I knew I wouldn't be able to go through with it unless you were here. And even now, I've had to talk myself into it.'

Sarah gave her another hug. 'Where does he live?'

'Percival Street. Number thirty-eight. I've never been there, though.' Donna dipped her eyes in shame again. 'That should have been a warning sign. Stupid fool.'

Sarah reached for Donna's phone again.

'What if they don't believe me?'

'Well, then they'll have me to deal with, won't they?'

Donna couldn't help but smile a little. 'Will you stay with me?' she asked.

'For as long as you want me to.'

Donna looked across the room. Outside, the weather was still as glorious as it had been when she'd first met Owen a few weeks ago. It had been the hottest summer on record.

It had been her worst summer ever.

Sarah touched her gently on the arm. 'Let me call the police.'

Donna turned to Sarah and nodded.

One month later

Since the attack on Derek, Keera had been doing a lot of thinking about their relationship. Derek was a lovely man, kind, and considerate. He would make someone a great partner; would it be so wrong if they did get together?

But she'd been considering, too, what other people would think about them. Would they see an older man after a younger woman because he was lonely? Or would they see two people whose friendship had turned into a little more than they'd bargained for?

One thing was certain, she was too young to think of settling down, especially with someone twenty-nine years her senior. And, more than that – she couldn't put her finger on what exactly – something between her and Derek had changed after the attack.

Had he become too close to her? She wasn't too concerned about the age gap between them, but that was because she didn't have romantic feelings for him … or maybe it was because she did.

She sighed. When had they started to get too close?

Even though she was getting along with her mum much better, she didn't want to stay at home forever, so the phone call she'd received last night had been a welcome relief. She decided to go and see Derek.

It was the first time she'd visited his house in daylight. He showed her through to the back garden and she sat down on a bench in front of the kitchen window while he brought them both a drink.

The weather was cooling now as summer turned into autumn,

and Keera was so glad that she wasn't about to start another shift at The Candy Club. Ramona had been upset when she'd handed in her notice, apologising profusely for her brother's behaviour. Keera had put her mind at ease, it hadn't been Ramona's fault, and she had got her own back in a way. She hoped Steve would keep away from her now.

She'd left with Ramona saying there would always be a place for her if she wanted to return. Keera knew she'd never go back there, no matter how desperate she became.

Derek gave her a glass of wine as he joined her.

'So, how are you feeling now?' she asked, as he sat down next to her.

'I'm fine. Stop fretting,' he joked stretching his legs out in front.

Keera looked at the gash on the side of his face. The stitches had been removed but the scar itself was still healing over. Tears welled in her eyes as she thought of the pain he must have gone through, all because of that lunatic Steve Wilson. Derek had refused to press charges, saying that he'd rather not be responsible for any trouble Ramona might get into. Ramona had been extremely grateful, but Keera had wanted justice. She'd finally given up pressurising him after Derek had persuaded her it was for the best.

Keera looked away before he could see how upset she was. But he must have noticed, because he leaned across and tilted up her chin.

'Hey, don't cry,' Derek told her, wiping away the tears that had fallen. 'I keep telling you that what happened wasn't your fault.'

She shook her head. 'If you hadn't met me, then Steve wouldn't have attacked you and …'

'Nothing to be done about it now. We can't turn time back.' Derek looked her straight in the eye. 'I've been thinking … I'm going to take a holiday. Get away for a while.'

'Oh?' Keera frowned. 'Where would you go?'

'To Australia to see the kids. I thought I might visit for a few weeks.'

There was a pause.

'You know you can't come with me,' he continued.

Keera looked at him. 'Of course I know that.'

'So we can stay friends for when I come back?'

'I don't think so.' She shook her head again.

'Oh!' Derek drew his head back and frowned.

'I'm moving to Manchester to be with Marley,' she smiled. 'Marley's mum says that she's sick of her moping around wishing that I was there. She says there's room for both of us if I want to go and stay.'

'That's great, Kee.' Derek smiled. 'Really, I mean it. You should get off this estate.'

'But who will give you a massage when you get back from Australia?'

'Oh, I'll just not bother going anymore.' Derek shrugged. 'My back hasn't been hurting me for a while now, anyway.'

'Why, you crafty bugger.' Keera thumped him playfully on the arm.

'You had no idea?'

She shook her head.

'Call yourself a masseuse?' Derek grinned.

Keera leaned forward and gave him an impromptu hug.

'I'll miss you, Mr P,' she said. 'You've been more of an influence than you'll ever know.'

Derek kissed her forehead. 'I'll miss you too.' He smiled. 'Be sure to keep in touch with the odd text message every now and then.'

Keera nodded.

'And maybe when you're back to see your mum, you could call round for a coffee?'

'More than once in broad daylight? What will the neighbours say?' she mocked.

Half an hour later, they said goodbye. They'd chatted about their friendship, and how it had been fun to get to know each other. Keera had long ago realised how much she liked him as a friend, but right now she knew that was all he would ever be. Their talk had cemented everything.

As she walked down the path, Keera also recognised that it would probably be for the best if this was the last time she visited. Derek would go to Australia and she would go to Manchester to be with Marley. They would be living separate lives again in no time.

She was glad that she'd met him. She was glad they'd shared a special friendship. But it was time to move on, in more ways than one.

Lewis stopped across the road from St Stephen's Church. Waiting for a car to go past before he crossed, he shoved his hands into his pockets. Facing his demons was one thing, but this? What was he letting himself in for?

Inside the grounds, he made his way along the gravel path beside the church, the September sun beating down on his back. He spotted a woman tending to a headstone, three young children charging up and down on their bikes, screaming at full volume. Life and death, all in one space, peace and noise as one.

He found the door that Josie had mentioned to him a couple of weeks ago and went into the building. Finding himself in a vestibule, the sound of laughter hit him immediately. The smell of delicious cooking did too, bringing back happier memories of family Sunday lunches. It was only half past eleven, yet his stomach began to growl.

Gingerly, he pushed on one of two doors and stepped into a large hall. Several round tables seating six at a time were scattered around the wooden floor, chairs stacked up around the edges. There were drawings on the walls from some of the local schoolchildren, a bright sunflower with screwed-up pieces of tissue paper stuck to its leaves taking pride of place by the door.

The laughter he'd heard was coming from the kitchen. Through a serving hatch, he could see two women, one of whom he recognised immediately.

'Lewis!' Josie beckoned him over. 'I'm so glad you came. I need an ex-soldier with a bit of nous to help me to keep this rabble in place.'

Lewis couldn't help but smile. Especially when the lady beside Josie gave out a whistle.

'Well, well, well, will you lookie here,' she beamed, wiping her hands on her apron. 'I'm Maura, and I'm *very* pleased to meet you. Please say you've come to help me. I can certainly find lots of things for you to do with those big hands of yours.'

'Maura!' Josie's tone was jokey. 'And you a married woman.'

'You'll be scaring him off too with that kind of talk, Maura.'

The voice came from a man sitting at the table closest to the hatch. Lewis guessed he might be in his seventies by his clear skin and his shock of white-grey hair, although the hands riddled with arthritis might indicate he was older. He wore a dark blue blazer, white shirt and tie. Polished shoes, Lewis noticed too.

'Ah, pipe down, old soldier,' Maura chided. 'That's Alf, by the way.'

Lewis nodded in greeting before spotting a young woman coming into the kitchen.

'Blimey, I don't know what you lot are gabbling on about but I can hear you all the way from – oh, hello.' She stopped short.

'This is Emily.' Maura shared a look with Josie. 'Emily, meet Lewis.'

'Hi.' Lewis waved. Emily's smile was shy and she dipped her eyes as he stared at her. He turned to Alf when he thought he'd stared enough. 'So, you were a soldier?'

'I'll always be a soldier, son.' Alf puffed out his chest. 'Wear my medals with pride, I do.' He lifted his knee slightly. 'See this? It isn't mine. I lost my leg below the knee in World War two.'

'World War two?'

'Yes, I'm ninety-two, son.'

Lewis tried to hide his shock. 'You must have seen some action,' he asked.

'Oh no!' shrieked Maura, loud enough to make Lewis jump.

'What's the matter?' he asked.

'It's like *Only Fools and Horses*, Lewis.' She laughed. 'You remember, Uncle Arthur's catchphrase line, "during the war?" Well, that's Alf's too. You'll never shut him up now!'

'Nonsense.' Alf waved his walking stick in the air. 'Us soldiers have to stick together, don't we, son? I'm sure you'd like to hear a tale or two.'

Lewis glanced at Josie, realising he'd been set up. She'd made sure that he could do something useful with his time rather than be bored enough to drink himself to oblivion – although he hadn't been near The Butcher's Arms for a while. At the same time, he could get to know another soldier. So what if the age gap was huge? That wouldn't stop them having lots to talk about.

'Come on round.' Maura pointed to another door. 'I'm sure Emily would like help peeling that massive pile of carrots over there.'

Lewis did as he was told.

'This place opens at twelve,' said Josie, 'and there'll be thirty-seven pensioners in, all wanting their lunch. 'Not one of them likes to be kept waiting. There'll be a riot if we're late.'

'You see,' Maura nudged Lewis who was already peeling a carrot. 'Never a dull moment here.'

Lewis wasn't sure what he was letting himself in for but the atmosphere here seemed fun, and so light compared to the dark that he had shrouded himself in over the past few months.

As he caught Josie's eye, he smiled again. Maybe in time he could make some new memories, perhaps leave the scars of the past behind and look towards a new future.

When Donna arrived at Mary's flat after her shift that evening, Sam was there. So too was Keera.

'What's going on?' Donna, eyed them suspiciously as she put away the key fob. 'I can't remember a time when we were all in the same room.'

'We just thought we'd get together before I leave for Manchester,' said Keera. Getting up from the settee, she came to give Donna a hug.

Donna hugged her back. She would miss her like crazy but she couldn't tell her that. Keera needed to stand on her own two feet, put the past behind her and start afresh. Donna couldn't have it on her conscience if she decided to stay here again. Manchester would yield more opportunities for her.

'Oh hi, Donna.' Megan came into the room, carrying a vase full of white carnations. 'I bought these for Mary. I thought after all she'd been through, it was the least I could do.'

'That's very kind of you.' Donna watched her son smile as Megan went to sit with him after she had put the flowers down. So far, they'd been out a few times, and it was early days, but Donna had never felt so delighted that he had found someone nice for a change.

'I'm glad everything is sorted and things can go back to how they were before,' Donna spoke to them all.

Megan hesitated for a moment before continuing. 'I never liked Denise, and gut feelings are always right. Isn't that so, Mary?'

Mary didn't respond as she sat in her chair.

'She'll stay away if she knows what's good for her,' said Keera. 'She's ruined any chance of working in this kind of environment again, especially being charged with assault. Serves her right, too. I hate bullies.'

'I'm glad now that I set that camera up,' said Sam.

'I was really nervous about it!' said Donna. 'Not about getting caught straight off, but about getting caught before I could get the evidence I needed to support my gut feeling.' She smiled uneasily at Megan. 'I owe you an apology, because I had my suspicions about you, too.'

'Me?' Megan frowned.

'Megan?' Sam and Keera spoke in unison.

'I'm really sorry.' Donna felt her skin flushing. 'It was just that every time I was here, you'd pop in and I … well, I thought you were keeping an eye on Mary so that she wouldn't say anything. Not that she would probably be able to say anything, but … Oh, you know what I mean. I thought you were trying to stop her from telling me.'

Megan nodded and smiled back shyly. 'I was trying to protect her. I like Mary, she's a lovely lady.'

'She is. Talking of which. I haven't spoken to her yet.' Donna tapped Mary on her forearm. 'Hi, Mum, how are you today?'

She was greeted by a smiling face. 'Hello, love,' said Mary. 'I'm good, how are you?'

Donna gasped. She looked at Megan and then back to Mary. For a moment there, she'd thought her mum had recognised her. But the blank expression had come back almost immediately. It was just a face that Mary had recognised – not the face of her own daughter.

Tears welled in Donna's eyes. 'I wish I could have Mum back, even just for one day.'

'Not a good idea,' said Megan. 'Because then you'd want another day and another day. One would never be enough.'

'That's very true.' Donna smiled. 'Well, at least I know she has you to look out for her. And that I am truly grateful for.'

'And she's going to look after me, too.' Sam nudged Megan. 'Aren't you?'

'You must be joking,' said Keera. 'That's a full-time job in itself.'

As everyone laughed, Donna took the opportunity to look round at her family again. Each one of them had been through some kind of ordeal, but at least they were all happy for now, and safe.

Except maybe her. She looked down at the floor.

Donna hadn't been surprised when the police had gone to Owen's address and found the property empty. Apparently, the landlord knew him as Simon Timpson. He'd been a tenant there for six months, but had done a runner owing three months' rent. She'd had no choice but to put it all behind her after that.

She'd be forever grateful to Sarah, for staying with her while she'd reported the attack. Like a true friend, Sarah had been there for her – was still there for her, constantly ringing her or texting her to see how she was coping, despite seeing her most days at work. She hadn't judged her; she had just supported her through it all.

More to the point, Donna had amazed herself by how strong she had been. She knew the incident would haunt her for the rest of her life but it was comforting to know that Owen might have moved on because he thought he was going to be arrested. And now that Keera was going to Manchester, she could worry less about him attacking her daughter.

She had kept the photos of her injuries on her phone, and the text messages that Owen had sent, just in case they were needed in the future. If it ever came to light that he had done the same to some other woman, she would do whatever it took to get the bastard behind bars. He'd done enough damage not to be brought to justice.

She looked up again. It would take time, and she would try to forget what had happened with Owen. And with family and friends around her, Donna knew she would survive.

But no one would ever see the scars that had been left behind this time.

ALSO BY MEL SHERRATT

Somewhere to Hide (Book1, The Estate Series)

Behind a Closed Door (Book 2, The Estate Series)

Fighting for Survival (Book 3, The Estate Series)

THE DS ALLIE SHENTON SERIES

Taunting the Dead (Book 1)

Follow the Leader (Book 2)

Only the Brave (Book 3)

Watching over You

A standalone psychological thriller

Thank you from Mel

A huge heartfelt thank you to Sarah Hartnoll for donating to the charity, Clic Sargeant, for Children with Cancer, and for permission to use her name in memory of Bill Hartnoll. The auction raised nearly £15,000 and I was honoured to be asked to take part.

As this is my eighth crime novel, I want to say a huge thank you to anyone who has read my books, sent me emails, messages, engaged with me on Twitter, Facebook or come to see me at various events over the country. Without you behind me, some of whom I call my Team Sherratt, this wouldn't be half as much fun. I love what I do and hope you continue to enjoy my books.

ABOUT THE AUTHOR

Ever since I can remember, I've been a meddler of words. Born and raised in Stoke-on-Trent, Staffordshire, I used the city as a backdrop for my first novel, TAUNTING THE DEAD, and it went on to be a Kindle #1 bestseller. I couldn't believe my eyes when it became the number 8 UK Kindle KDP bestselling books of 2012.

Since then, my writing has come under a few different headings - grit-lit, sexy crime, erotic crime thriller, whydunnit, police procedural, emotional thriller to name a few. I like writing about fear and emotion – the cause and effect of crime – what makes a character do something. I also like to add a mixture of topics to each book. Working as a housing officer for eight years gave me the background to create a fictional estate with good and bad characters, and they are all perfect for murder and mayhem.

But I'm a romantic at heart and have always wanted to write about characters that are not necessarily involved in the darker side of life. Coffee, cakes and friends are three of my favourite things, hence I write women's fiction under the pen name of Marcie Steele.

You can find out more at melsherratt.co.uk
on Twitter as @writermels

You can find out more about Marcie Steel
on Twitter as @marcie_steele

18432374R00160

Printed in Great Britain
by Amazon